gather the weeds
by
Patrick T. Kilgallon

ISBN 978–1–7358998–5–5

Acknowledgements

I thank the following people for assisting me with this book: George D'Amore, Jill D'Amore, and Kevin Mundey for helping me with the American Sign Language (A.S.L.) dialogues in this book. If there is any mistake, it is my fault, and the printed version will never substitute for the real life dialogues among the Deaf. I thank Abnel Ortiz and Cristina Rodriguez Alma for helping me with the Spanish and Spanglish dialogues. Again, any errors are mine. I also thank Steven Barish, Willy Conley, Harvey Grossinger, and Jennifer Nelson for their input, along with students in my creative writing classes. Finally, I thank Mr. Sparano for editing my book.

Dedication

This book is dedicated to Mom, Margaret Kilgallon, and Dad, Michael Kilgallon Senior, with love.

Contents

Right Now...i

Part One: Start of Day……...................................... 9

Bell and Blue Light 11

The Fight Outside.. 23

Memory In Dream..28

Words To Live By.. 35

Roll Call 39

The Little Boy.. 65

The First Few Movements 90

The Message On the Terminal Billboard.................... 166

Stillness 167

Part Two: The Dying Daylight..................................... 173

A Visit From Past 175

Duck…. Duck…. GOOSE!.. 221

The Last Few Movements 230

Early Light 240

The Monster At The End of the Book.......................... 268

Right Now

—Hurts. Cold, oh Jesus, seventeen and cryin', a baby. Great, should hold my breath until my face turns blue. Whysees would want that.—

He weeps. It is a lost, bewildered sound in the bare room. The smears of ice blur the glass window, turning the streetlights from the plaza into a pink fog. Cold drifts under the cover and trickles weary sighs across his shivering form. Harsh air rasps against his lips. His teeth chatter. A sticky odor, from lonely spent nights, rises from his tattered sheet. The blanket, which used to belong to Henry, is too thin to hold the bitter weather at bay.

—All wantin' good lookin' girls and go home to play hockey. Blanket stinks of spaghetti sauce. Whysees takin' away from me. Whysee Henry chokin', Whysee Henry stupid way of dyin'! Stinks, smells of Henry's B.O. Meats, Whysees takin' hidin' at Monkey House. Sickin', why they doin'. Sam… no thinkin' of him; will be screamin' 'bout him. First, poor Henry, we all turnin' on him and all. Pushin' him and end. No one cares. Me hurt. Here. There. Everywhere. I'm holdin' on. Not my fault bein' deaf, bein' bit stupid. Don't be cuttin' me down. That's Whysees' job, yuk, yuk, yuk.

Can't get no girls. Someone pretty to be with, someone to touch warm skin and Whysee takin' that from me. Takin' my own time! And stuck with Paul, Jose, Nancy, and Gertie draggin' me. Paul is mad at me and no one cares.—

Self–righteous, he sniffles to himself.

—Nobody cares. And Whysees gray uniforms, flat, white cop hats, bossin' the wards and goin' out with well—shaped girls. Oh, first few days of September. Feelin' real good. Kickin' blockhead Richie Trunk's ass good. Sam, why you gone now? Can't help nothing happenin' to me. Here, wish not remember home.

(Mom signs over the glow of the tablet from the eBook, *Peter Pan*, on her lap. She pretends at being a lost boy as she holds onto the bedpost so she does not fly away. She sits on the edge, giggling. The mattress yields to her soothing weight, her presence of comfort and joy. She reads from the book signing, the inflection of words unknown without voice.

And Michael believe longer than the other boy, though they jeer at him; so was with W–E–N–D–Y when P–E–T–E–R come for her at the end of the first year.

A tear slides down your cheek.

Michael, are you crying?

Mom, other girl and boy in my class, they laugh and yell at me. Not fair to me.

Just the way now. Just bear it. At least try. It will be O.K.

She signs the word *bear*, as the animal, which is alright with you. It is an ongoing family joke to sign words according to their literal meanings. Patience is a portrait of a plodding creature with its head stooped toward stubborn pain.

You make her promise it will be okay.

We will see, she answers. *Alright? That the best we can do. We will see.*)

Don't go back now. Everything is gone.

'Klin.'

(It is the last time you can go where people are. The frost of vanilla ice cream at the Dairy Queen tastes cool and sweet. Under the twirling light of the hologram ice cream cone, Mom wipes the fudge from her mouth and glances over her shoulder. Remember mounds of grass, marble crosses, and the round stones through the fence across a two—lane road in your town? Much clearer is the taste of melting sugar, cream, and vanilla. The evening grows late, twilight colors riding the sky.

Dad's smile strains from his haggard and hollow–eyed face. The shadow of Dad's half–full chocolate milkshake inside the *Dennis the Menace* cup slopes as he holds it. Mom is signing.

Michael, last day we can go out. Now on, you and me must stay in the house.)—

In his bed, his restless feet kick at the torn blanket. His eyelids close and he sleeps to dream of more life.

—(*Why, Mom? Not right! What about Peter? Can he come over and play?*

Mom shakes her head. Dad's face turns somber as he talks. Mom shifts away, her smile vague.

We must hide you and Mom, Dad signs. *No going outside and playing hockey. All bad now.*)

Where is home in PA?

(The letters in scrawls, teacher shows the paper of where your house is: 119 CLOVER LANE… letters with word TOWN at the end before PA… then numbers.)

Don't know for sure now. Fading remembers of paper. Me cannot see it too good now. Could hear them, though.

(Children giggle when the teacher's hand rattles the paper during class. Teacher's voice chirps but inaudible what she is saying. They have no interpreters anymore. In the school hallways, older boys in gray shirts have pleasant faces only for others, not you. They walk the hallways, saying things over and over. No more Mrs. Cradle to sign at school. A hearing friend pedals his bicycle on the street past your house, his shoulders hunched.)

Peter, gonna get you for this, you dirty double crosser! We supposed to be friends!

(Weeks before the Gray Man comes to see whether Mom and you are deaf, Dad makes Mom and you lie and pretend to be hearing.

'Remember, Michael. Watch your lazy tongue. Remember and practice! Watch D and T.'

'Woch out for the Gray Man.'

'Good, Michael. Watch your speech.'

A tap and Dad opens the door. Gray Man stands there waiting. He comes in and tests you. An hour after, the stranger signs, hands stiff and awkward. You lost, you and Mom got caught. Mom's eyes become dead as the front door snicks shut behind the stranger. Dad's sniffles turn to light sobs. His fist keeps circling on his chest.

'Dad, what's happening?'

They are taking you both away. I am sorry.

Dad stops signing and buries his face in hands, his shoulders shaking.

You and Mom must live at the Chateau Peak Resort. A large decrepit hotel in the Pocono Mountain has been converted into an internment camp. Dad says on one visit, *All need B–A–R–B wire around the place. Instant A–U–S–C–H–W–I–T–Z.* You know that Dad's joke is tasteless. What happened in 1933 Germany is an evil so profane that today it is still wrong to joke about it. Mom laughs, her face hard and angry. She makes him promise he will not post the comment on Profile, a public social media.

Years later, the listless rocking of the train is no comfort. Mom's face fixed as the plastic people in the clothing stores. And you sit next to her on the padded seat, asking her questions. You remember that nice lady in uniform at the station platform who beams and fingers spells that *you 2* will be with *T–H–E–I–R–K–I–N–D–S.*

Where are we going, Mom? Why do we have to go?

We will wait and see.

Mom forces a hard drawn smile and tea–colored bags borne in under her bleak eyes.)—

Tonight, at the Gate Institution, he lays with an arm flung across his face. In his sleep, he smiles. All the ghosts in his head call out their names.

—Sam and poor Henry. Sorry, we didn't mean to! Kasy, too much to see that. And even poor Gertie.—

Through the icy glass, the dark morning sky grows a timid shade of gray.

—*We will wait and see… wait and see…*—

Patrick T. Kilgallon

His disturbed mind recalls bits and pieces of this year. Streams of thoughts, floating scattered images and murmurs with them, and signs he had seen, echoes of voices heard through his hearing aid, faint but audible, and no telling the exact dialogues and moments of these times.
—*We will wait and see... wait and see...*—

Part One: Start of Day...

And whatever their illness and pain or if they were possessed by demons or were insane or paralyzed—he healed them all.

—Matthew 4:23

What has happened to me? He thought. It was no dream. His room, a regular human bedroom only rather too small, lay quiet between the four familiar walls.

—Franz Kafka, The Metamorphosis

Bell and Blue Light

It should have been a nothing day. It began on this soft morning when the siren from the Bell Chapel rang, although Michael Poole did not hear it, the sound carrying from the tower clock to the Galton Dorm. Blue lights of the wards' daily wake–up alarm invaded his sleep.

—Flas lights! Eyes! Goddamn–duh! Ooh, sorry Jesus, lights hurt! —

Phosphorus lights stole beneath his eyelids. He blinked at the blazing bulb above the closet. Across, Henry struggled out of his own bed. Light blipped again, showing his roommate's red hair, his lolling long head, and his puckered mouth.

—Henry here, retard, why not me room with Sam or room with Paul, just me here with retard, no fair 'cause me deaf, me with him. Don't say nothin' to me, Henry! Time drains away, just stayin' in bed. Henry's goin' slow. Slow talk, slow thoughts, he is not so fast. —

Michael (whose name sign is the letter M above his shoulder to show his longish mussed hair) sat up, his body bathed in the neutral air of the first few false summer days. His dry stomach clenched from hunger as he buried his face in hands and groaned. Henry waved at him to get up from his bed. At the doorway, the shadow of his roommate thinned, then disappeared. Lights from the wake– up alarms filled the room from the hallway. While he dressed, he saw wards passing the window, signing, and forming crowds on the plaza. Bodies skirted around in the easy air with no heavy heat to bog them, nor cold to carve into their skins. Four or five looked in at him. Two had smug grins on their faces.

—Stupid asses. Think you're smart enough gettin' out. It's nothin' to wakin' up to another day. —

He felt the worn carpet beneath the soles of his clammy feet through his dank socks. The light flashed, showing his sneakers. One on the floor and one under the bed. He crammed the first on his foot, hopping on the other. The room teetered from loss of balance, and he collapsed on the bed, wrenching his foot into the first sneaker. He dipped himself to snag the second under the bed. His fingers stroked the hockey stick hidden under the bed before he put on his second sneaker.

—Think got time. No Gray Boys comin', nuh–huh not bein' here when lights goin' out. Goin' getcha outside, getcha outside. Almost forgot my hearing aid. —

His inside–the–ear hearing aid, the most durable and finely programmed hearing aid available, attached to the worn and nicked charger, was on the bureau with two missing drawers. He unattached the hearing aid and pressed it into his ear. First squeals, then sounds of the world.

—(Eeeeeee Braw! Braw! Braw! Along with the bell. Own Braw! heavy Braw! breathing Braw! the click Braw! of Braw! world Braw! Braw! Braw! into motion Braw! from Braw! Braw! sound. Braw! Flas Braw! still popping Braw! into Braw! eyes. Braw!) Hurts. Braw!)—

He groped for the handle to pull it open and stepped into the hallway. White and blue lights scattered and lapped against worn tiled walls. Doors lining the hallway opened closed as distorted and unfinished images passed, seeming to float. There, the chubby face of a boy. Next, a face, unfocused eyes, a snarl, uttering what Michael believed to be curses. It was the blind boy from three doors away. From another opened door, two flat hands shook at the flashing bulb.

—Oh yeah, Jose, the deaf retard sayin' *FINISH! FINISH!*—

They moved toward the door at the end of the hallway. A high, sweet voice sang. Michael knew the words. His mind had labored to piece these words together. Same as many mornings before, he worked to follow the words on the singer's lips:

Rock of Ages cleft for me
let me hide myself in thee
let the water and the blood
from thy wounded side which flowed
be of sin the double cure
save from wrath and make me pure

A giant teenager danced, his voice carrying. He bounced on the toes of his sneakers. His graceful marching made his body whole in the light. The worn soles of the boy's large sneakers made the brown skin around his ankles appear smeared. More figures moved, and Michael nicknamed them to himself. The exit door stayed open for them before it shut again.

—Black retard. —

A weeping giant head on a small body followed.

—Baghead. —

The heavy head hung; the mouth pulling into a frown deep as a sick elephant's lips. After him was a boy with hairy breasts peeking from his unbuttoned shirt.

—Girlman. God with his toes pointy and everything ugh. —

The curly–haired teenager walked alone among many, no matter how skilled he was at American Sign Language. The last door near the exit clanked open, and a blonde seventeen–year–old boy strutted into the hallway. He carried a battered flashlight, swinging it as if a baton in his right hand.

—Nattheasshole, high and mighty with his swishin' gray armband and a crappy flashlight, not important. Better not be pushin' me. —

"Out!" Nat's lips hollered.

He poked the flashlight against Michael's chest. The cool metal dug in through his shirt.

"I'm movin', Nas," Michael said. "Besigh, only dummies carry flaslighs with all lighs blinkin'."

Nat's mouth mimicked his voice, and he raised the flashlight to Michael's chin, his face contemptuous. It clunked against his jaw as he squinted into the dull glow. His chest tightened as he fought to keep his chin from quivering at the sight of Nat's enraged face.

—Oh great, Nat, the block guard and lord over everyone. Don't show him you're scared, okay? —

Nat grunted with satisfaction and stalked to the door. He yanked it open, and his duct taped sneakers disappeared behind the closing door. Michael gritted his teeth. He followed but stopped when a form in a wheelchair pulled at something. It was Paul, who doubled over, his face aggrieved. Another familiar body thrashed by the footrest. He attempted to bypass them. A hand snagged the tail of his shirt.

"Michael!" Paul shouted and signed, his hands choppy in the flashing lights. "Stay and help me!"

A blip of blue reflected his gray eyes through the lens of his glasses.

—Dead in tummy, swallow a walnut whole. Yeah, that's me, a ward leavin' his closest friends for the boys in gray. —

"I gotta go, Paul! I gotta jus go!" Michael gestured at the flashing lights.

Paul swung his body with his arms, balancing on his wheelchair. The bent deadweights in pants that were his legs bumped against Michael's hip.

Help your friend too, Paul signed.

Michael sighed hard and got on his knees. Sam's shoulder flopped out of his hands so he could not grip him. Thoughts hurled.

—Too fast. Get—get the… get… oh that Sam. Stay still, damn it. The boys in gray, they comin.'—

The muscles in Sam's shoulder slammed on the carpet, a dull thoink that jarred at Michael's fingertips. A door, the corner covered in mold, opened in front of the shaking body. Another ward stepped out, and Michael could see a flimsy string tied around a soft biceps.

—Oh, just Eggy the retard thinkin' he's boss over the rest of us. Because of bitty string. Just a dog for Nat.—

Eggy's genitals peeked out from between stitches and small holes on the worn crotch of his pants, jiggling over Sam's racking head. His spidery arms rose, and he chanted something that meant nothing more than a frog croaking. Michael gave him the finger, and the form fled, hollering. The door opened closed again as the sound of the bell waned.

— (Braw! Braw! Bra! Blip! Blip! Blip.)—

Hurry! Paul signed.

Sam's eyelids fluttered open. An outline of Paul raised his hands in frustration in the last flash.

— (Blip. Blip. Bri…)—

All the lights snapped out. In the dark, Michael could see only Paul's seated figure and the stirring body of Sam. Hums from stuttering lights faded. Footsteps clunked from the other side. The handle of the door turned. Paul shouted something, his voice pleading. Sam blinked, his dark eyes still glazed and his face gleaming with sweat. His mouth moved, mumbling something. Michael could picture in his head well–scrubbed faces, above gray collars, hardening. His face tingled with shame.

—Stupid, a stupid baby peein' pants, makin' a beautiful mess, sendin' ripples into the shiny pond of what should have been just another day. Stupid. Stupid. —

The exit door opened.

—Don't hit! Please, we tryin' don't hit me, oh d– —

No blows rained on his head. The morning dusk shoved through the square window. A thick head tilted above him. Against his back, the door thudded. As he crab-crawled to let it open wider, the carpet rasped against his hands. He struggled to lip–read the murmurs.

"Please move. Move a little more."

It opened wider as Michael scooted to the side. Dusty and neatly laced army boots passed as bodies of the Whysees filled the hallway. They wore running suits and stank of sweat. A painful twinge landed on Michael's hand from one boot. The Watchers (signed as *WHYSEES* with a scornful expression of puzzlement) filled the hallway. The brown–haired one with a red bar on the patch sewn onto the sleeve was the leader. Mild brown eyes looked at Michael. More Whysees filled the hallway.

—The leader, a boxer with a face–cake, soft and sweet. Talkin' just babbling. —

A blonde Whysee's face filled the ceiling above, his rosy–cheeked face pinched with disgust.

—Blonde looks kinda pretty if a girl. Wouldn't say that to him though. —

The Whysees' rough hands dug into Michael's arms and hauled him to a standing position. Between two other Whysees, Sam teetered on his heels and muttered. A narrow–faced Whysee thumped him in the stomach, and he sagged, clutching himself. A lanky Whysee said something, his voice cracking. The blonde one poked Michael hard in the lower ribs and spoke. He watched the Whysee's mouth form each word, breaths cinnamon.

—Onnnnneeee… ow…OnOWMo…Monkey House. Oh… Jesus no! No, please, I'll be good! —

Someone giggled while Sam tried to struggle. Another blow to his stomach sent him to his knees, and thin saliva dribbled from between his lips. Black hair spilled over his friend's bleary, resentful eyes. Michael's thoughts flitted.

—Stop stay. Don't start nothin', no big *mucha mierda machista!* Last year here. Remember the *barrio* outside. That's what you always sayin', 'Last year, then *barrio* outside!'—

"Paul?" Michael asked. "Whas up?"

Whysees' faces turned toward him with looks of weary contempt.

No house. Boss Whysee said, 'No lunch,' Paul signed.

16

The Whysees filed out as the blonde one butted Michael's shoulder upon leaving. The hall tilted as his legs shuddered. Only one stayed to give orders. The top of the last one's head only reached beneath Michael's chin. Sam moaned as he pulled himself up, using Paul's wheelchair for support, and they both went back to their room. The short Whysee turned to Michael, raised a hand, and jabbered. Michael took Paul and Sam's cue and headed to his own room.

He scuffed over to the bed and removed his hearing aid, a pop in his ear. He placed it on the carpet and lay the weight of his head in his linked hands. His eyelids closed. Opened, then closed. His right wrist tickled. His left hand closed upon the wrist, and his fingers brushed the barcode etched into his skin. The number 123 was beneath the fine lines. His eyes burned, and he stamped on the mattress, his body bouncing with suppressed rage. His hands twisted around his blanket, and he stomped his heels.

—That's all? No words about me, no nice things, no name, nothing, just 123 no me. No! No way! No right talkin' down at me. Make me dog, woof good dog Michael, good dog! Them! Them like dogs! Kill off all of you, just off you, oh! You all die, get off me, get offa me!—

The door in the room rattled hard, and Michael stopped. He reached to the carpet to scoop his aid and put it in his ear. He could hear heavy pounds from the other side. The voice cried out through it.

"Own it en there! Umber un entee ee kee own in ere!"

"Okay," Michael said through clenched teeth. He took it off.

—Stupid short, stupid high squeaky voice thinks bigger than me, big bad ol' Whysee.—

His eyelids were ladened with sleepiness.

—Can't go like this. Why no girl love me? No smooth, fleshy girl to touch, stroke, and rub. (Supple tanned limbs, sweet dirty smells, the flesh of female hips around the waist to bury up and out and up and out.) Whysees, why won't let me out? Let me have one, oh please God! Just one! Get somethin.'

Nobody loves me. To sleep with a warm body, long hair, round bare shoulders, swells of boobs on my face, and my hands on her…—

No dream of a female body but only of home, dead and forgotten except in sleep.

—Seven me. Me is seven–year–old. Seven years old, age seven…—

His crusty eyes opened.

—Too late, nothin' to go to. Mom… Mom! Is someone cryin'? Dad's hand goes *sorry, sorry*. Me sayin' over and over, Clean. Cleeeeeeeean.' (A hockey stick with a red blade leans against the closet in the bedroom.)—

The last image faded from his morning slumber. The late noon sun poured through the window and onto his face. He shifted and held back from bursting into tears. Instead, he reached to the floor and put on his hearing aid. He got out of bed.

—Here again? What the… oh, Sam fell again and then they got us. Needles hurtin' my insides, heart putterin.' The hockey stick! Where did I drop it?—

Michael leaned over and reached under his bed. His hand brushed the dry wood of his hockey stick. It skidded as he pulled the stick and contemplated it. It was in a weary condition, and age had yellowed out the stick, the blade dark with oily stains.

—Might be its last year. Damn, a crack runnin' from handle. What am I to do now?—

He remembered the sensation of three years ago, winter biting into his skin, the hollow sound that a plastic blade makes scraping on the icy surface of the plaza. Then a whisk of a rock slab. The world slit as eyes find the target, a space between two stones, the goal posts. Three years ago, Sam's voice cried out, cracking with the onset of adolescence. His dark lips formed the words in his language. He held a flat board to block the shot.

—('Aha, *porqueria de* player!'

Then I go 'Just watch me, Sammy!')

He 'bout gonna copy my funny talk, maybe goin' 'Jus wath me!' I give that rock a whack. Then his eyes poppin' open and he duckin' his head, lookin' past between his legs, and the rock snug there in the goal behind him. Hockey stick in the air, me yellin', 'Ha! Goal, Peter!'

Sam looks at me funny and he goes, *'Por qué me llamas Peter?'*

Then my throat gets gummy and tries tightenin' my teeth not to cry 'cause daydream picture comin' up hard in the head.

(The image is Peter wearing a Flyers sweater in the wintertime. Then at school in spring, he wears a junior Watcher T–shirt. Mom's face comes up, crying, and she's signing, *please don't go over to Peter. They won't let you see him. He won't see you.*)—

His head lifted, his eyes damp.

—Freak.—

His body trembled.

—A freak, a shoelace body and a child's wobbling voice. Get out of here. Get me home. Don't know where I am. This place's all weepy and tired.—

He hauled himself to the window, the childhood sport equipment still in hand. His forehead pressed against the warmed glass, and the soft sunlight bore into his eyes.

—Past the fence, the *barrio*, the leaves don't rot. Bet they are bright, cracklin' when walk on them (red, yellow, burnt orange, peeking from between tobacco colors.) Should be fallin' soon. This time around September. Out there. No one to go, 'Ward, pick that, do that, ward take that there.' A girl lettin' me touch her body all over. Yeah, right. How could Mom let me get here?

'Mikey!' Dad yells and signs. 'It's not Mom's fault. It just happened.')

Yeah, Dad, everything. It's all tastin' bad in my mouth, needles of pain shootin' in my stomach. My belly all shriveled up. Dinner ends soon. Gotta go now.—

Kneeling as if in a prayer, he tucked it beneath the bed. He had to go now, soon leaking at the tip. He hurried out of his room. The door barely opened a crack, and the short Whysee trotted up, squabbling at him. Michael raised his hands in protest, mumbling.

"Sorry, I gos to go bathroom. Bathroom. If I don's I'll pee ous the winnow."

The Whysee guffawed at Michael's speech. After a friendlier wave toward the bathroom door, halfway through the hallway, Michael nodded. Another chuckle and the word, "winnow" from the short Whysee's mouth before Michael left him.

In the bathroom, he unzipped his pants at the urinal and let go, liquid streaming out and bladder emptying. Behind him, the odor of blood or metal. He twisted around and looked at one stall. Underneath the door of the stall, bare feet thick as hooves swung. A muffled sob came from there.

—Ungh. Why can't clean self? Sounds of a girl.—

"You all righ?" he called. He tucked and zipped up with care.

A high–pitched reply came, and he answered.

"I'm sorry buh I'm deaf an' can nos hear you. Gos to ree your lips. I will go now, sorry."

The stall door opened. An overweight girl sat on the toilet, sobbing. He washed his hands, thinking.

—Smart girl. Hooked her feet under the door and got me involved. Now gotta put up with her. Ugh, fat spreadin' out on the crapper. Why she not stay at the girls' dorms?—

His glance dipped, and he noticed dribbles of blood between her melting thighs.

—Guh! Say something, don't get into it, not your trouble. Might be retard girl. Not knowin' what is going on.—

Her mammoth body shivered and her swollen eyes, bloodshot from crying, looked up at him.

—Ugh talkin' slow. She knows I read lips sometimes.—

"Please," she blubbered. Her voice caught. Her gullet quivered as she tried to speak again.

"The Whysee..." she said, and several words after that. Then her lips blubbered. "Now look at me!"

Her blubbering tumbled into fresh tears. Michael kept his eyes averted from the girl's nakedness. Still, he could see rolls of flesh, the bloody wrinkled opening, and a tuft of damp pubes hair.

—Great, just great. How come she not plug it up?—

He moved to the next stall, grabbed a flimsy roll of toilet paper, and stepped in front of the girl.

—Hope she knows enough to do it.—

"Um, you gotta roll up like this."

He showed her by miming the pushing of the roll up into his crotch. She had her head lowered and her eyes wet.

—The stink. Why don't they clean more?—

Her thick fingers reached to the other roll of toilet paper hanging in the stall. With a snuffling noise, she rolled up her own paper. Her eyes fell upon him again. She questioned something, and he answered.

"Yes, yes. You gos to pus is up there."

"Where?" she asked him, her hands raised.

"You gos to do this," he said and mimed pressing it inside again.

"Eew!" she squealed. Her hands lowered to cover herself. "Will that, um, plug my hole?"

"Yeah. At leas I hope so." He became inspired to get away from her. "Hey, I'll ges the Whysee guy an' he'll help."

She begged him, saying something how she does not want them to know. He let the door shut behind him, cutting off her protests. The Whysee came up glaring.

"Please," Michael asked, his voice soft. "A girl in there with a perios. She's scares and confuses."

The Whysee groaned and rolled his eyes.

—Damn hungry. Nothin' there when I get there. Cafeteria better not end, just better not. Wait, he's sayin' something.—

"Ard?"

"Yes, and with a perios," Michael added right before he rushed away.

The Fight Outside

"Then I sae, 'Look you little shis, why don's you go in there an' check is ous yourself?'"

As he told his story to Sam Rueda and Paul Flounder, he looked past the cool spaghetti, one slippery strand on the scratched plastic plate, and saw inside his mind's eye a moment of childhood that appeared before him. From a strand of noodles to a worm in his memory.

—(Mom, on the lawn chair, mock threatens you to stop whining or she will have Dad put a worm in your mouth so it will slither *down your throat, wriggle around, tickle your tummy and make you laugh again.* Dad's palm holds out a tiny clump of grass. You believe that there is a worm wriggling among them, and he will do what Mom says. You stop crying. The sunlight bakes your bare back while the bricks and a black shingled roof pasted against the cloudless sky are behind Dad's grinning face.)—

The curdled milk on his tongue brought him back to Sam and Paul again. Sam kept nodding to Paul, his eyebrows raised, his face composed in fake earnestness.

It was hard to be friends with Sam, his lean arms crossed, a thrusting jaw, and a sloe–eyed gaze finishing with a droopy left eyelid. His face made him an older boy, the violent sort that demanded respect if not kindness. He only knew finger spelling, and whenever Paul's hands flitted in signs, he often looked away in discomfort, as if sign language were a display of an artistic or a feminine nature, a *pato*. But Michael had grown accustomed to Sam's dialogues that he could try seeing the words in rapid curls, raging red, cautionary yellow, burnt orange, in easy go–go green when he cooled to mild, and in times of helpless sorrow, shades of gray. He might have misunderstood Sam's entire speech but could track most words as if they were colors on a toucan's feathers from the years that he had spent with him. Besides, his hearing aid could pick up Sam's illegitimate *ingles* or/and *inglañol* if not his inflection.

Michael continued to search in his memory for what happened or what he wanted them to think happened, his mind running the images.

—(The short Whysee shrinks back from a hardened ward you, and he nods, a bobble–head doll.

Then you go, 'I best get movin' if I were you and don't want a foot up in my ass.')—

"An' then–" Michael continued, still caught up in his story.

"You *noquea al piso* outta of *de puro terco* your *novio*, and *los mistels* realized they shouldn't put *afflicciones* into *penas*, and we all lived happily ever after."

"No, no, I physically intimase him."

Paul raised his eyebrows over his glasses. He spoke and signed.

"You banged him? That's a clever way to get someone to help."

"No!" Michael shouted. "I use my size to push him aroun'."

Sam pretended to be in awe. "Your dick that big? *Ai!*"

"No! Jesus' sake-"

Paul helped Michael out. "He means intimidate."

"Yeah, shus up, Sam, whas Paul means."

Sam pointed at himself with a lazy grin and said, "Gonna make me?"

"Um no," Michael said. He stayed silent for a second. Then he asked, "Um… do you think someone can ever ges ous of here?"

"Ges ous of here?" Sam asked. Paul signed for him. "Hmm…., *pasas por Nat* and he'll ask the Whysees to let you

24

out and then the Whysees will check the general *populacion* and if they say, '*oh–key!*' then *zap* you're on your way home. Me, I'll ask St. Christopher Hospital to review my case, and they'll say that '*oh–key yo no naci un gen malo.*' Maybe we'll share a cab on way to home."

"I'm serious, Sam. Whas will iz take to ges ous?"

Sam spoke to Paul. Michael did not know what he said.

"Lot of memes," Paul intoned. His fingers spelled it as *M–E–M–E–S*.

Paul differed from Sam, able to flow through the days as a hearing who knew home signs he had picked up from Michael. He worked as a ward clerk at the Whysees' library inside the London building. Paul could shift in his mind and rationalize, in spoken and sign language in a way Michael's own cluttered mind never could. He was the connection, or the *el click* as Sam called it, between the spoken words and home signs when they could not understand each other.

One time Paul explained to Michael and Sam how memes work. An idea or a single meme exists in a person's mind. It fades with the person's death if the idea does not take hold. If that person records this idea online, then that meme becomes viral, planted in many minds. With luck, the memes can spread to the entire population, and they occur in a period of despair and hunger. It was just a theory, or a simple fused picture in a joke on the antiquated internet before they became government policies. It made Michael think of a germ. A starving germ.

Now Paul was laconic as Sam was. Hurt, Michael glanced at the windows. Through the glass, a small group of wards formed. Michael recognized Nat's bouncy blonde hair and the bald head of Eggy. Paul turned his head to follow Michael's line-sight and stopped laughing. Outside, the group spread. Their bodies separated, showing a quiver of heavy flesh between clothes. Sam's face hardened, and Paul clamped his hands on the rims of his wheelchair. Paul asked Sam something, his face bleak. The siren on the ceiling flashed, signaling lunch's end. Sam and Paul did not clean their plates, so Michael left his as he hurried after them. Soon, the doors of the cafeteria closed behind them, and Sam started shouting and moving up the concrete steps.

—What are they sayin' what they sayin'? Hey, that's Jose there and that girl from the bathroom.—

A deaf boy with a face like the underside of an iron jumped again, signing, *STOP! STOP!*

The girl huddled by the shrub. Someone had torn her dress along the strap.

"Paul! Whas everyone sayin'?"

S–A–M said, 'Leave her alone or anyone with gray armband going be hurt,' Paul signed while Sam voiced his threat. *'Nat said, 'B–U–T–T out Shakey.' Sam said, 'Oh? Cute name, how many year that take for you to come up with that? Go before you get on my nerves.'*

Above them, Sam advanced toward Nat. A large blockhead climbed the steps on the opposite part of the plaza, swinging his hammy arms. The bulky square face of the blockhead cleared the cobblestones. A moment later, Michael could see curly hair peeking from the collar of the blockhead's undershirt and his funny walk in size fourteen hiking boots, tattered and worn at the heels.

—Look, trash can with legs. So dumb know nothing except for the word deaf. But no one to fool with.—

Richie Trunk came up, signing to Sam.

NOT PLAY ME.

Paul interpreted as Sam above, exclaimed with his usual tact.

Oh great, a fat ugly deaf signing to me.

Trunk scowled at that, although no one told him what Sam had said. Nat and Sam circled each other, Nat's voice was high and stringy while Sam's own lowered into snarls. Sam reached out and grabbed Nat by the throat and shouted something. Trunk stomped behind Sam with his hairy hand knotted into a fist.

—Sam, look too late.—

Trunk had his left arm wrapped around Sam's neck, his fist hammering him, and Nat started spitting on him.

—Those scabby…—

He felt a tug on the tail of his shirt.

"Michael!" Paul shouted.

Below and to his side, he saw Paul's irritated face.

You want to watch them or see me sign?

"Um, both."

Sam grimaced as Trunk's fist thumped his back.

—Sam's in trouble now. See what you got yourselves in stupid… get to help him.—

Michael thought to move, but his legs rooted.

—Just run the steps and give a few hits. They won't know it's you. Should I? Should I not?—

As if his feet decided for him, he started moving. The fight had looked slow and stiff before Michael helped Sam. Now everything moved fast.

"Michael!" Paul shouted.

The stairs hurled beneath him.

—Hope I can jump really high, a wild yell then oh! Right on Trunk's back and spinning, owiiee!—

Trunk's body fat vibrated with his grunts of pain, and Michael's hands dug into his thick face, rubbery and firm clay. Something heavy pounded his back, and he felt Trunk's fingertips digging into his spine. The world flipped, concrete slamming into his back. He saw Nat falling too, holding his bloody nose. His back wrenched, he could not breathe.

—Can't think, UhhuhUhhuhHUHhuhhuhhuh, yes, can breathe now, thank you, Jesus.—

The stomping shoes broke apart, and a brown haired Whysee's face appeared above everything, his brow lowered in confusion.

—Oh, great. Here we go again.—

Memory In Dream

Before the hallway, the girl in the bathroom, and the fight in September, he dreamt. He was at his home back in Pennsylvania, and it moved to its swift end, so it was too late to change a thing.

—Michael was seven years old. 7.

(Scent of soap on female feet, legs firm and supple.

'Hey Michael, you know... smells of *oceano* up there, mmmm. Oh, *lo siento*, didn't know I was talkin' to the Virgin *Marcos*.')

Oh yeah, Sam? Well, you.... shut up.

You are seven. (Warm light from window turns shady.)

God, God, God... wish I can... where am I?

(Dad sits across the round kitchen table, his rough hands signing. *Michael, everyone is asleep now. Walking around as if wonderful thing happen, face shining.*

Mom sits on the other side in her red dotted dress that she wears to church. Her wavy hair covers her inside–the–ear hearing aid. Dad shivers, his lean arms bunching, and he has a grim smile.)

No! They are coming for you. Oh, God! Help! Help! No, no, no! We lost! Melting away! It's gone! Too late! Too late!

(Somewhere a child's high laughter etches through the windows of the kitchen. The table, Dad, Mom, and the kitchen cabinet fade.)

Children laugh all the time in school. I hate them. They make my days just not alright or bad. No fair.

(On alright days, the classroom door is closed and harsh discomfort wafts underneath. The class stare and here's you all over again. Watching them and Mrs. Lowenna's eyes feint hard at you. Gotta sit apart from the others, right? Don't wanna be within reach of the grownups. Her talk, everyone else understands. Why can't you? You lost! You and Mom. Then the stranger came over to take you away and you're gonna lose. Mom... when that day near the fence... no more Mom.)

No! Don't wanna think anything. Lemme alone! Lemme alone!

(You are apart from others. And we're back to you, a little boy on the carpet. A spider spins a web near one window, the narrow kind with metal handles. The colors of the books on the shelves capture your gaze. No one will sign what Mrs. Lowenna said. Mrs. Lowenna gives her lessons in a bright sing–song voice, her eyes shifting to you, not upset but uncomfortable. You sit alone.

Some children point at you and whisper to each other about you, you think. Ahh hick! You. Ah tick! you. Woch your T and D. One time on a bad day, Douglas is hall monitor. He does not let you use the bathroom that's around the corner. No, you gotta use far bathroom on first floor, the one for the retards and dummies. You run hard, but your legs burn, and pants dampen. Children point at you. Douglas, his face twisted, pushes you away. Others crowd around, faces awash from light shining through the glass entrance door. You all spill outside, you cryin', a little sissy Mikey.)

Shut up! Shut up! Lemme alone! Hurts!

(They sing nursery song, a new one, and you huddle against the white brick wall and try to sing along so they'll like you and stop bothering you. You blubber nonsense that the children sing except theirs are words while yours are gobbles. Let us see how it goes? Oh yes:

Ah! her eh Eeeeee
Uh the Eeeeee
Or In Oooooooohhh

And you look and sound stupider. They laugh and you wanna fall into a big peaceful hole, deep and dark in you go. A tan station wagon pulls up near the parking lot. Mom! The door slides open. First, her sandaled foot shows, then the rest of her scrambles out, her mouth a hollering O. Her legs and waist wade into the crowd, and you cry harder reaching up to her. Grown—up hands pull you up from the mass of children and you bounce on her stomach and breasts as she carries you away, the violet in the air from her soap. Her hair tickles your face and you just put your arms around her tight as she carries you to the waiting car and puts you in. As other parked cars and trees roll outside the side window, Mom steers with one hand and signs with the other, her face tearful and angry.

I look and look for you everywhere. I D–I–D not see you until you come out with the children. Let it out, cry it out all you want. We never come back here.

You love her so much you forgive her for the times she made you stay in and eat dinner when you want to go out to play hockey and hollering at or slapping you for saying 'Ffff… or Shhh…!')—

When Michael napped, his face became more troubled. He moaned, and his empty stomach clutched.

—(Mom and Dad sit there around the table again. Their features twitch, both trying to hide their fear.)

Oh, Mom and Dad. We're going to lose. I love you, but we're gonna lose. Gray Man is going to bring out that big plastic picture with the gold seal on it to take me and Mom away. Poor Dad is crying on the couch alone.

(A sharp knocking.)—

The eternal sound continued. It breached time itself to exist in Michael's dream; bad old days gone but still locked inside the cavern of his mind.

—(Dad's head raises, and he talks, his tone flat without signing. The acts of a careful stranger.)

'No signing today because the tester is coming. Woch your T and D Michael.'

30

'Okay.'

Mom's hand clutches at yours. God, it hurts how hard she holds it. The kitchen melts, and you are in the living room. At the window of the front door, a sallow man stands outside. His knuckles tap on the glass and the sun shines bright behind him, so his figure turns dull, even gray. Dad's hand pulls the door open and lets the stranger come in. The stranger blocks the doorway with a briefcase and a retro mini camera in either hand. His smile is wide, but sharp eyes glint through the steel–frame glasses from his round, hollow–cheeked face. Iron–colored hair plasters across his brow, and he looks boyish although he claims sixty as his age. He'll say such as he turns around in the passenger seat and signs *6–0*. You are on your way to the local authorities for *T–A–G*. The driver is a blonde man who is the Gray Man's younger partner. Mom will smile and sign.

6–0–old. A 6–0 man fool us. He must be wise to get such a smart boy.)

Wait, that comes much later. We thought we could win, but we lost.

(Dad steps aside and the Gray Man… his name is Dennis Speeling. Don't call him the Gray Man! Mr. Speeling moves in with a wide, jovial smile.) Oh, what does it matter? (The Gray Man's overcoat brushes you as he sets the camera on top of the grandfather clock Mom hates so much. The red–light blinks on from the antique machine. Mom is first.

He directs her to turn around, reaches into his briefcase and pulls out a tennis ball, a chalky green ball with two wavy lines, swollen with malice. So fearful he holds yours and Mom's world as he hefts it. He lets it drop.

Pitt.

You hear the sound and oh, God, yes! Mom hears it too as she nods. From the opened case, he takes out a baseball and drops it.

Clunk.

Mom tilts her head, and she laughs, saying something. Dad nods. Time to get out of the test.

'Mis tick! er Speeling, can I go ou tick! and deh—tick! play?'

The tester's own hands move.
Go now. You are excuse from test.
Ooh, a trick.
'Mister Speeling, can I go play?'
'He said, 'Wait for test first.'' Dad says.
'Okay, Mr. Speeling.'

Mom sniffs and says something. Dad says something. Mr. Speeling speaks, his finger pointing at the camera. When it makes music, it signals the end of every hour with chimes. Which means once music plays, it will be over. Mr. Speeling speaks to Mom and Mom nods. One more thing, just one more, and Mom will finish. Mom turns her back and the old man raises the tennis ball. He bounces it. One. Two. Three. Then he lets it dribble four or five times, and it rolls near the couch. Mom's face tightens and her lips purse. You scoot and kick the ball under the couch. Mr. Speeling's teeth show.

'Goal!' You crow as you lift your arms toward the ceiling.

Mr. Speeling's thin lips move.
'Don't do that, young man.'

Dad snaps at you. You, strong and brave, walk over to the Gray Man and kneel by the couch to hunt for the ball. The fuzzy green ball turns into a planet eclipsed by the unseen space of the universe as you reach in and grab it. Someone picks you up, and it is Dad.

'Listen to him,' Dad demands. His face hidden from Mr. Speeling; he gave you the slightest sober nod.

The old man's bright eyes fall upon you.
'Your turn,' his lips say.

Then Mr. Speeling mutters something to Dad and Mom's face brightens. Not waiting for Dad's reply, Mom strolls into your room and comes back with your favorite eBook, *Poems and Rhymes*, downloaded on your tablet.

Oh, that stupid Gray Man! Doesn't he know you practiced speech and listening using that? Why, you know the words! You snort as the old man looks at the tablet and says the lines as you pretend to listen and repeat them.

'Own en urree.'

'Brown and furry,' you say.

'Aerpill n urree.'

'Caterpillar in a hurry.'

'Ae or all.'

'Take your walk.'

'Aye ye.'

You don't know that word. Quick, what is it? Something… something about a tree, um…

'Don't know that word,' you say aloud.

Mom shouts something in a voice. 'Adee! Like a tree!'

Mr. Speeling glances at Mom's sheepish face and then back.

'Or uh ot.'

'Or what not.'

'It aw be osen ot.'

'Which may be the chosen spot.'

'Oh, roe to I you.'

'No toad to spy you.'

'Overin ir of ray as by you.'

'Over in bird of prey pass by you.'

Dad's two fingers shift from his closed hand to sign H behind Mr. Speeling's back.

'Hovering!' you shout.

Mr. Speeling continues.

'In or I. Ooh ive a utter rye.'

'Spin or die.'

'To live a butterfly.')

You're finished. And you are safe. No, I am not.

(Dad takes the tablet from Mr. Speeling and goes to your room. Mr. Speeling raises his head, dismayed at the clock. The clock hands are at three and the long hand at twelve. He glances at his watch. He closes the briefcase and walks to the camera. Mom reaches to turn the doorknob.

'Goodbye, Mr. Speeling,' Mom says in a clear, manifested tone.

At that moment, you can hear the moans of the clock playing a distant lost tune, a ghost. It gongs three times. And gone is all hope.

Dad comes into the room and sees Mr. Speeling collect the camera from the top of the clock. He tucks it under his arm and grasps the suitcase from the couch with his other hand.

'What?' Dad says his voice faint.

Finish. I have on tape. Your wife and son don't hear the music on the clock.

Mom's face turns sullen.

Good try, the Gray Man signs. He steps outside, and the door snicks shut behind him.)—

Words To Live By

Thin men stand in row
Cool hard won't let me go
E–I–E–I–O
Let me go!
Thin men in row pinch my hands
What are they? 1

Crystal clear
Colors of black tears
Lines around number
Wanna make me holler
Go away chain!
Out of my hand!
Holding me here
Under my wrist
What is this? 2

Eater of sky
Between day and night
What am I? 3

They got brooms
Sweep us in rooms
Drum down
Not my own
Black brooms
Black booms
Roots halves splitting in middles
Can you answer this and riddles? 4

Chunky tomato soup
Falling out of ears
Where I am near
Jumps the leg log
Move like the bug
Pete is my name!
What I see not game!
Break away from thin men
One dances east
One falls south
Two follow meet west and north
Black broom sweep
Boy jump east cheep
And weep
No place to cradle in. 5

WARDS' WORK SCHEDULE

0600 TO 0700 WAKE UP
0810 TO 1210 on Saturdays ROLL CALL
0710 TO 0910 BREAKFAST
10:00 TO 1410 on Sundays WASH
0910 TO 1110 LABOR
1110 TO 1310 LUNCH
1310 TO 1610 LABOR
1610 TO 1800 DINNER
1800 TO 2100 LABOR
2100 TO 2200 HOUR OF REST
2200 TO 0600 LIGHTS OUT

RULES

1. Always obey a Watcher.
2. Check the Workboard for the task that matches your barcode number.
3. Do the work assigned to your number and complete it.
4. Always cooperate with blockheads, the wards with gray armbands.
5. OBEY ALL RULES ORDERS AND REQUESTS OF WATCHERS.
6. DO NOT argue, plead, shout, infer with a Watcher. No stalling, no pleading gestures, or facial expressions showing displeasure.
7. DO NOT fight, bite, hit, pinch, kick at other residents, block leaders, and the Watchers. If so, punishment will be swift.
8. DO NOT stay in the cafeteria after the flashing siren goes off.
9. DO NOT protect another ward from justified punishment. If so, punishment is on you.
10. DO NOT LEAVE. GENERAL POPULATION IS HOSTILE.

THE MESSAGES ON THE BATHROOM WALLS

WHEN GETCHA OUT
WILL FUCK PEFECT BITCHES IN ASS
FROM HERE TO L.A.
MAK SUCK THERE SHIT FROM MY DIK!
SHOVE IN HOT BITCHES ASHOLES
hear! hear! Ha ha!

I luv suck cocks!
me too.
met me room 209
wear something red.

unsoft broken bitter
without muchrooms and
catapillars close by bees
flowers and butterflies
a hive to die Wish I fly
What am I? <u>6</u>

HANDYTOWN HERE I COME!
LEROy here. Wish I wasn't.
Me name Joseph
I am afraid.
      Me too E.K.   I have baby in 209!

Roll Call

After the fight, the Whysees came in their gray tunics with the same leader. The leader jotted their numbers in the notebook that he had produced from his pocket. The only thing that stood out was the leader's look of mild irritation when Michael clasped his hands and said, "Oh please, no respors, oh Gos, please." causing Sam to bite his lower lip in stifled laughter. The leader's shaded eyes had glittered at him from beneath the brim of his hat. Then he spoke in a soft, heavy voice, a promise of consequences to come. That had made Michael's body turn into a brittle husk. The blonde Whysee was the one who shouted and pushed.

The daily life got to Michael. In five years, the surroundings grew to feel like home. The faces of the strangers grew known, and their voices. The way they spoke settled in his memory and words anticipated, if not signed, by them yet. The female ward was still too learning the *A–B–C*, and Michael avoided his roommate, Henry Trotter, for now. Soon Michael will grow to know Henry and Nancy and be able to fill in brief guesses of words that his deafness prevented him from knowing. It started with a tap on his shoulder, a timid tap on his shoulder.

—Oh great. What's she lookin' at me for? Just a retard. Nothin' much.—

Her eyes squinted beneath raised eyebrows as she smiled.

—Bet she's scared of botherin' me. Ought not wear same dress. Oh great, openin' her mouth talkin' to me.—

Michael had made up for his lateness yesterday by coming out early today. Pride swelled in him as Whysees gave him crisp nods of approvals. But now, he had to tolerate her. She looked up at him, her hands plucking at the dress she had bled on yesterday.

"Hi," the girl squeaked.

Michael nodded and turned to the dorm. His throat tightened.

—Don't they gotta hold separate places for her and Huh–huh–huh–Henry? Why not keep them away from me?—

There was another tug on his shirttail, and he turned, his arms twitching.

"Hi." Her puffy lips framed each word. "My name is Nancy Wellfil. Do you have a name?"

Michael nodded again and turned away. The flashes stopped as the last few wards streamed out. Her plump hand touched his elbow. Nancy smiled at him. Her eyes glimmered. Her chapped lips moved again. She spoke several words, and Michael did not understand. She continued talking, oblivious how he kept glancing away. Sam finally came out, his face untroubled by their warning yesterday as he pushed Paul in his wheelchair. Michael felt another poke in his side.

"Does it feel you're standing in a graveyard?" Nancy asked, her gaze direct. Her eyes scrutinized him as her face turned somber. Her cheeks bulged again for her uneasy smile.

—Fog rolls in. Way she gets me sad.—

"That's how I–" Nancy said.

"I see my friens now, gos to go."

Michael hurried away.

The day lagged as he lugged the wheelbarrow loaded with bricks from the ruins of one building by Farrow Field. He lugged it through the underground parking lot to the receiving dock. Since the wards who labored by the ruins had to pass through the parking lot beneath the plaza, two Whysees have been stationed to watch them. So far, there have been no complaints. At night during free time, he ventured out by the football field to run hard. He needed to release suppressed rage from seen and unseen forces repressing him to the air. It only made him more tired, but at least he would not lie awake thinking helpless, angry thoughts.

When flashing lights woke him on Friday morning, he subtracted himself one day from the seventeenth year of his life. From morning to noon, he swept the sidewalks around the ruins of old buildings, his mind numb from boredom until he spotted the few hearing wards among them reacting to the bell from the tower. Relieved from his shift, he leaned the red dusted push broom against the pile of broken bricks for the next shift and plodded to the cafeteria.

He stood in line behind Sam, who picked up two plates, one for Paul and one for himself, and plopped them onto his tray. Before Michael could reach for his own tray, he felt the timid tap again, and Nancy peered up at him.

"Thank you, thank you. You helped me back then. I was real scared," she said, her eyes threatening to fill.

Michael noticed Sam's sly grin and said, "Thas okay. Jus some advice." He turned to pull his own tray from the stack by the serving line. Nancy started babbling about something to Sam. Michael tried to ignore her.

—Stinkin' of pennies and sweaty. Same ol' dress again should be keepin' clean. For Chris'sake.—

A damp, soft hand fell on the crook of his elbow. Sam raised his empty plate over his mouth, holding back a snicker. Michael tugged his elbow away from Nancy's grasp. She repeated what she might have said before, "If there's anything I could do, anything" and picked up a tray.

Sam gave Michael a slow wink.

"Thas all righ," Michael said. "No problem."

"No *hay problema*," Sam echoed, his eyebrows raised. When Nancy turned away from him, Sam pretended to swoon with a dreamy sigh.

"Anything I do," Nancy repeated.

She reached over for her own plate, brushing Michael, and he froze. Sam tilted into Michael's line of sight, pointed to her buttocks, and made a grabbing motion, his face urgent.

Michael shook his head, and Sam looked away, covering his mouth as Nancy straightened and smiled again. They got their food and Paul's food, too. Michael, holding his own plate of mysterious gray and orange meat with graying potatoes, followed Sam to where Paul waited, reading a book. Sam nudged Michael, almost spilling their food.

"She likes you."

"Sorry, I'm nos into retars."

Sam grimaced and looked past him. Michael turned and saw Nancy brake in her track, her eyes wide. His hearing aid picked up the sound of the plate clattering on her tray. She whirled and carried her food over to where people same as her sat. Her body hunched, she sat and munched at her food, still gazing at the floor. Sam's face twisted in disgust.

"Whas Sam? Jus the way is."

Those in wheelchairs and braces sat near the entrance, except for Paul, who was with Sam and Michael. Nancy and Henry sat near the center of the cafeteria, an island of uncertain faces, a few with wrinkled eyelids and most with sluggish bodies. The blockheads, the ones with the gray armbands, had entrenched themselves close to the serving lines. Nat ate his meal, stringy blonde hair dangling about his face. Eggy sat right, plucking at the string and probing his meat with a fork. Others, along with Richie Trunk, ruled their tables. The two blockheads for the female wards were Kelly, her pug nose snorting as her thick lips slurped at her potato, and Terry Dimitri, her name sign a finger tracing the outline of half her face to define her beauty and use the sign for the letter D. She nibbled at her meat.

—Who could fear her? (Blue shiny eyes, tanned skin, and dolly lips.)—

The largest group by three quarters were the deaf. It was full of moving hands and rapid faces as they talked. At Michael's table, Sam put a plate of food on the table for Paul and sat to his own meal. He whispered something to Paul, who put aside his book. Paul tried to keep his face composed but broke and giggled, his mouth spraying a spit of gristle.

"Whas you sayin' whas!"

He tell me you S–T–U–D, Paul signed.

"Thanks Sam. Thanks a los."

Sam covered his mouth in a fake alarm and leaned back, smirking.

"You're sus an ass."

Sam nodded, eyes and mouth wide in eagerness.

"You seriously are!"

"Well, I don't go about snobbin' retards." He pushed his nose up and pointed at Michael.

"Thas because you wool go for anything with a hole."

Paul snorted.

"Do I?" Sam asked Paul.

Paul nodded.

"Oh serious, Michael? *Oh–key*, maybe you have a point there."

Michael burst into laughter.

Sam asked, "How come you let her down?"

"I don's do no retars." He picked up the plastic fork and speared his food. "I don't think they fis with us. In here, ah leas I gos my standars."

He gestured with his fork toward the ruins seen through the window. Paul made a slashing motion across his neck. Michael looked to his side, where someone stood glaring. A scrawny girl with eyes that swelled through buggy and thick lens glasses rocked on her heels. She hitched her pants and screwed her face, her knuckles to her waist.

"Not funny!" she screeched.

—This is what you are: (a mousy boy cringing from a retard girl who keeps dominating him with her voice.) Don't back down now. Not when Sam is talkin', 'Michael goin' *loco* and jumpin' on Richie's back.'—

"So whas you goin' do abou it?"

Nancy called from her table, and the skinny girl shouted back and flounced off.

"Whas was thas all abous?" Michael asked.

"Not funny!" Sam pretended to pull up his pants and glared at Michael. "Stop laughing, not funny!"

They, except for Paul who rolled his eyes, laughed. Sam's head twitched, and he stopped. He pushed himself away from the table and dropped himself off the chair.

"Flas," Sam said, his eyes far and gone in their sockets.

Paul winced and rolled himself back as Michael rushed to Sam's chair to move it from the bucking body.

On Saturday, the air remained tepid. Wards, most deaf and accustomed to scheduled routine, awakened to blue lights again and were herded to Farrow Field for roll call. Again, Michael's puckish flesh was poked at, and he was prodded in the hallway, this time by Richie Trunk,

—Trunk. With a head of tree trunk. Stump. Stumped Trunk. Should rip into his fat face with my fingernails.—
only to stumble onto the plaza with the other harried wards.

Tendrils of faded morning light crept into the tattered and stained clothes, meaty stench pungent with sweat on sallow flesh. Whysees wedged in and out from clumps of crowds, their faces remote and their slashed mouths muttering impatient orders for the wards to hurry to the empty bleachers that lay dull under sunrise.

Michael waited with the others near the chain–linked fence, odorous bodies of others smearing his senses. Vague faces bulged too near, and mumbling voices jammed between unbearable silences. The crowd from the highest steps pushed forward, the skin on his chest mashing against the numbing wires of the fence. Michael grinded his teeth.

—Watch the front, retards.—

At each open gate, two Whysees stood, optical scanners ready in their clenched hands. Paul was being carried down the steps, his face set, and his hands clenching the rims of his wheelchair. The clinks of the metals and braces jangled through the hearing aid, tickling his ear.

—Can't take more of these halting lousy stupid hummingmmmmmmmmmmmmmmmmmmmmmmmmmmmmm mmmmmsoundsoooeHuhnnnOOOooooooooooOoooooowee ooooEEEEEEuuunnnghnnninside my head so bad you wanna claw right in bony head and mash them in.—

Michael wondered how long he could rely on the battery without charging it and he needed to do it after dinner because the electricity gets turned off along with lights. He groaned, pressing his hand to his forehead. The blocks of lines rippled as wards in the front wandered to Farrow Field after the Whysees checked their codes. He stumbled once in the late morning, and Paul, on the field, signed to him to ask if he was okay. He waved back and nodded. Exhaustion numbed his head, and hunger dulled his mind. Each second of the seventeenth year of his one life ticked away, robbed by the slow movements of the wards in front. It seized inside his chest, second by second gone and hoping nothing would come of this: not a rebuke, a hard stare, nor a grab from a Whysee.

A deaf ward near the first opened gate signed to an indifferent Whysee how he is the one who gets up first. An obese girl by the next gate submitted, her head stooped and docile as the Whysee ran the scanner over her wrist. Michael was jostled, and he moved down one step with the others in his row.

—Oh, here we go. All eager and nice to be helpin' the Whysees. That get them to like you? Yeah, uh–huh, right. They still think you're the best of us?—

Steps below, the girl turned to look at him and smiled.

—Oh, her. Don't encourage her. Name is… oh, yeah, Nancy. Just a retard like Henry. Should remove them. Damn it! Waiting for everything.—

Each minute lost; the sun shone higher in the sky, warming the damp field ahead. Michael could study the Whysees. The Whysee at the gate ahead (Michael assumed) focused on keeping his face smooth as he passed the scanner over a chubby boy's wrist. Further away and below, Nancy waited to go on the field. The Whysee waved her past and her

45

row marched onto the field. She smiled and joined Jose, who signed a greeting. Her fingers formed letters, but she was too far to tell what. The newcomers on the field soon swallowed them. Faraway figures in uniforms strolled along the crowd of wards, faces blurry from the distance. An iron fence had been put up opposite Farrow Field, further away. That fence ran around the Gate Institute, separating the compound from Handytown District. Seen through the bars, older youths of Handytown walked the avenues, signing while others kept their heads stooped or stared.

—Next year gonna be walkin' the streets like them in the *barrio*.—

Someone pulled his arm, breaking into his overlapping thoughts.

HURRY! A scrawny boy signed, *HURRY MOVE!*

His thin fingers were spidery with speed, and he made a funny buzzing noise as he signed. Even the boy's cultivated mustache vibrated with impatience.

Michael mimicked the boy's voice. "Mmmurreee mmmmm ammmm moooove immm."

He turned and stepped down. The line moved. Someone poked him on the shoulder, and he whirled around, breathing hard.

NO SNOB. The same boy signed with a toss of his head, peering downward at him, mimicking superiority. Then the boy folded his arms and nodded, his mouth pinched. *YOU NO ABOVE YOUR SIGN SLOPPY.*

So what?

MAYBE YOU WANT SAME HEARING. The boy jerked his head toward the Whysees. *WHY? FRIENDS WHOOSH!* He finished the insult by sweeping his hand across his mouth as if mocking dust.

Michael reassured himself by looking at Sam, who stood near the top of the steps. Then Michael took the last step, held out his right arm, and fixed an easygoing smile for the Whysee. The Whysee grabbed his hand to pull him for the scanner. He grunted as he was jerked downward and to the side. Then he was let go and the guard, face twisted with impatience, waved him toward the field. He tried a nod, looking for any sign of friendliness in the Whysee's eyes but finding weary scorn. He trudged toward the field and waited with Paul for Sam.

I am sick of this, he signed to Paul.

Paul glanced toward the iron fence separating Farrow Field from the Handytown District before he replied. *You and everyone else. Try to stand this one more year. Then we will be out here and over there.*

Just another place with a fence around us. Wish not have to be here.

Careful what you wish for. Look, let us not get into this.

Paul's head turned to stare up the slope, where Sam waited. Michael looked too. The crowd parted, the wards behind the chain–link fence spreading out. Something had happened to Sam.

Hope Sam not get into another fight, Paul signed.

He wheeled himself toward the fence where many more waited. Michael followed and saw Sam's jiggling body between the legs of the wards.

—Oh, again third time this week?—

Michael's walk broke into a run, and the Whysee boy held up his hand. The run came to a stop.

"Please les me see my frien' okay?"

One Whysee near him regarded him while the other Whysee made shooing gestures. On the steps above, Sam's pants blurred in convulsions. Paul rolled up and spoke to the first Whysee. A circle of gawking wards formed around Sam, the backs of their heads craning. Paul's voice rose in frustration. Someone brushed by, and it was Nat, his face snotty with pitiful authority. Paul shouted at Nat, and the Whysee shouldered between them and stuck his finger at Paul's face, ordering him.

"Is over," Michael said, peering at Sam's legs, which had stopped moving.

Paul backed away and maneuvered his wheelchair closer to the fence. Nat seized the handlebars, giggling. The Whysee shouted at Nat and whirled, his boot kicking at the metal plates of Paul's footrests. Paul hollered, grabbing the rims of the wheels to keep them from turning him. Michael exploited the distraction and pretended not to see the second Whysee shouting as he clambered for the fence. His legs swiveled over the bar. A piece of his shirt caught on the chain-links and the bar. He stopped to tug it off the wires.

—Keep movin.' Pretend you don't know they are yellin' at you.—

He teetered on it and freed himself. His ankles bones rattled as his sneakers hit the ground on the other side. He stumbled when he broke through the crowd to Sam's prone body. His hand pressed upon Sam's shoulder. Sam's eyes opened and his face filled with misery.

"*Mierda.* Again, damn it. People looking at me."

"Is all righ. People look when they sign."

He helped roll Sam to the side and up, grunting from the weight. By then the gray uniforms surrounded them, faces irritated. Sam held up a free hand to signal that he wouldn't inconvenience them further. One of them grabbed the hand and ran the scanner over it. Then another Whysee waved them through to the field. On the way to Farrow Field, Sam moved Michael's grip off him and stopped, his face troubled. Then he grabbed Michael's elbow.

"Talk to you later, Michael?"

"Yeah, okay."

"I got to see the doctor first."

Sam did not answer as he looked toward the bleachers. Michael could see the crowd dwindling to a few wards.

"I hope we don't have to wae long."

Paul wheeled himself to them.

I can see the car, he signed.

Michael looked up the slope where the trimmed hedges stood behind the bleachers. A white Oldsmobile pulled over and parked. The shaded figure inside the car opened the door.

Limp strands of blonde hair and a wrinkled face appeared over the roof of the car. Michael knew him as Dr. Broom, who checked the wards' health once a week. The doctor made his way on the steps to one gate and, with a low kick of his leg, saluted one Whysee. The Whysee snapped a salute before opening the gate. Two other Whysees set up a coffee table by the goal post.

"I got to see him," Sam said, and he followed some others to the coffee table.

On Saturdays, the doctor would visit the Gate Institute to check on the wards. All female wards were encouraged to see the doctor if they had stomach pains, experienced nausea, or missed their periods. If any female wards do, they must visit the Health Center before next week. Sam tried patience and waited near the group around the table. Most of the deaf wards found the doctor who used gestures charming. Dr. Broom clutched his stomach in pretend agony for the first ward, and for the second one he acted as if he were vomiting. Some wards got into the game and acted out their illnesses. Sam, at the side of the crowd's edge, stood on his toes and tried peering in between the shoulders of the other wards.

"Is Sam all righ?" Michael asked Paul.

Paul looked over to Sam and signed, *He don't have more medication for his seizure.*

Michael saw the back of Sam's lowered head when the crowd shifted. Paul straightened in his wheelchair.

"Whas Paul?"

Four Whysees hustled over to the crowd around Dr. Broom.

Wait, he is yelling something.

Speckles of gray waded into the crowd.

"Whas with Sam?"

I don't see him now. Wait, they move him out.

By the card table, two more Whysees surrounded Sam, who kept yelling over their shoulders. Sam stalked away and plopped on the grass, his head in his hands. He started pulling up the grass, his mouth twisted.

"Shool we go to him, Paul?"

Paul's eyes were wide behind his glasses. *If you want to, be my guest. I will let him cool off, though.*

Michael swallowed hard, his throat clicking.

"Nah, better les he settle a little. Besigh, will be a few minutes 'til he calms down some."

He sat and stretched out his legs.

—Nice to sit or lay down if want to do it. Only in fall. In winter, long time to wait in the chills after chills.—

While the last wards pantomimed their sickness, the sun was a quarter past the zenith of the sky. Sam's shoulders lowered, and he sighed.

Finally, Paul signed.

He pushed himself toward the fence to be carried up the steps. While the Whysees carried the wards with mobile disabilities as if they were sacks of potatoes to the road, Michael waited. Sam sat further away, picking bits of grass and tossing them. With the first group placed upon the road, the rest can go. Michael walked with the crowd.

He felt a poke in the shoulder, and he turned to see Sam giving him an awkward grin.

"Hi, Michael."

Michael gave him a querying look. Sam shrugged.

"That? That's just the *medico* not giving me prescripts for my pills. They said they can't give me pills unless prescribed by a personal *medico*, and who gets one around here?"

"How mush you pay for them?"

"*Que gracioso eres.*"

Sam stalked ahead. Michael caught up to him.

"Sorry, I was jus foolin'."

"Yeah. Hilarious."

They walked in silence.

"Umm, Michael?"

"Yeah?"

Sam looked into the distance, then back. "How long we know each other?"

"Sunno, guess four or five years."

50

"You know the pills I am taking?"

"Yeah, for your seizures."

Sam paused with a smile, shamefaced. "I keep *avanzando* without *los mistels* knowing."

"Sam! If they knew…"

"See, I'll be up the ass without a condom. But I can't stand this." Sam shook his arms. "I feel stupid when I wake up. But they're watching me. I just got caught two days ago."

"Whas dis they do to you?"

"Sent for *los mistels*. It was my first offense. Well, first time I got caught."

"Sorry 'bou tha."

Sam burst laughing.

"Whas?"

Sam nodded and held up his hand. "Just thinking about when you jumped on that dickhead Trunk's back."

—(Wild–eyed deaf coolly leaping on Stumped Trunk's back.)

Would've kicked his ass if Whysees hadn't come. Yaaaaaahhh! Don't take me down, man. Nobody can take me. Too fast and wild.—

"I saw you jumping, and I went…." Sam's eyes bugged out, and he did a double take. "Holeeee– *mierda*, *loco* Michael, aww man you so *loco*, you even me *asustaste*."

"I dis?"

"Yeah, you're *loco* man. Messed up in the head."

—Yeah, once me get messed up, just stay out of my way. Yarrrgarrgh!—

"Nice."

"I think, here this *amigo loco* messed up, he'll just walk into the health clinic and stroll out with Die lay tin pills. He can bang a female nurse or fucking two just for the fun."

"Ah…"

"You're *loco*, right? Michael. I always told Paul that. 'Don't push Michael. He's *loco*.'"

"I guess…"

"Yeah, you can do it."

"Um…"

"Yeah! It's the one in blue box and it's spelled *D–I–L–A–N–T–I–N*…" After fingerspelling, Sam showed him the measurements with his hands. "And this big… and in it, triangular pills." He showed him the shape using his hands.

"Aw, come on, Sam. Don's call me thas…"

"And it's room one oh two, in the cabinet above the sink."

"How wool I get in?"

"Easy. I took the trouble to think it out for you. Just pretend you're hurt or sprained your wrist or something at work. It's in Health Center. You know where?"

"Bus I'll ges in frouble."

"Life's full of risks. It's up there at the corner…"

"No, Sam."

They stopped by the plaza. Sam stared; his hands open.

"*Vamos*, Michael. You can come through. When I flas fall and I opened my eyes and I saw your face above, I felt you are there for me."

"I can's. Sorry."

"I need you."

"Sorry, man. I wool like to bus I don's wanna frouble."

Sam blinked.

"*Oh–key* then," he said. His eyes brimmed. He twisted away to stomp the stairs to their dorm.

The Girlman headed for an empty table and sat by himself in the corner of the cafeteria. The blue shirt was open, so the areolas showed through his undershirt.

"I los my appesie."

Michael let the fork clink on the table. Half–eaten bread joined the fork by the grayish meat. He pressed his eyes with the heels of his hands.

"God, is wool be grae if I leave this place."

Sam made his way to the table. He stepped as if walking on glass barefoot. He gave a crestfallen glance at Michael before he sat across from him.

Last year then Handytown, Paul signed.

"Neas, maybe we'll paree or something."

—Yeah party. Sam with *chicas,* Paul playin' DJ music 'cause can't dance. Girls. Music playin.' One girl passin' by round ass jiggling through her shorts, and she'll turn and say, 'Ain't you that *loco?* The one who saved Sam?' And I'll say, 'Yeah. What's it to you?' And she will say…—

Michael looked at Sam, who faced the window.

What is with him? Paul asked.

"Nothing," Michael said.

The eyelid that hooded the left eye of Sam twitched. He leaned over to mumble something to Paul.

"Whas you sae whas?"

Sam enunciated, "I am not telling you."

"Sam!" Paul said.

Michael shrugged.

"Why don't you party with him?" Sam said, jerking his thumb over his shoulder to Girlman, who looked up from his table.

"I don't hang with fags who wans to be women," Michael retorted. His eyes shifted to Girlman.

Girlman kept his gaze toward the window. Paul sat, the vein in his forehead pulsing.

"Come on, all right?" Paul said.

Sam held out his hand, his face weary and earnest.

"Sorry, Michael."

Michael shook the offered hand and brought his attention back to his food.

"Michael?" Sam's hand waved in Michael's view.

"What are you talking about?" Paul asked.

Sam talked to Paul, his voice urgent. Then he leaned over, his right eye wide and his left one sleepy. "Come on. One time?" He held up one finger. "Just once."

Michael stared at his plate. His throat became too dry for him to swallow. Paul muttered something harsh to Sam.

—Sam walkin' on tiptoes, ruinin' my time with his baby needs. All others deaf smiles and signs, faces not bothered. Why can't I just be like them?—

"I told you to leave him alone," Paul said to Sam.

"Shut it, Paul."

Sam's hand kept waving. Michael looked away and tried to pretend not to see him talking. Sam leaned into view.

"*Vamas por favor.* I'm tired of being sick."

Michael turned in his seat and kept his eyes on Henry, who sat with Nancy. They were practicing the alphabet together, going from *A* to *D*. Henry squinted at his hand while Nancy's cheek bulged from her tucked in tongue. Sam pushed himself off his chair. He walked on his knees and grinned as if in a joke. Desperation crawled in his eyes.

"Please. P–p–please," Sam sang as he pressed his flat hand to his chest and made it circle.

Paul's hands covered his glasses. "Oh, stop it, Sam."

"Puh–puh–pleeease Mikey? Pleeeeease!"

"Look, I sae no okay! I go in too mush frouble with the Whysees boys, an' I'm in deep shit all righ?"

Michael drew out the last word louder than the rest. Sam staggered back to the chair. Others looked at them. Sam bit his lower lip, and his eyes became wet. He got up, leaned on the table, and spoke. Michael could sense his disappointed gaze. Sam's left eyelid flapped. Paul reared back, his mouth agape and eyes wide. Sam turned and walked away.

"Whas dis he sae? Whas?"

Paul signed what Sam said.

You nothing to me. Worthless.

They avoided each other for a while. Sunday morning came. Naked bodies, except for towels clutched around their waists, filled the hallway. Paul was behind Michael, a towel draped over his shriveled lap, his face vulnerable without glasses. His reddened eyes squinted. Sam stood behind Paul, looking away from Michael.

—'Cause you're chicken. A chicken! Wish me built tough like Sam.—

Sam's lean body inflated with hard muscles, his stomach ridged, while Michael's own just had a fine line running from his chest to the belly like a boy.

The line started moving. The door opened, and the Whysee stepped out, dripping in his damp T—shirt, shorts, and sandals. He waved several wards in the bathroom as the line moved several paces. A heavy hand lay on Michael's shoulder. Michael turned his torso and tried to ignore Sam, who kept pleading, hands clasped, and his eyebrows raised over his widened eyes. He faced away, trying to ignore Sam's pleas. Then Michael's towel whipped away, and his chin pressed to his neck. Cool air tickled his pubic hair and his bare buttocks. He jumped at Sam, who twirled the towel, taunting him and grinning.

"Sam! Give back!" Paul shouted.

Michael grabbed for the towel, making Paul grimace and cringe back to keep Michael's privates from brushing his face. Covering himself with his hand, Michael made for another grab. Sam stepped away, yanking the towel back. He stuck out his tongue and waggled it. Michael looked to Girlman. Girlman had observed their antics, his own towel wrapped around his upper body. Then Girlman turned and raised his head in irritation. Michael whirled back to Sam and made for another snatch. Sam jerked the towel away and snapped it into his face. The corner whipped into his eyes, stinging them. His exposed genitals felt shriveled, the size of an acorn. He stopped reaching and turned away from Sam.

—Keep head down so nobody sees you cryin.' Not cryin'! Just eyes hurt from towel.—

The towel dropped on his shoulder, and he felt Sam's fingers brushing at the back of his neck. Michael took the towel from his shoulder and wrapped it around his waist. After a few paces he was at the bathroom door. It opened, and he entered with Jose and Girlman.

The Whysee, a tousled–haired boy, stood in his shorts and sandals with a dripping hose dangling from his hand. Attached to the faucet, the hose somehow had the coldest water running through it. A head jerk from the Whysee toward the shower room, and one by one, the three wards stepped into it. Michael, his movements automatic, took his towel off to wrap it around the showerhead that had never sprayed water for two years. He turned and hunched toward the wall, covering his privates. A sidelong glance showed Girlman next to him covering his own privates and breasts, his arms crossed, acting as if a modest, naked girl. Jose stood on the other side, his penis a bulbous stem and cap of a mushroom. He scowled as the hose sprayed water. The Whysee sprayed Girlman first, causing a violent shiver, and Michael could see how he clenched his teeth. His breasts jiggled as the water hit them, and Michael turned, embarrassed for him. Done with running the hose on Girlman, he turned to Michael. Michael squeezed his eyes shut and braced for the spray. His teeth hurt as icy water stung his back.

Later, after he dressed and went outside, Richie stepped to block him.

—Oh nice. Real great. Right out of the shower and dress for lunch, then squeeze in getting your ass kicked by your friendly blockhead at the nearest location right outside the dorm.—

Nat came up the steps with a grin as sloppy as his wet hair. Eggy followed. Kelly, leaning on the concrete balcony that overlooked the grass by the underground parking lot, straightened. Several other slight Deaf teenagers with hard faces came. The hangers–on for the block leaders. Kelly stared over Eggy's shoulder. With a narrow, monkey shaped head, hair smooth as a burr, and her teeth were jagged, as Richie's teeth were, her looks repelled him.

You guy a couple? Michael signed, trying to be meek.

Kelly glared and signed; *NOT PLAY.*

Nat's eyes skittered back and forth. "Hey, wait, what are you saying? Come on!"

Michael told Nat what he and Kelly had said.

Eggy, after listening, pretended to laugh. "Haw. That's funny, real funny."

"Listen," Nat said, stepping toward Michael. "Enough with talks. I know what you do every night."

"Whas? Sleep?"

Kelly made a masturbating gesture and signed with the other hand, *YOU D–O* "det."

She formed the sign for the word "that" with her lips. A short black–haired deaf to her right laughed. Eggy gave a headshake. He motioned to show running with his arms. Nat gave a reproachful nod. He spoke as if mulling over his thoughts. From the years Michael spent in proximity, he understood most of what he said.

"What I should do? What shall I do?" Nat sighed as if the hardest decision he had to make. He searched the sky, trying to find a meaning. He smiled. "Maybe report you…"

Michael shrugged.

"Or penalty?"

"Whas?"

Nat's face brightened. He pointed at Richie and made a hugging motion. Richie lumbered over. Michael sidled, but Richie grabbed him by the arms and pulled him. Sleepy eyes stared from Richie's piggish face. Michael struggled, but his arms were clamped.

"Come on, Nas. Please."

Nat dipped his head toward Michael and made a kissy face at Kelly. Michael looked over. Kelly licked her lips as dogs would lick their chops.

"No! No! Repors me, repors me!"

Her face darkened, and she lunged, clamping her mouth onto his own. Decayed breath from her rotten teeth clunked against his own. He squirmed. Her tongue darted in and raped his throat. Richie released him. Choking, he stumbled against the trash can by the doorway and dry heaved. Nat, laughing, scooted in and rammed the battered flashlight into his stomach. He groaned as he slid down the door, clutching himself. He felt Richie's grips stopping his slide, and a knee jutted into his groin. Nausea spread from his legs to his stomach, and he fell to his knees. Another hit rammed his head, shiny black spots swelling in his vision.

"Gooooaaal!" Eggy shouted from far away, his thin arms thrust to the sky.

Needles of pain spread from Michael's testicles to his stomach and legs. Worn, torn sneakers and shoes clapped away on the concrete and the blockheads' laughter waned. As Michael gasped on the ground, he hoped that some beautiful female ward would come and hold him.

—Would be nice if she pressin' my head to her breasts stroke my face. Would be nice if she holdin' me.—

Someone shook his shoulder. His eyes opened.

—Oh, my beauty, oh my love, oh ugh. —

Nancy's face above him sagged. The only thing that he liked of her features were her eyes. They made her bunched face look gentle if sad. She wore a green dress, not brand new, but it was not as worn out as her sneakers. A long, knobby face appeared next to her. It was Henry, his roommate. A smaller face moved by Henry's shoulder, and it was that deaf boy with the face pressed in tflat.

—Jose, right?—

A narrow face hovered over Michael's forehead. Her face was familiar, with a turkey neck and glasses smeared with stains and dust. She was the girl who had scolded him a few days ago. Four faces crowded over him, breaths sour.

—Get away from me!—

"Michael, get up. Muh–Michael," Henry kept saying.

58

They moved back as Michael groped behind and moved to a seated position. His stomach complained and his legs felt slack from the assault. His rescuers spoke too fast for him to understand. Jose grinned. The other girl with the glasses grunted.

"He's okay!" Nancy shouted.

"Duh, Nuh–Nancy," Henry said, rolling his eyes.

Nancy snapped at him, pointing her stubby finger at Henry, who brayed. The other girl also screeched at him. Henry said something back to her. He dipped his head at Michael, who finally focused on Henry's face.

"That's Gertie," Henry said. "She's a puh–puh–pain suh–sometimes."

The girl named Gertie glared, but Henry ignored her in favor of Michael.

"H–uh–hu um hey, this is nee–neat, muh–me talking to you, we don't talk mu–much."

"Grae, maybe we shool do this again sometime soon."

Michael leaned over and propped himself to get up. His arms shuddered, forcing him to stay in an all–fours stance.

ME NAME JOSE. ME AGE EIGHTEEN, Jose signed.

Henry's head bobbed with joy, and he moved behind him. Michael felt himself hauled up by the armpits.

"Come on, buh–bud. It's lun–un–lunch time."

Michael struggled to stand.

"Okay," he said, and staggered away to check himself. He raised a hand to them. "I'm okay…. I think."

He limped a few steps and noticed Henry, Nancy, and Jose standing there as if waiting for permission. Gertie grunted in disgust and stalked to the cafeteria. Henry, Nancy, and Jose's faces were so bright with hope. He swept his arm at them in a come on gesture, and they followed him to the cafeteria, Henry grabbing his elbow to check Michael's steps. Inside, Nancy helped Michael to one table as the others got their food. When they came back, Gertie flounced to the far table and plopped herself there, staring at him with sullen eyes through her buggy glasses. Michael noticed with delight that Henry got Nancy's food for her. She should stop giving him adoring looks from now on with Henry. The pain ebbed as he looked around with despair, seeing them with their vague smiles and lolling heads.

—What Sam and Paul say if saw? Maybe think me a deaf and dumb loser for having only retards for friends. Never said nothin' to Henry all this year.—

Jose moved to join them but looked off to the corner and squealed. He hurried with his tray to a table where a willowy girl sat with her large, muscular boyfriend. The muscular boy signed, H–I, and Jose chattered in signs, oblivious to the boy's unsure grin. Michael looked and saw Paul sitting where they sat at the usual table. Paul gave him a weak grin. Then Sam placed the tray for Paul and sat where his back could block Paul from view.

"Who cares about them?" Nancy said. "They don't know how to be nice."

"They're my friens."

Henry said something, then clasped his hand to his forehead and spoke, pausing at each word.

"Have yooo–you met Nancy?"

—(Damp pubic hairs cling around crimson vaginal opening and breasts flop, udders.)—

"Yeah, yeah I meh her all righ."

Henry announced with a broad smile. "She's muh Ma! Mm–my girlfriend now."

"Yeah, yeah, tha's nice."

Michael ate bread and spaghetti, sour and bland.

"I am learning some sign language," Nancy claimed. She put her hand up to form the letters A, then B, then C. She stopped and froze, a winded–down doll. Henry showed her D.

"I am learning signs too," Henry said. "Helps me. Meeeee. Me tun–tuh talk right."

—Poor Henry. Tryin' to learn signs to talk to me, me snubbin' him.—

Henry gave Michael an uncertain smile and stuttered several words.

"Me too!" Nancy chimed.

"Well, not as much as I am," Henry said, stroking his budding beard. "Boy, it's t–t–t–tough to live in deaf sk–shh–school." His face contorted as he dug his words out.

—Sounds like a muh–muh–muh–motor b–b–b–boat.—

Nancy tilted her at Henry. "I'll do better!" she said and grinned. "Henry is so jealous that you saw me with no clothes!"

"Sorry abous thas, Henry." His ears flushed.

Henry spoke, scowled, and pounded his open palm.

"I won's mess with you," Michael said.

"Fuh–fine. I'll not fight with you only because she said so."

"Sure. Okay."

Nancy clasped her hands. "It would be terrible if two of you fight over me," she said, but her face showed otherwise.

Gertie came to the table. She sat with Nancy and bent her head toward her, whispering. They giggled when they glanced at Michael. The siren on the ceiling flashed. Michael got up with Henry and Nancy. He saw Sam walk toward him. Before he could say anything, Sam's shoulder bumped his before he moved past to put his tray along with the others on the conveyor belt by the partition.

During his shift, he couldn't push the wheelbarrow without getting stuck. Crumbly red pebbles slid off. The wheelbarrow handles twisted. A Whysee overseeing the wards glared at him. Michael knew him as the same smiling boy who had pushed him a week ago. Fighting for grips, he struggled to keep his grim hold on the handles.

"No, no, no," he hissed.

A brick fell, cracking on the red–streaked sidewalk. The next one scattered on the concrete. His hands were slippery with sweat, lost hold, then grasped again. An orange dust–covered hand moved into view and snapped at his face.

"*Ahora mismo*, let's go," Sam's voice hollered, and his form moved past.

—(Before, Sam's surer hands would grip the handles and right the wheelbarrow with his stronger arms. Sunlight might hide his face, a hood shade and what can see was his reproachful headshake.

'*¿Que pasa? Michael?*' he would say. '*Mijita* needs help?'

'Get the bricks over to the dock, dork!'

'Ooh, Michael, how rude!'

His hard laughter.)

Here I go now.—

The wheels squealed.

—Wait, no, wait no!—

It toppled, buckling his arms, compressed cores of muscles and bones, and the bricks crashed into a ruined pile.

—Okay, okay, now kick at the bricks and say a bad word 'cause Whysee's face twisted. He'll go easy if thinks mad at yourself.—

"Oh, you mother…"

The Whysee stalked over, hollering. His smooth hand grabbed Michael's shirtsleeve.

—Keep your head down, for Chris'sake. Down.—

The mouth prettiest in its symmetry moved in an uncomprehending squall over the neat gray collar. The Whysee kept shouting, his face icy with rage.

"Clean!"

His spittle sprayed. Michael cowered. He made an awkward snatch for the handles while gazing from the piles of hard–burnt clay and saw Sam, now a doll–sized figure in the distance. The click–clacks of other wheelbarrows moved past him. The Whysee marched back to his post by the sidewalk. Michael righted the wheelbarrow and started putting the fallen bricks back in it.

He waited back outside his friends' room, already dreading the lights of tomorrow. He raised a fist to Paul and Sam's door and held it there. His knuckles rapped. It opened a half an inch, and his face glared. It slammed shut, and the hearing aid enabled him to hear the shouting.

—Great, Sam takin' over, keepin' Paul away from door.—

He bit his knuckles in frustration hard enough to taste blood. He pulled back and saw crescents of cuts on his first two knuckles.

—Just out of here would be heaven. Out there, won't deal with stealin' to keep friends or be a stupid dog like today. Only to do whatever I want. Just me.—

The next few mornings, Michael started walking the sloped road along a different side of the Bline Memorial Building. That road stopped at a small concrete and brick bridge near the library complex. He didn't use that road often, but he knew Paul always used that route.

"Michael?"

Paul, on his way to work as a clerk at the London Library, wheeled alongside him a pile of books on his lap. A cluster of wards walked ahead, signing.

"Whas do you wan?" he asked and shivered.

"Just hi," Paul said and signed.

"Why do Sam push us aroun'?"

Paul's lips curled into a smile.

"Whas?"

Paul slapped the armrest. *He tell me this morning, 'Just because Michael the E–L click to here and still can read lips, he act like we can't survive in here without him.'*

"Oh yeah? Well, you tell him—"

Paul poked Michael in the side. *You tell him. I am not your secretary.*

"I am sure he'll unnersann' if you 'plain him real slow."

Now you make fun of his intelligence.

"Oh, like he's so funny makin' fun of me tawkin.' Bes he'll look so cool goin', '*Estup*–unnnngh!'" He wobbled his head hard, imitating Sam's seizures.

That low, Paul signed, although a small grin dug into his mouth.

They passed the mammoth building where Whysees go to classes. Michael drew a deep breath.

"I'm jus scare of stealin' an' goin' in deeper frouble."

I will be too.

"A real frien' wool'n force someone to ges in frouble."

A real friend will risk trouble to help.

"Yeah," Michael snapped and then he stopped.

—(Sam collapses from a Whysee's hit in the hallway before the fight with the blockheads later.) Did he say something for me?—

"I guess the worl los a grae lawyer when you decize to be born a cripple."

Paul checked about himself. Then he grinned at Michael and laughed. A ward ahead turned, his face puzzled. Who could laugh in such a place?

The Little Boy

Michael's labor assignment number 123 on the terminal billboard was with 169, Sam's number. The job shown was RAKE LEAVES COURTYARD. On the other side of the concrete bridge leading to the courtyards, moist brown and black leaves blanketed the grass.

Now he turned from his rake and watched Sam attack the leaves, his mouth moving into what he guessed to be curses. Michael grinned to himself and raked the leaves. They worked for a few minutes, the rasps of the leaves loud in the tense silence. Sam swore again and threw the rake onto the ground by the trash can, half-full of leaves. A step toward Michael and a step back to the rake. Then he kicked it aside and walked up to him. At last, a wave without a smile.

"Goo sign."

That got Michael a smile from him. Then Sam frowned. He opened his mouth, grunted, and looked toward the fence, where a Whysee stood guard. He spoke.

"You talk to Paul?"

"He's righ. Bus I can's jus go in there an' steal. Nos in a place like this."

Sam slapped his hand against his pants.

"Eh, *muchas gracias*," he said to Michael and turned back to raking after picking up the discarded rake.

Sam stopped halfway and looked past him. Michael sensed someone and turned. A little boy, seven or eight years old, waited. He wore ragged overalls, and the undershirt beneath spilled, a cloth tail that hung to his knees. His curly, filthy hair reached to his shoulders, where the ends feathered. Bright brown eyes looked from beneath dusty eyebrows. He smelled foul, as if not washed for days. His hands spewed sign language.

ME WORK TWO HOURS. MUST.

Slow, Michael answered, *I am most Signed Exact English.*

NOT KNOW A.S.L. MATTER? YOU DEAF!

Sorry. My name I–S M–I–C–H–A–E–L. What I–S your?

ME NAME R–O–B–B–Y…. S–Q–U–A–L–E–R.

Michael noticed Sam's envious face.

—Oh, now you wanna know signs?—

"What are you talking about?" Sam demanded, putting his hands to his waist.

"I usually help my frien', bus since you nos one, I won's say."

"Why should I care for stupid signing?"

"Grae. You besser go back to work."

Michael turned to Robby. He turned back to make a shooing motion at Sam. Sam's mouth opened to deliver a retort but became at a loss for words. He gave a baleful glare and stalked back to the rake again. Michael ignored the crunching sound of leaves being raked with vengeance. Robby wrinkled his brow at Sam.

Never mind him, what do you want?

WANT? NO WANT THEY INFORM ME HELP YOU WORK.

Why?

ME NOT SPEECH GOOD. ONLY SIGN. Robby gave a rueful grin and showed his reddened knuckles. *TEACHER RAP. ME SIGN. SHE RAP.*

Why hit you? You are in deaf place.

TEACHER WANT PERFECT DEAF LIKE HEARINGS. ME NOT PERFECT DEAF.

Not right for them to do that. No one in trouble for signing.

ONLY WAY.

Robby's face was mournful as he signed that. Sam dropped his rake and came up to them, his face irritated.

"You know, you can't be cutting me out like this."

Michael had lost count of how many times Sam and Paul had carried on voiced conversations without including him.

HEARING BOY MAD FOR?

"Well, you leff," Michael said.

"Well, you leff," Sam retorted.

"Oh, have fun trying to lissen to signs."

Sam's mouth tightened, and he twisted toward Robby.

"What you looking at?"

WHAT TELL?

"Kids shouldn't be here."

Robby signed back. Sam turned back to Michael with a dazed smile.

"What did he say, huh? What he say?"

"He sae whas a hearing person like you here for? You got wrong directions?"

Sam's face whitened beneath his tan, and he advanced to Robby.

"Wanna know what sign I learned all these times?"

He thrust the middle finger at Robby's face.

HE TELL 'F–f–f–f–f' T–O ME? HE 'F–f–f–f–f' ME?

"What has he said to me, huh? Why he's trying to say F?"

"He wans to know if you sae F wors."

HEARING PERSON HERE FOR?

"What did he say, huh? What did he say?"

Michael raised his hands. "I'm ous of this," he said, trying not to laugh.

He felt someone tugging his shirt. Robby let go and kept lipping the word, meaning "that" as he signed.

WHAT "det" MAN TELL? WHAT TELL?

Forget it.

"This is stupid," Sam snapped.

He pushed Michael aside and knelt, so he was facing a small but defiant face.

"You see my lips? Nobody.... just...."

He paused and Robby nodded, his eyelids scrunched shut. Michael sighed.

"give...."

Robby's head nodded, his lips going, "Uh–huh–uh–huh..."

"a damn.... about.... you." Sam had on a wide smile when he said that.

Robby pushed him. Sam flailed but caught himself from falling on his buttocks as he planted his hand on the grass behind him. He struggled to his feet and wiped his nose. His face became murderous. Michael tried to step in between them.

"Sam, come on."

BIG HEAD NOW? CAN'T BEAT SMALL KID.

Michael stifled his laughter at how Robby mimicked Sam's behavior and the way he lipped words for big and small as "chow" and "mo."

Sam grunted, pushed Michael aside, and picked up Robby by the pants. He lugged the kicking boy to the trash can and dumped him headfirst. Robby's wriggling legs kicked feebly in the air. His leg pushed against the inner wall of the trash can, and a few seconds later, he worked himself upright.

ME OUT FINISH!

Sam stepped toward Robby and pointed at him. "And you better–"

His finger trembled and his eyes rolled back in their sockets. Before he could fall, Michael heaved himself over and caught his shuddering body. He slid on one knee from the weight. He braced the jostling body as leaves scattered and some clung to them. Something thumped. The body slapped against his hands. A stain spread on the crotch of Sam's pants. Far away, the Whysee gave a dry chuckle as Michael struggled to prop Sam on his side so he would not swallow his saliva. Sam's torn shoes thrashed, kicking the pile of leaves and more swirled around them. The Whysee still stood guard by the fence. Sam's unfocused eyes looked upward as a squelched sob came.

"Michael, I don't know, I just don't. I'm *estancao* being this stupid shaky."

Sam bit his upper lip, his way of keeping from crying. Michael looked toward the trash can to tell Robby everything was fine. It lay on the side, the leaves spread into a decayed fan shape on the ground. Neither had not seen Robby shrieking and climbing out of it. The thump had been the can falling. Far away, Michael spotted a tiny figure running back to the dorms for children.

At lunch, Sam hadn't come yet, so Michael had a moment's peace from the guilt. He waved Paul over to join them.

"Wow, our group is growing," Nancy repeated, her face awestruck. "Another person already."

Paul, out of his element, smiled, his lips stiff.

"How you—yo get into the wheelchair?" Henry asked.

"Thas nos polite, Henry."

Henry lowered his eyes. Paul pushed up his glasses.

"It's okay," Paul said and signed. "He's just curious."

He lowered his head and started talking and signing at the same time.

"I never knew to walk. My father, a teacher, and my mother, a nurse, had me late in the years. It was a demyelinating disease from birth, and these days, it was not wise to see a doctor about it. My legs never improved at six, and by then they knew not to check me into the hospital. They hid me until the neighbor down the block found out and called the state's disease control center, then the office of standard health. The disease had mysteriously stopped as it started, but it was too late. I remember my Mom and Dad standing on the lawn when the health official came to pick me up to take me to the 30th Street Station in Philadelphia. They clung to each other while the car pulled away. I could see them out the back window, they huddled like chubby children lost in the forest to me.

Even if they did not fight, they cry neither. I guess they must have accepted it and resigned themselves to being childless. They were acting as if well–behaved children. As if they could forget a child like me."

"Sorry," Michael said, staring at his stained plate.

Paul remained silent, then he clapped Michael's shoulder. "Hey, don't be. Otherwise, I wouldn't have met such a cutie as you."

"Aw, shus up."

Knuckles mashed Michael's left shoulder. He looked up at him.

"Eh, hey."

Someone had smeared a foul residue across Sam's sweaty forehead. He did not notice as he sat. His left hand shook as he picked up the fork. The fork rapped on the table as his hand continued to shake. After a while, his hand stopped its tremors. He scooped the colorless meat and ate. Paul's face became puzzled as he looked at Sam's head.

"Sam?" Paul asked, gesturing at his forehead.

Sam's response was an angry shrug.

"You, okay?" Henry asked.

Sam looked at Henry, his eyes worn. "Yeah, sure. Never better."

Her thin arm shoved in, and her hand slapped a blank paper on the table. Beady eyes glared through glasses over pressed lips.

"Help now," Gertie said. She held a piece of crayon, and the paper was a piece of cardboard rescued from trash. He recognized it from the discarded ones thrown into the dumpster after use of keeping first year Whysees' uniforms smooth in their plastic packages.

"Hey, come on," Michael said, shifting his chair away.

"She's an artist," Nancy explained. "She came to college so she could study art."

Paul leaned back to look at the ceiling and grimaced.

—Sure, Nancy. I came to college on a hockey scholarship.—

Sam had his head lowered and kept concentrating on keeping his fork from shaking.

"Give me your bowl, Michael," Gertie said.

Her pale, gnarled hand seized his bowl and placed it on the paper.

"Thanks for asking," Michael said.

Paul laughed. Gertie stuck out her tongue and traced a circle around the bottom.

"What are you drawing?"

"Shh! I'm drawing." Gertie sniffed at Sam and leaned back, fanning her nose. She took a spoon from Paul and placed it in the crimson circle. She traced two jagged spoon shapes on the paper.

—Looks like bloody eyes.—

Gertie used the impressions where the handle of the spoon narrowed as tear ducts. A hand seized Michael's wrist.

"Thumb out," Gertie said, her cheek bulging from a tucked in tongue.

"For Chris—"

"Just do it," Paul said and signed.

Michael sighed and let her. Her crayon skittered around his thumb, and her thin clammy hand let go of his wrist. The outline of his thumb remained encrusted in red on the drawing. Her hand clenching the piece, she drew a thick line to the bottom.

"A balloon with eyeballs?" Michael asked.

"No," Gertie muttered.

She reached across and grabbed Sam's wrist. He did not resist, his smile weak. Soon, the outline of a thicker and calloused thumb in red appeared. Gertie worked on the paper, coloring in the spoon outlines. She used the floral disc as a face. Then she made crescents around the circle. She finished by marking streaks of red on the bottom.

"It's a flower," Paul said.

"No, it's not!" Gertie squalled.

"A face," Michael guessed.

"A flower with a face?" Nancy asked.

"No, it's a face," Gertie snapped.

"But what's that?" Sam said, pointing to the slashes.

"It's the grass, stupid."

"Oh."

Paul's lips pulled into a smile, but his face grew still, and he gazed at Sam's forehead. Gertie snatched the drawing and hurried away with it. Sam lowered his eyes. Michael twisted at the sense of movement from behind him. Nat and Eggy stood nearby. Richie, behind them, gloated with his piggish eyes and signed.

RECENT ME SEE YOUR FRIEND DORM.

Sam hunched over his meal with a grim look, keeping his eyes from rising to meet theirs.

WHAT FRIEND DO ON FLOOR?

Michael pushed back and stood. A hand grabbed his shirttail, and it was Paul, shaking his head. Michael turned to Sam, who was still sitting.

"Hi Michael," Nat said. Then he held out his arms, one holding the flashlight, and jiggled them. He stopped grinning. "Get it?"

Laughing, he walked off with his gang, swinging his flashlight. Michael waited until they left. He turned to Sam.

"How come you didn's do anything?"

Paul stared at Michael, his face slack.

"Well?" Michael asked.

Sam slammed his hands on the table and stood. He pressed his hand to his forehead, and his finger brushed the dripping streak mark. He glanced at his hand and sniffed. With a strangled cry, he pushed past Michael and fled.

"Whas with him?"

"It's nuh–nnh–not good to fight them," Henry said. "They're the leaders."

"Sam coulsa handle 'em!"

"What did you think happened?" Paul shouted and signed. "They took it from the bathroom and put it on his head while he was out! He had another seizure. We should've been there for him!"

Michael's mouth unhinged.

Paul nodded again, his mouth twisted and bitter. "They sure fixed him."

The next day's sun hung behind a cloud, an obscured silver coin. Michael did not notice, for his eyes flicked sideways at the short Whysee. He hoisted the handles of the wheelbarrow.

—Gotta look real. Get ready.—

He lugged the bricks laden wheelbarrow away. Feet away, Sam tottered as he used both hands to heave bricks into another wheelbarrow. He, despite the cool weather, sweated from the exertion.

—Won't be fallin' no more, Sam. Don't have to, gonna be over. Fallin' so others can see him and Whysees.—

The Whysee turned, and Michael grunted aloud as he began rocking the wheelbarrow by the demolished pile.

"Oh no, is falling!"

The bricks did their part. A hit. Pain shot from Michael's instep to the rear of his calf. He was not acting as he screamed and clutched his right foot while falling. The faces of others surrounded his vision. Through the blur of tears, he caught Sam's own panicked face among the others.

DO? DO? One ward signed.

"Health censer! Oh Gos! Health censer!"

Faces looked at each other, expressions vague. Sam grabbed one ward and pointed toward the Health Center. Hands grabbed Michael's legs and arms. He was carried from the site. The world wobbled from the sidewalk to running sneakers and shoes and then to the above harsh blue sky.

"I said...." The doctor said later, "You must be popular for the wards to help you here."

The nurse shifted Michael's foot. He kept staring at the blonde nurse. When she stared at Michael, her face hardened but softened when she gazed at the doctor. As she breathed, her breasts swelled beneath her garb. She pursed her lips at Michael, who turned his eyes away from her.

"Okay," the doctor said. "Let's see." He hummed under his breath. A few acne scars dotted his forehead, and he looked fresh out of medical school.

"Hurts?" the doctor asked, pushing Michael's toes back.

Michael yelped.

—Just go. I need to take care of business in 102.—

The doctor peered at Michael's foot. "Just bruises and swelling. Your toes mashed."

"Is always like this."

"You need new shoes." The doctor said, pointing downward at his own.

The nurse added something, rolling her eyes.

"Jus because you're ugly an' stupis doesn's mean you can take is ous on me," Michael said.

The nurse hissed through her teeth, and she flicked Michael's foot.

"Now, now," the doctor said as Michael screamed.

"Sorry, slipped," The nurse said with a small smile.

Michael tried working an earnest expression for the doctor. He turned to the doctor. "Will need bandages or tape?"

The nurse snapped at the doctor.

"Well, if the nurse sae so," Michael said, with the right amount of scorn in his voice.

The doctor disagreed, admonished the nurse in a few words not understood. With a wink, the doctor turned on his heels and left them. She crossed her arms and stared; her face a stone.

"Though you dis nos have time for this," Michael said.

He lay back on his palms and stared back. He tried a feral smile, and when it felt right, he widened it. After a while, the nurse turned and stalked away.

Alone, Michael brought his legs around and lowered himself to the floor. He hesitated, then stood. The bones inside his right foot ground. He stifled a groan and limped to the opened door. To keep the weight off his injury, he listed to port and crept the hall. Around the next corner, he peeked and saw more doors.

—102.—

He slid alongside the wall, reading the numbers. 108 106 and then... a sob rang out from behind the door.

—Jesus! Jesus.—

The wall felt cool against his body. The sound continued through the door. He pushed on past and reached room 102. From 104, he believed the sound had subsided. He snuck into room 102.

The steel cabinets waited above the sink. A metal bin nestled in the far corner of the room, across from the hospital bed. He shut the door behind him. There was a tapping sound, and a confused warble. The door moved inward. Michael hopped, rolled under the bed, pressing his lips to not to cry out, and huddled beneath it. A female ward walked in the room. Michael glimpsed her feet encased in battered sneakers. When the sneakers turned, Michael peeked out. Her face looked hard and smooth, but her blue eyes glittered, and her soft lips pouted. Her fine haired arms cradled a bundle, and her mouth cooed at it. A baby–shell shaped hearing aid dangled from one tanned ear. She moved like an animatronic poised in a clean blue smock.

—Kind of lady in songs and poems. Be nice if she finds me, fall in love with me and then we can be a pair. Nice.—

Her back and legs shifted, and she showed her profile. The side of her face remained fixed toward the bundle as she stared at the bin, her face doleful as a toddler. When she lifted her arms, Michael glanced at the gray armband on her sleeve.

—Oh, not Dimitri. Oh, come on.—

Her smooth hand moved inside the bundle and withdrew. She pressed her fingers against her lips. Then she stepped to the metal bin. Her sneakered foot stamped on the pedal and the lid clanged open. A fetid odor wafted from the bundle. She plucked the cloth wrapping, and something tumbled into it. It appeared a discarded doll, the arms and legs just rubbery sticks before the lid closed. Her lips turned upward into a blank smile. She left, sniffing at the cloth. After the door closed behind her, he slid out and got to his feet. He sidled up to the cabinet and opened it. The hinges squeaked, making the handle vibrate under his hand and he cringed. Nobody came in the room. He scanned the room for boxes of medications.

"Die lay tin," he mumbled.

On the top shelf was a blue box, and he read the first few letters that were spelled DILAN. He pressed his hands on the counter below and pushed himself up on it. His head slammed the bottom of the cabinet.

—Thanks. Thanks a lot Sam.—

He let himself back to the floor and bit back a cry as his ankle grinded. His good foot bent up, and he stood as if a flamingo. If anyone walks in, it would be obvious what he was trying to do. A hiss of pain through his clenched teeth. He lifted himself and hunched over until he knelt on the counter. Cramped and folded in, he feared that if he reared his head or moved too fast, he would take a tumble. He hooked his hand over himself and felt for the box. His fingertips brushed the corner and lowered. His hand closed around the box's edges to guide it out.

—(What if boxes after boxes clatter to the tile floor below him?)—

He inched it outward and took the free box.

—If cover not blue, I will just scream to let them take me. Please, for Christ's sake, let it be blue.—

He looked. For one terrifying second, he stared at the box, the red leaping and burning his eyes. A dull roar rushed through his mind.

—Whoa, whoa, wait, wait. Just red letters, the red part just letters on the blue box.—

76

His breath skipped. He wriggled his tucked legs off the counter and shifted himself halfway to the floor to unbutton and slide the box inside his pants. With his pants zipped over the bulge, he stood.

—Either get caught or impress everybody.—

He closed the cabinet and made for the door. His eyes fell upon the waste can.

—Sam gonna ask if I look. Can see him asking me that.

('I been in there before. I looked in the can. Nothing much to talk about in there.'

'Did you look *en la canasta?* Did you, Michael?'

'Nah, I don't care what's in the damn can.'

'Aww, *nina* afraid to look? *¡Poc–poc–poc–pooc,* Michael *es un gallina!*

'You just watch it, you lousy…')

Okay, okay, I'll look. You just watch me, Sam!—

Michael crept to the bin. His foot hovered over the pedal and stopped.

—Shh.—

Instead, he squatted and pressed his fingernails under the rim of the lid. He lifted to look inside it. At first, he saw splatters of blood and flesh. Small faces with fixed unseeing eyes and tiny hands, feet, and torsos filled the bottom of the plastic bag in the bin. His own eyelids stretched in terror. The newest one, entangled in the mound of torsos and still faces, started twitching. Its bloody mouth strained to breathe. He lowered the lid and backed away. He crammed his knuckles into his whimpering mouth. His other hand fumbled for the handle and turned it. He leaned over and pulled the door open, peeking outside the room. The hallway was empty.

Stepping out, he leaned against the wall. A hand fell upon his shoulder, smelling of pine.

"Are you all right?" Dr. Broom asked, his lips forming the words. Blood dew had spattered across the collar of his white coat. "You looked peaked, young thing."

"Who, me?"

The other doctor hurried to them and spoke to Dr. Broom, his voice cracking. When he frowned at Michael, his lips formed unknown words.

"Oh, I though you sae to walk is off," he answered, pointing at his ear ashamedly.

Dr. Broom nodded at the other doctor. He said something and moved his hands, gesturing toward Michael. Then he beamed and tapped Michael on the chest. He walked a few feet away, his face miming a grimace of pain. The younger doctor nodded and added something, making a stay gesture. Dr. Broom nodded and murmured. Michael nodded too. The other doctor said a few words. Then the doctor fidgeted as if playing the game, charade. Dr. Broom suggested something, and the doctor nodded, then his face brightened. He pointed at Michael, who stayed, his smile growing wan. The doctor put up a hand for stop and made a wrapping motion.

"Wae an' I'll ges banages?" Michael guessed. Still standing, he crossed his legs.

Dr. Broom chuckled, and his hand clasped the younger doctor's shoulder. The young doctor appeared flustered.

"Okay," the doctor said, still gesturing toward Michael. His mouth gaped wide in a pretend scream, and he covered his mouth, peeking over his hands.

"That's good," Dr. Broom praised.

—God, just make them shut up, please.—

Michael tried to sidle away.

"Hello," the younger doctor said, "I'm not finished with you." He pointed toward the room that Michael was in before his trip to 102.

"Thas okay," Michael said. "My foos feels better."

The doctors laughed. Michael turned and pretended to adjust himself. The corner of the box jabbed into his groin.

"Well, I'm fine now. Thanks."

The younger doctor snapped something, stopping him from leaving.

Later, Michael waited on the examination table. He was back this time with Sam's pills still poking his testicles. The surly nurse came in, and there were some dime–sized drops of stains on the front of her garbs. She spoke, her face dour.

"I though to take a walk, I guess," he answered.

The nurse sighed and said, "Why can't you talk like normal people?"

"Normal like you? God, I hope nos."

The nurse gave a last scowl and flounced away. Michael waited until the sound of clomping shoes echoed to quiet outside the examination room. He reached in and pulled the box aside.

—Just givin' an old friend of mine a little breathin' space, that's all.—

His hand pulled out as the doctor stepped into the room with the bandage.

"Ah–ha," the doctor muttered, now good–natured. He started binding Michael's foot after cleaning the grime and dust off with a wet towel and an antiseptic cleaner. He remarked something while rubbing just his thumb and first finger together, a universal signal for cash. "Okay, just put some ice…" He crossed his arms and shivered. His lips shaped the word again, "… ice…" Then he pointed at Michael's foot. "Ice."

Michael nodded, although he knew he would never see ice.

The doctor spoke and Michael tried to read his lips and caught only "like a horse, y'know?" Michael's face must have shown confusion, so the doctor mimed holding a gun to an imaginary crippled horse lying and pulling the trigger.

"Boom. You know?"

The doctor almost laughed and gave him a thumb's up but stopped when he saw the expression on Michael's face.

That night, Michael stood by Paul and Sam's door.

—What say? 'Hey, Sam, you better get to kissin' my ass 'cause I–' No. No, no. 'Okay Sam, I got 'em for you so now about Nat and Eggy'… wait that's not right.—

It opened. Paul pulled back and behind him, Sam hunched on his bed, clutching his frazzled blanket. Michael said nothing as he stepped inside their room, cradling the box. He held it out to Sam. His *amigo's* hands reached out and accepted the box.

"Robby is a real pain," Sam said, but he kept grinning.

Michael felt better after gaining a few notches of respect. His foot was healing, and it was just back to old times.

—Yeah, that's right. Badass deaf *loco* strollin' in the Health Center for his *amigo* Sam. Nobody's better be messin' with me or I'll uh… um get them.—

They walked toward the playground. Michael had told Sam how his seizure had frightened Robby off, and Sam decided to visit the boy at the children's dorms. A throttle linkage in the engine of the flatbed truck a mile away had become disabled, so the wards won an hour of freedom. Most passed their time waiting by the wheelbarrows for their next order or discussing what's a throttle linkage is. Sam had just whooped aloud and grabbed Michael.

"*Vente*, maybe we'll see Robby."

Michael had looked back before they went. The Whysee had said nothing and just gazed at them.

They approached the waist–high chain–linked fence. Inside the playground by the corner, a rusty slide sagged under the weight of clambering children in old clothes. An empty folded wheelchair leaned against the ladder. Farther inside was a rotting wooden jungle gym. Children covered the playground, chattering and squawking. Even though their hands twitched, they used their voices.

Michael looked at the slide for Robby. His eyes shifted to the jungle gym, swarming with more children. Not there.

Around the corner where the bottom concrete steps spooled from the second floor, there he was running, and a cluster of bigger children ran after him. Robby's wide, tearful eyes had that detectable fear in them. The children ran after him, shouting, their hateful faces intent on him. Robby raised his bulging eyes to Sam and Michael and put an extra burst of speed until he hid behind them. Taunts and laughter stopped. The children, once sure of their sizes, now looked up at the two older wards. The tallest boy, although his head reached just beneath Michael's chest, asked them something. Sam kept lifting his hands, unable to reply.

What doing? Michael signed.

"He's signing! He suppose to tawk!" A girl with a scab on her chin shouted. She stamped her torn sneaker on the dirt and crossed her thin arms.

Sam held out his hands again and gave a helpless shrug. Other children climbed off the slide and the jungle gym. Soon the playground was a sea of small inquiring faces.

"¿Los niños y niñas abandonados?" Sam asked.

"Ousize worl took children too."

While looking at their round faces, he kept wondering what became of their parents. He looked behind at Robby. He was sticking his tongue at the others, and…

—Heh.—

his thumbs stuck in his little ears, fingers wiggling at them. When Sam tapped the boy's shoulder, Robby jumped, startled. He lowered his hands, and his head stooped in guilt.

Why you chasing him? Michael asked.

The tallest one spoke. Thin as the others, his blonde hair had grown to below his shoulders. His brown eyes hardened as he enunciated something.

"Yeah…" the girl with the scab on her chin said, although her eyes glistened, and she frowned.

Michael turned to Sam.

"He said signing is not allowed," Sam said.

Michael checked on Robby, who stared at the children, his face fierce.

81

ME CAN'T SPEAK BUT TEACHER CAN'T CORRECT ME SIGNS.

Michael nodded and smiled.

—Sam's same as Robby at his age.—

Robby's face swelled with relief at finding an ally.

"Aw gee," the blonde boy said, "I don't know buh Mrs. Luggin sae we have su encourage him su tawk righ." He said the rest slow and careful to make sure everyone understood. "Dere was the resar children, one in wheelchair and they not here no more." Small eyes rose. "Mister? You know where they gone? They're here as beginning, bus they're gone."

Sam's face became serious.

—Room 1. Oh no… (Still tiny faces, airless and no life.)—

A little girl piped up, her voice questioning. Incoherent question after question spouted from her, eyes shinier with hope. Most took up her cries of queries. All Michael could do was to put up his hands and shake his head.

"Brother… Down's buh…. don't… him… no… more."

"Tell… mom… get… me… home."

Some pulled on Sam's sleeve, distant babbles that he seemed to understand. Michael pried one of the insistent hands off his shirttail and looked back at Sam, who answered their questions as best he could with grimaces and gestures. Most were shrugs and headshakes.

One boy shouted and signed; *WE SIGN MAYBE DEAF MAN HELP.*

Small hands moved, some A.S.L. and others' mixed English and home signs. Michael could understand most of them.

ME SAW B–I–L–L DEAF YOU KNOW WITH CRUTCH? NOW NONE.

Dad tell me he was coming to pick up me.

SCHOOL FINISH NOW?

Are there monster outside that eat bad children who go out of the fence?

"I don's know abou you all," Michael said. He raised his hands in surrender. *I don't know.* He tried to disentangle himself, but the children pressed closer.

MY DAD WITH YOU? DAD DEAF.

When time to go home?

Their faces creaked and small eyes filled. The few sobs in the playground were hopeless sounds that carried through it. A few faces twisted into anger and fear. Most went to the slide and jungle gym, playing but without a game.

"How can they live like this?" Sam asked, unbelieving.

"Like us, day affer day."

Beyond the heads, Robby was kicking at the pebbles.

"Now, children, what's wrong?" someone shouted above them.

Sam raised his head. A scowl came across his face. An elderly woman squinted her eyes at them from the second–floor concrete balcony.

"Why are all of you crying?" she shouted again.

Some children shaded their eyes while others squinted at her. She put her finger to her chin and spoke in long pauses.

"Recess....is....over."

She clapped her hands.

"Now.... is.... the.... time.... to.... go.... inside."

Murmuring, the children climbed the stairs stalling as much as they could. The woman held her hands up while Robby started after the others.

"Robby.... Robby.... you.... can't.... come.... in."

Robby looked up at the woman who shook her head, her face severe.

BUT COLD, Robby protested. He shivered and grimaced.

"You.... are.... talking.... in.... baby.... signs."

She beamed at the children passing her as they marched inside the building. Her gnarled finger touched her chin again.

"You.... two.... both... must.... learn.... to.... speak.... more.... properly.... to.... come.... to.... my.... class."

"Come on," Sam shouted.

Her face turned stiff. Her lips pressed together, she responded, "Do.... you.... have.... ward.... work.... to.... do?" The hoary finger remained on her pooched lips.

Michael saw the wicked look on Sam's face and his left eyelid widening.

"Um... les is go, Sam."

Sam's own finger pressed his lips.

"I.... believe.... a.... fat.... bag.... like.... you.... needs.... to.... get.... some.... But.... I.... doubt.... there.... will.... be.... a.... line.... for.... that.... ma'am."

Colors bloomed in the teacher's pasty cheeks.

SHE NOT HAPPY, Robby observed.

The old teacher whirled, and Michael could hear the clops of her shoes into the building. Michael started laughing. Robby frowned, his expression wary, and then grinned.

ME STAY OUT GUESS.

The soft wind of the coming winter blew through their hairs. Robby looked toward the building, dejected.

Wrong? Michael asked. He stepped closer. *You O.K.?*

Robby pushed Michael hard enough for him to take a step back.

"Why's he doing that?" Sam asked.

SEE? Robby's signs chopped the air. His shoulders shrugged and his hands splayed in outrage. *YOU MAKE ME THINK NOTHING ME SIGN. LOOK! ME TROUBLE.*

What I do?

LOOK!

Robby raised his swollen redden knuckles. His tiny thumb on one hand jutted out, bruised. *NOW CHILDREN CHASE ME. BEFORE ME HOME WITH PARENTS NOW ME HERE.*

Robby turned and stood by the chain–link fence. His face pinched. *THEY,* he pointed to the surrounding emptiness, signifying the entire world. *THINK RIGHT. WHY THEY HURT ME IF THEY RIGHT?*

Sam still had his lips pursed in confusion at Robby's signs. Michael walked to Robby.

Wish I know, he signed *but stuck here.*

They walked away until they could view the dome of the capital turning whiter as the sun rose. Robby pointed behind. Michael turned, and a seagull twittered on the trail that ran along the playground. The gull cocked its tiny head at them. With a tweet, it took flight and lit upon the streetlight that never glow.

"Day affer day huh?" Michael said to himself.

It was not a big deal to see one seagull or a dozen. What could it do that stirred him. The gull spread its wings and noted the silvery sky. It took a casual flight, leaving everything behind it. At the next breath, it was a plump dot dipping over the crumbled row houses further away. Someone behind stepped closer, a voice calling out his or Sam's numbers. For a time, they ignored the source of the irritated voice.

It was the Whysees who caught them and made them go to their shift by the wreckage. As Michael dropped the bricks into the wheelbarrow, he saw past his hands, roughened by the broken bricks, beyond the wavering road, and while he lugged them to the receiving dock, he saw Sam, young and thin at fourteen. During that better time, the food was fresh and nourishing, and the Whysees patient. He listened to how Sam's voice must have sounded, urgent and cracking, as his friend told him about *el indoro en el baño*. It was the only bathroom in the house. The memory happened in spring after the winter when he shot a goal between his friend's legs. He had just learnt the word *barrio* from Sam and kept being reminded of it everywhere he saw. The sunset that day shone an orange light through the windows of the lobby, creating tangerine squares on the tiles, and back then they were made to wait; for what, the wards never knew.

After he had picked up the new battery charger from the Health Center, Michael had spent his time exploring the underground parking lot until a Whysee, his gestures gentle, shooed him from the gleaming aerodynamic–shaped cars, bidding him to go upstairs and not come back here. After a few seconds of guesswork, Michael had gone upstairs to the plaza and into the Galton Dorm. Sam lay on one of the golden orange squares of light, his hands clasped behind his head, staring at the ceiling. Michael's father had trained him to hear almost like a hearing person, so along with his fine–tuned hearing aid, he could pick up Sam's voice and fill in the blanks, the words that his ears didn't catch.

—(A disjointed view, as if Sam is hanging on the wall, behind his head remaining to be seen. There is a brief step to an earlier time, the upside–down house in the fun park. Inside, there's Mom next to you, Dad, a group of other grownups and children sitting in the middle of the room, several feet up from the floor on a giant hanging bench. The lights darken and you watch the table with the lamp on it goes up, the couch next to it up, the chair too, up, up, up, and they all are above Mom's upside– down laughing head, and the room goes light to dark to light to dark, screams and laughter.

You bring that up when you come in and sit next to him. His head lifts and peers at you.

'See, Michael. That was ut on der lan.'

You repeat that back to him.

'No, no, Dutch Wonderland…. Won–der–land. Right, me and my *hermano* go there once or two times.'

'With that rabbit, 'What's up, Doc?''

'See, with Fred Flintstone and Dino, when we were young and dumb to believe Bugs Bunny and his friends go there.'

'Yeah, I remember. What you doing lying there?'

'Whas you doin',' he mimics you in a falsetto. 'Whas up, Doc?' and he laughs.

The ceiling high up the four floors of lounges, staircases, railings, all the same as pipes of a squat tunnel, same as the one on the road underneath the Wilson Dorm that leads to the receiving dock. All floors, built the same, appear different from the play of orange lights jarring through the grates of the rails. The edges fall on the crooked blocky spiral staircase that leads to the fourth–floor lounge. It is as if the lounges were balconies set on the side of a building turned inside out. You turn your head to Sam to tell him about the inside of here. Instead of laughing, he turns his face to the ceiling, and his eyes are getting wet. He says something in his language, and it looks as if he is going back in time in his own head.

'Bathroom?' you ask.

'See, *baño*,' his lips pronounce. 'Right.'

'What about the bathroom?'

'Oh, it's in my home.'

'It's bad to do that. Will mess you up. Got to think of now. That's all,' you say, even though you break that bit of wisdom many times.

'See bas to do thas.'

You sigh. You hate it when he makes fun of your speech.

'What about the bathroom, Sam? That's where you spend your life there?'

'Ha, ha. It's just the way light hits the floor. It's *mi baño en* home. Our home is in a row house, between other narrow houses. Narrow houses with narrow rooms inside cluttered but warm rooms with heavy chairs and clunky tables for people to come, sit, rest. And center of the house, *el inodoro en el baño*. Such hollers from *mi familia*, who gets to use it first, who uses it longest, and who stinks it up the most. When I get in, I appreciate my time there, pissing in *el inodoro*, taking a dump in there.

El baño is long and narrow and the tiles are in chalky squares. The ceiling rises in the form of a butcher knife. The walls are milky colored, and we have a built–in shower stall with three broad wooden shelves. One shelf, a clay pot with a red flower on it. I do not know the flower, but it had red petals, big as my palms. And the soil, in that whiteness of the room, looks clean and dusty. Around the corner, beyond the shower stall, is a towel rack on the door of the closet. *Mi Mami* keeps a daisy–colored towel, and on it or doily, I'm not sure, there's plastic doll babies' heads attached to the hanging cloth. Rows of fake rosy lips puckered in teeny kisses. And above everything, there's a skylight where you get a piece of the sky. And the color of the room, with white walls, changes, whether red, yellow, or orange. On moonlit nights, the beam form a column, a house in Greece. I see this bathroom in my dreams, hot on summer nights, cold on winter mornings, and in many sleeps. I could touch the door, but my fingers only brushes. It won't open.'

A teardrop glistens on his cheek and his lips move slower.

'That's I keep in my thoughts, just this one room. And I couldn't get out there to *mi familia*, *mi Mama*, *Papi*, even Luis, *mi hermano* in his Jockeys posing with little muscles in the bedroom mirror. Just me and this room in the house in the middle of *familia*, middle of many fights, and now I have *baño* and I couldn't get out of there.'

He thrust his palms against his eyes and rubs them.

'I just want *mi familia* back. That's all.'

'You can't get out.'

'Why not?'

Propped on his elbows, he looks directly at you, his eyes narrow.

'Um… because if the door opens and you go through, there's gonna be nothing. A hole you fall in. I get dreams this sometimes. And you fall, you die, and when you die in a dream, you die in sleep or almost.'

'Almost huh?' he says, his smile wan. 'A long *pesadilla*.'

'La what?'

'Nightmare.'

'Daymare.'

'*¿Que tal?*'

You sit up to see him better. 'Because happens in real life.'

'Michael?'

'Hmm?'

'You know, *barrio?*'

'No clothes naked?'

He shakes his head. '*Barrio* neighborhood district. Like projects in Philly. No *reproduccion.*'

'Black houses?'

'See, closed–in places. Places to separate and sort. They say for our good, but it's for them. *Limpiar estandarizar y otorgar esplendor.* Almost same here.'

Sam once explained that to you a few weeks after the first time you met him. Paul had to spell everything for you. Clean, sanitize, and grant splendor. You stare at a fixed point on the wall opposite you and Sam.

'*Barrio* means to keep here?'

'See, Michael.'

You shake your head and let out a grim sigh. 'Jeez, they sure didn't cover that in the brochures they sent us.'

A burst of laughter startles you.

'Ah, Michael, you say the funniest things sometimes.' He lounged on his elbows. 'And the Watchers are *los ángeles* among us.'

At last, three years later, you watch this seagull flying over the rooftop and beyond, from the *barrio* to the outside. Then the Whysees come and make you go to work.)—

Michael's sore muscles welcomed the bleary red of the sunset, and somewhere inside him, the dry hunger grew. It made him canny enough to wait. It trembled, giving him enough resolve to see Paul before dinner and find out where he got these books.

The First Few Movements

Before Michael entered Sam and Paul's room, their door opened and Sam almost collided with him, a flimsy mask in one hand and a sheet wrapped under his arm. Back on his medication, Sam had become surer of himself and solid on his feet.

"Hey *loco*," Sam said, "Seeing Paul?"

"Yeah, I gos to ask him something. Whas you doin'?"

—How long gonna be, Sam? Before you go 'Whoa ho *loco* Michael gonna swipe more Die lay tin for his *amigo*, eh *hombre?*'—

He remained silent while Sam handed him the mask and said something about the Halloween party the next week. Michael inspected the mask. It was a PhtoneSkin product that displayed bulging, heavy–lidded eyes and a toothy grin. The entire material can congeal to the face, a second skin.

"Whas this?"

"It's a deaf demon. I got it from the clothes that the Watchers collected for their charity thing. I think a Black guy wore that. You can be like Blacula or Deafcula or both."

"Neas." Michael gestured at Sam's sheet. "Whas happens? Too crispy from many nighs?"

"Why Michael, it would be your bedsheet then. But isn't. Gonna be a bride. The pillowcase is my *mantilla*."

"Whas?"

"See, Michael. Part of my culture."

"Didn's know you guys were gay."

"Aw, you love it."

Michael tried to get past Sam, who backhanded his behind before hurrying off to the lobby.

"Sheesh, Sam."

His laughter trailed. Michael sighed and flipped the light switch by the door. It opened and Paul peered out.

"Hey Paul, can I come in?"

Paul opened it wide and backed up from him. Before Paul could wheel himself to the window, Michael skirted past and placed the mask on the ledge below him. He examined a square shape imprinted in the dust beside it.

"Paul, whas happenes to the book?"

Finish.

Paul guided Michael from the glass and faced him, his arms crossed, his head tilted. Thin light hit his face, edged with wariness. A flush building the rear of his neck, Michael attempted conversation.

"Neas, whas the book's name?"

The Human Zoo.

"Nice. New or ole?"

New to me. Can you sit so I can see you better?

"Nice, how ges them?"

Paul shrank back in his wheelchair.

"Maybe I can ree is! Where ges is? Come on Paul, I'm jus curious."

Why?

"Curious, come on."

Stop playing me.

"I'm nos!"

Yes, you are.

"Nos!" Michael giggled.

—Jesus, just like kids. Nuh–uh! Nuh–huh!—

"Michael!" Paul signed and shouted. "Stop playing! You're trying to use me!"

"Whas you 'cusin' me of?"

"Michael, you keep pacing, and you wouldn't sit down. Plus, asking me for books is like Sam coming in and asking me about flower arrangements!"

"Well, Sam gonna be bri," Michael attempted to joke.

Get out. Leave now.

Instead of sitting or leaving, he stepped closer. "An' you'll do whas?"

Paul gripped the rims of his wheels, and his face creaked. The door clunked into Michael's back. He could sense Sam behind him, trying to work his way in. When Michael twisted to look, he glanced at Sam, who had been talking to Paul, his smile confused. Paul explained something to him, and then his eyes narrowed.

"Sam, whas you wans?"

"That's what I want to know," Sam said back.

"It's okay. Please go now," Paul asked.

Sam's lips pressed.

Paul ticked his head toward the door. "Go on now. Please."

"Fine, but I don't like this."

The door slammed behind Michael.

Hope you are happy, Paul signed.

—Assholes! How long before Sam goin', 'Hey, whoa ho *loco!* How about stealin' and riskin' you neck, helpin' *amigo* Sam keepin' strong.' Paul with his big shot books.—

Paul must have read the anger, for he swiveled himself to the window, so Michael only saw the back of his neck, his stooped head, and the way his arms draped over the armrests.

"You want honessly, huh?" Michael shouted. "You jus coverin' your ass so you can be keep gettin' your books. Maybe I wans something too."

Paul faced him again.

Fine. What do you want?

—Just sick of this place.—

"I wans ous, Paul."

Paul gave a meaningful glance at the door. Michael collapsed on Sam's bed and switched to sign language.

I want out.

We all do.

I want out because I get run of bad luck here being at wrong place at wrong time and you know how to get book, and you get them and get to pretend you far from here. Me, I am stuck here in real time. I want to die than live just one year and only go outside to another fence.

They won't make it easy.

I know. I want to run for it and if they get me, beat me, I get bit of grass, smell, and feel real outside. They will see I like out like real people, and I will try. At last, they will see I will try for it. Please P–A–U–L? My life.

What about…?

Will explain. Sorry I push you. Get mad and scare.

I need to think first. After dinner, I will let you know.

The door swung open, and Sam walked in with a stiff smile.

"Everything's fine now? Going to dinner?"

Paul nodded at him and swallowed. Sam looked at Michael, his smile faltering. When Michael left them to drop off the mask in his room before dinner, he remembered the look on the face, the way his friend's brown eyes had become dull.

After the shift, Michael stood by the door to Sam and Paul's room. Dust clung to his clothes, and the grist of turkey and watery lemonade fizzed in his stomach. Throughout dinner, Sam and Paul had argued in voices, and when Michael asked what they were talking about, Paul turned exasperated, and asked Michael what he thought it was about. While waiting again in the hallway, he could hear their urgent voices. The door flew open, and Sam stalked out.

"Have a nice talk with Paul," he spat, stomping away to the door for the lobby.

"Come on…"

Sam thrust his palm out and kept moving. Michael winced when the door to the lobby slammed. He entered their room, and Paul waited by the window, his face still. Michael sat on Sam's bed.

"Okay, Paul."

Paul nodded and began.

The man who get me book is the P–O–S–T–M–A–N.

We get mail here?

Paul's head tilted; his eyebrows arched. Then his face turned hard. *Now, what I am about to tell you is for few to know. If you tell or all talk and no act, I will cut you out. I am not playing ...* He crossed his heart.

Alright! Alright!

If you are stuck, I can't help you, not S–A–M either. You will be alone.

Yes.

The man pass V–I–R–G–I–N–I–A A–V–E in what S–A–M call the B–A–R–R–I–O. He come by every week. I will let you use my time one time. He will get what you need: playing cards, soap, string, a milkshake from D–A–I–R–Y Queen. But you must pay with what you get. You must know his look: cap, sloppy beard, and long ponytail out back of cap. For what you want, it will only be once.

Why?

Either free or dead.

—Just what I need. Wish Paul and Sam get small so I can carry them in my pocket out of here.—

Michael was about to express his wish aloud when Sam stuck his face in from the opened door.

"Now can I come in?"

"Sure, Sam."

"*Gracias*, Michael, *oh muchas gracias*, Michael, *de nada.*"

Sam stepped close and Michael threw up his hands involuntarily.

—Real great. Real tough. Are tough now, *loco?*—

Paul barked out something. Sam turned and raised his hands in supplication as he slammed himself on the bed next to Michael, the muscles around his jaws bunching.

"I gos to go now," Michael mumbled. The bed creaked as he jumped up and left. He berated himself as he retreated to his room.

—Stupid and selfish, already cryin' freedom.—

He lay on his bed. His worn eyes refused to remain closed, and he waited for the sun to come up, his mind worn.

He could not get to the Postman sooner. Five times this week, he lost half an hour of dinner dawdling near the fence as Paul instructed. The dust and sweat clung to his skin, his issued denim pants and shirt smelling of zinc. All for the Postman. Today was the same.

Michael gazed through the fence at the passersby of his future *barrio*. A chubby man with orange hair and a sloped forehead loped past him. After him was a bony Black woman with horsey teeth who swung her knobbed hips at him. She urged him in signs to poke a part of him through the fence to make him happy in exchange for a bowl to be filched from the cafeteria tomorrow. He lipped the word, "no" along with a headshake. The woman snorted at the way he blushed before moving on elsewhere. Another resident came around the corner. Michael clung to the bars, cool and dry.

There was no ponytail on the back of that man's head, but frazzled hair on an old lady shuffling along, her smile uncertain. Tucked under her arm was a worn pillow in the shape of the smirking cat, *Garfield*. Right after her was a blonde man with fat lips and reptilian eyelids who stuck his tongue at him before jogging after the old woman. Michael sighed.

Another man came from the south end of Virginia Avenue. Michael peered harder and gratefully saw the narrow eyes, the beard, a ponytail poking through the back of his cap, and a potbelly sloped over his thick leather belt that had a ring on it jingling with old keys. He watched through the fence as the man continued his loping gait, grinning, his hands stuck in the pockets of his torn windbreaker. When the man drew nearer to the fence, Michael fell in step with him.

"Nice day, huh?"

—Way to figure that one out, Michael. Jeez.—

The man who might be the Postman was sharper than in imagination. He could have been fatter or thinner, darker or lighter, taller or shorter, but he was there now. His head turned and nodded; his face mild.

You get thing, right? Michael asked.

The man tilted his head with a puzzled smile.

Are you one?

The man stumbled forward, stopping his fall with a hand planted on the sidewalk, and grabbing one bar with another, his keys clinking.

You O.K.?

Michael leaned closer to the man, who had not answered but stayed on all–fours, breathing hard. Small eyes glinted at him from beneath the brim of the cap, and the head nodded. He held out his hand, gesturing for help. Michael put his hand between the bars and grasped the man's arm. Two hands grabbed at his arm and pulled hard. The iron bars mashed against his face, his ears stinging. One of the Postman's hands still gripped Michael's arm.

NOW ON, the Postman signed with the other hand *NO STUPID.* The pupils in his eyes contracted.

"Whas!"

The hand, still holding his arm, squeezed harder, twisting tendons. *NO STUPID. TRY SMART. NO...* His face turned dumbstruck.

What can I do? Michael signed with a free hand, grimacing.

The putrid odor from the Postman's rotten teeth flooded his nostrils, making him want to retch, but he forced himself to relax.

BETTER. The man's grip loosened.

Michael moved his head back.

WHAT NEED BOY?

Out.

WANT ME WORK FINE. YOU SAME. ME WARN YOU WORK WILL. The Postman signed with strain the word *WORK*, and grimaced, which meant it would go harder for Michael. Then he mimed pulling down his pants, his eyebrows up, questioning. *FOR ONE WHYSEE?*

—Old queer!—

STRUGGLE FINISH! An aw–shucks grin from the Postman and he continued. *ONLY ASK ME MAKE DIFFERENT ARRANGEMENT THURSDAY. ME NEED YOU DISTRACT THEM TEN MINUTES THURSDAY TIME TEN. DO FOR ME. YOU ME AGREE THIS THURSDAY.*

Doing what?

THINK YOURSELF. THURSDAY NIGHT. TEN DISTRACT WHYSEES.

Try.

WAIT.

Michael did. The Postman gave an abrupt sign, finishing with a sweeping flip of his palm over the roof of his other hand, still gripping Michael's own.

—Did he say die?—

The Postman sighed and signed slower. *YOU WORK UNDER ME OR DIE.*

Michael yanked away from him, rapping his elbow against the bars. It stung along his forearm.

"Asshole," he muttered and walked away, breathing hard.

Over his shoulder, he saw him walking away as if nothing had happened. Michael winced, rubbing his shoulder, and headed to the cafeteria.

After dinner, it was his and Sam's turn to rake the leaves. They worked silently. Michael turned to Sam.

"Sae, whas wool you do to mess a guy from bas neighborhoos?"

"The blockheads?"

"Anyone you don's like."

"Dunno, heet him."

"Whas if bigger than you?"

"Doesn't take much against someone who uses size."

"Whas if he's better, faster, smarter?"

Sam put down the rake, eager to share his experience.

"If you get into a fight, you got to keep your fists up." He appraised him. "Besides, you can count on me anyway to watch for you."

"Hey, teach me."

"Come on, you got me to do that for you."

"Yeah, buh something migh happen an' you may nos be aroun'."

Sam snorted and picked up the rake. "Nah, you're stuck with me."

"If I was myself, how I go to protes myself?"

"Just run."

Michael put up his fists. "Betsha, I cool kick your ass."

Sam glanced at him, his face quizzical.

"Come on, you shicken?"

"Michael, what you gotta prove?"

Michael took a couple of swipes at him. "Come on, tough guy."

He swung and Sam's hand caught his and twisted it behind Michael's back, one–handed.

"You got to learn to swing without your eyes closed," Sam said before letting go.

Michael rubbed his arm.

—Like someone tied it into a knot.—

"Man, I wish I am tough as you."

"Careful, you may get what you wish for."

"Still do."

He laughed and held up his fists. "Put them up. Come on."

"Like this?"

"Weak. Got to be ready."

Michael bunched his hands, nice and tight, and tried glaring over his fists. His hands still felt loose, and his thumb kept sticking out.

"Better. Now, when I take a swing, block it. Ready? Now watch out, here it comes, now block–block–block!"

Michael raised his arm, and it connected with Sam's arm.

"Block with your forearm."

"Yeah, I see. Wish I knew karate or something." He chopped the air, shouting nonsense.

Sam snickered. "Guy you're fighting with gonna die laughing."

"Guess he wool."

"Want to know how to fight for real?"

"How?"

Sam ran his hand along his forearm. "Use this. Keep your elbows high."

Michael nodded. "Yeah, nes time Whysees come you can punsh them, an' I'll give them this." He swung his elbow at an invisible enemy.

"Hah, that'll be the day."

Sam turned back to work. Michael picked his own and watched Sam before raking. A steady dull pain grew in his chest.

Later, he did a practice run from the cafeteria to the dorm. He trooped back and checked two avenues of escape. One was a gravel path through the basketball court to his dorm. The second avenue was under the parking lot. It took sixty–five Mississippi getting there after the trial run. The next day stretched before him. He found himself excitable, easily irritated. One time, he snapped at Sam for dragging his footsteps with his wheelbarrow and received a slacken grin of shock on his friend's face as he passed.

—Why not just hit him, moron? Last few days and givin' him a hard time? Tired of everyone here. First Paul judgin' me 'cause I'm leaving this place. Blockheads now lookin' at me funny eyed when passin' them on the plaza. All's fuzzy now. And now the Whysees, yellin' more and more.—

Michael entered the bathroom before lunch. In the bathroom, he saw two bare feet squirming underneath the stall door. His stomach could not decide whether the odor of sausage from the stall should make it retch or rumble. The toilet flushed and Henry got out of the bathroom. Henry's hand chopped out the T as he signed *toilet*, and he whinnied at that.

At lunch, Sam jabbered about that day when Michael jumped on Richie's back, going "and dere's *loco* Michael all crazed up, wildly screamin', 'Son of Bis! Son of Bis!'"

Sam giggled at the memory. Nancy harped on about coming to college here and what she was learning today, listening to the classes while cleaning the floor of the Bline Memorial Building. Michael's mind drifted.

—Wish they stop foolin' themselves. Better get that straight 'cause I'm out. And right now, before this run, scared now. Of runnin.'—

Thursday night, Michael stared at himself in the bathroom mirror. He saw his cloudy blue eyes wide and his lips jerking into a nervous smile. The reflection showed a curly–haired boy walking in wearing a bathrobe, a toothbrush brush in one hand and a bar of soap in another. Then the image put them on the counter.

—Oh great. Aw, not right. Messin' me up when all shaky and ready runnin' with big chance.—

Girlman's hands moved in the reflection, signing something. Michael could see his sloped breasts between the parting of his robe.

MY NAME WHAT? Girlman signed, skilled.

Not know. Sorry.

A wearisome sigh from Girlman. *ME K–A–S–Y.*

How you? O.K.

Michael stepped from the sink and felt a sharp grab for his elbow.

"Whas?"

Girlman's face had purple bruises under his baggy eyes from the lack of sleep and the tight curls around his soft face hardly moved. His lips moved.

"My name."

"Kasy all righ? Leave alone."

ME TELL SOMETHING. His eyes squinted with self–righteousness.

"Fine. Go ahay."

YOU NOT LOOK ME LIKE… He swiveled his head, his face snotty.

—Talkin', signin' same time, hummin' at me. He's bitchy for Chris 'sake.—

YOU NOT MAKE FUN ME, Kasy signed.

I don't.

YOU LIE. YOU TELL 'Ooo I lost appetite?' HOW ME FEEL?

"Thas fine, I don't care. I gos stuff to do."

Michael let the bathroom door swing shut on Girlman's weary face as he hurried out. He went through the lobby and into the cool, damp air of the night. He fought to think of nothing but thought too much.

—Doors should open at night. Gotta be. They lockin' night? No. There you go. Ready? Goin' over to the Whysees. Dark night. Good. No moon, good. You run this before, right? Know this area better than Whysees. When runnin', run hard. No thinkin', hard run. Time, do not know, wait and see. Watch dorm lights, when goin' out, time to start.—

He waited until the lights winked out one by one. Soon the windows of the Osborn Dorm peered like blind eyes.

—Ready. Set. Go.—

He started walking, his motion quiet and formal. Far away, he recognized the gray shirts of the youths walking toward their dorms. He crept closer, keeping to the side of the wreckage of the building where he hauled bricks. He sighted the doors to the lobby in the gray building at the end.

—Whysee building starts with O... not know all the word but use O building.—

He dashed to the door, keeping to the dark, his sneakers skittering on the tar. He entered the building, even brushing past a Whysee who only cocked his head in puzzlement. Michael lunged for the first red he saw, which was the fire alarm, and his fingers dug in it. The lever was too stubborn to move, so he pulled harder. It peeled. In the flashing lobby, another Whysee popped up from his seat in the front office, and Michael caught the stunned face through the glass partition. Lightning struck all over the interior. The Whysee shouted.

"Jus stupis I guess," Michael muttered as he dashed out.

—(Braw!) Funny (Braw!) same (Braw!) sound (Braw!) every (Braw!) morning makes. (Braw!) Could (Braw!) hear (Braw!) runnin' (Braw!) feet (Braw!) between them. Getoutjustgetout.—

Giggling from terror, Michael body–slammed himself through the double doors and he reeled into the night air. His head bent, he pumped his arms, sprinting in a straight line past the three Whysees' dorms. With an exhilarated look over his shoulder, he saw the first clumps of Whysees shivering outside in sweatpants, pajama bottoms, or boxer shorts, arms crossed over bare chests. Over the steps, he leapt and tore across the road that led to the children's playground. To the side, two Whysees waved their arms at the others. Four or more took after him, mouths open in aggrieved rage.

—Oh, Jesus, more coming after me.—

One Whysee was even in his briefs. Michael flung a hyena laugh over his shoulder when the faraway figures shouted at him. He took the slope, grass sliding under his pedaling feet, and twice he skidded on the dew. Another shout from Whysee, who slipped and landed on his back.

—Oh snsssk! Funny! Do not laugh. Laugh about it later. Now get to work.—

He measured the fence coming ahead with his eyes. He did not think, but threw himself over the rail, tucking his legs up under him. The ground slammed his left shoulder, and he rolled to his knees. He stumbled and ran harder up the steep hill. Several Whysees had made it to the waist–high fence. A few climbed over it. He noticed a ripped piece of underwear flapping on the rail. Further away, a naked and aimless Whysee wandered around the children's playground, his hands cupping his privates. Michael made wide steps, skips, and jumps on the way to the top gravel path to gain purchase on the steep slope. The gravity pulled at his back as he leapt over a narrow ditch to the path. He staggered to the top behind the children's dorms and ducked into the darkest shadows he could find. Then he wove his way back through the underground parking lot.

—Good dark now. It is a can't see me hood to cover me with. No one up there yet. Get out. Don't wanna get caught now.—

He scrambled up the stairs and tried the door.

—Oh no. I'm fucked. No! Don't do this to me!—

Michael pulled hard at the door, rattling it. He looked over his shoulder. Hundreds of Whysees who did not chase him waited for the alarms to stop so they could get back in the dorm far away. Thank God, they kept their gazes on where the chase began. He guessed they expected the ones who gave chase to drag the chastened ward back. He stooped and crawled to the window that investigated his room. His neck cricked as he scuttled to his and Henry's window. He raised an arm and rapped against the glass. Through the window,

Henry's face appeared and reared back, eyes bugged and mouth open. Michael pointed at the entrance and hissed.

"Ges door!"

Henry looked behind, debating.

"Now, please!" Michael made begging gesture.

Henry's face moved back, and Michael peeked over the windowsill. Through the glass, the dorm room was empty. He inched his way over to the entrance. No cries of notice broke the terse silence. Henry's silhouette appeared at the front entrance. There was a click and,

—Thank you, Jesus. Think got away with it.—

Henry held the door open for Michael. Henry, goggling at Michael, asked nothing even though the knees of Michael's pants were damp with dew and he kept gasping hard. They made their way through the lobby to their room.

—One messed up but smart *loco hombre*. Hope Whysees likin' their wake–up call.—

They crept into their dorm room and Henry, still shaking his head in wonder, climbed into his bed. Michael lay back in his own bed, grinning at how the tide had turned.

That morning, he told Paul what he did and gave him the day of Halloween to go outside the compound. Paul met with the Postman and came back to tell Michael to return there to pick up a note the next time he comes by. On Saturday he waited, acting as if he was just watching the passers–by of Handytown *barrio* after roll call.

The roll call ran late because earlier, Whysees had prodded Paul to the front of the throng to interpret that automatic locks would be installed after Halloween and all wards would be expected to be inside before 9:00 p.m. and could not exit until the early morning. One–minute past nine, any ward caught loitering outside would be put on report and meals be withheld the next day.

While he waited for the Postman, Sam stopped by before heading to the terminal Workboard.

"Why you not going to the dorm?" he asked Michael.

Michael looked through the fence where the *barrio* began.

"Jus checking our future home."

—Sam's future home. He's the one left behind.—

Sam told him, "Later, Michael." When he left, his grin faltered.

Michael clung to the bars. Soon a familiar cap came into view among the residents of Handytown, and the Postman's quizzical face turned toward the fence as he walked along it. A flash of white fell to the ground, where a clump of grass struggled to grow in the damp weather. Michael bent on one knee and made as if tying his sneakers. His hand darted and retrieved the paper. He stuffed it in the guise of putting his hands into his pockets.

A Whysee shouted something and laughed amid a crowd of other Whysees. Michael pasted a vague grin on his face and strolled toward his dorm, his heart hammering. He made it across the football field and past the bleachers without an outcry. Agony settled upon him when he spied Nat and the usual gang crowded around one bleacher. Richie stood and signed.

YOU HAVE SOMETHING.

Michael tried to pretend ignorance and kept moving. One, then two started following. Richie fell in steps with the others. A pat and Michael turned. Nat sneer at him and then stepped up his pace to a hurried walk. Richie hurried next to him, his thick arms swinging. Then Richie signed across to Kelly, and Michael missed the signs.

ME KNOW YOU HAVE SOMETHING IN POCKET. Kelly signed, grinning.

What?

PAPER, Richie responded.

Michael twisted and ran from the hollers and slapping of heels. He made it halfway into the underground lot when a foot swept under him. His knees hit the concrete, and his palms skidded burning. A familiar bald head blocked the pipes under the underground parking lot and was about to speak when Michael's own foot lashed out and caught him in the groin. Eggy grunted and staggered back. Michael struggled to rise, but another heavier shoe shoved into his ribs. Richie beamed as Michael lay on his side, coughing.

WEAK, Richie signed.

Legs in worn pants and holey sneakers surrounded him.

—Goin' be stuck for the rest of my life rest of my life restsmyliferestmylife!—

A hand reached into his pocket, searching, and seized his testicles, a sickening pull below his guts. It was Kelly's hand. Michael screamed hard and croaked from the nausea bubbling in his guts. The hand traveled to the paper and plucked it out of his pocket. Kelly stood and whooped, showing her prize. She handed it to Dimitri who read it aloud, signing with one part while she voiced the message.

"Night Oct thirty one. Go time nine thirty. Find wait Seventh Street far away one Washer. Washer leave nine forty forty five seconds changing of Washer. Red shirt help with danger fence."

Dimitri glared at Michael, who moved to a seated position, clutching his crotch.

Trying to leave us? She signed before resuming her reading. "Red shirt watch at you. Will tell to you what to do."

Dimitri turned to Nat and voiced something. Nat grabbed the paper and read it aloud. He looked at Michael.

"Don't think you are going to make it," Nat began and screamed.

"I don't think you have anything to say about that," Sam said behind Nat and pulled the blockhead's arm higher, twisting it.

Richie advanced but stopped when Sam cocked a broad thumb under Nat's eye.

"One step, he's losing an eye," Sam said.

"Don't!" Nat hollered. "Stay away hurts!" His other arm flapped at the others to stay away.

NOT FAIR CAN'T DO THAT. Kelly signed.

Sam answered with a shrug and pressed his thumb under Nat's bulging left eye. A rim of blood ran beneath his nail. Sam's own left eyelid rose. "Don't try me. Just don't."

Michael stood and staggered to Sam's side, rubbing his stomach. Nat mewed, his twisted face seeming to frighten others.

"Get paper," Sam said.

Michael moved over and tugged at the paper. He looked up at Sam.

"Let go, Nat."

Nat did. Michael plucked the paper and folded it back into his pocket.

"Okay, Michael is going first. I'm next, and Nat's coming with us," Sam instructed, as if he was conversing about the intricate design of the pipes beneath the ceiling of the parking lot.

When one tried to move closer, Sam pursed his lips in a frown and his brows furrowed in a warning. That blockhead backed up, hands raised. Sam nodded toward the steps and gave the rest of the blockheads a death stare. They drew away as if Sam were a beagle panting blood.

"You okay?" Michael asked.

Sam's head bobbed with impatience. Michael obeyed and marched up the steps but waited by the entrance door.

Through the entrance, he saw two heads, one blonde–haired, the other dark–haired, bobbing into view. Then he saw Sam's face. His arm was around Nat's shoulder and he kept smiling as if just a joke. His hand crept up the arm roped around the blockhead's neck, then shoved him down the steps. Nat disappeared, grunting. Sam ran upstairs and around, his frantic hand waving at Michael to get into the dorm. Michael moved, hands raking at the door handle and pulling it open as Sam crashed in behind him.

They scurried across the lobby, Michael yanking the next door and both running in the hallway to Sam and Paul's room. They stumbled inside and Sam giggled.

"The Whysees, they come over only to see Nat falling on the others. They come running and now yelling at Nat and others." He controlled himself. "What's so important on that paper?"

"Nothing."

"Nothing," Sam repeated. "Nothing that almost got you be beaten and me having to almost kill somebody. Nothing is causing this. Paul is telling me nothing. Oh, nothing."

"I'm sorry."

Sam's tone softened.

"Look, I didn't do this because I like to hurt," he said, although his shiny eyes said otherwise. "I do this 'cause *tú eres mi amigo*."

"You're righ."

"So, what is it?"

Michael handed him the paper and shifted.

"It's just the time, and someone something with a red shirt."

"I'm getting ous."

"Huh?"

His eyes felt wet. "Away. Is's jus' thas I'm tire of them taking my life."

"They're not killing you."

"No, buh they're taking my time away."

"What about you, me, Paul?"

"Yeah, buh these Whysees, they sae I am nos human, bus I laugh an' I ges hurs jus like they do."

"But it'll hurt Paul."

"He knows. Thas why he din's tell you."

"But we're going to play hockey out there and be together in winter in the *barrio*."

"I'm sorry. I can's live like thas."

He stared at him, his eyes wide. "Fine, Michael. Go away, please."

"Sam?"

"Get out. We're not enough for you."

"Come on, Sam."

Sam flapped a hand at him. The room blurred as Michael backed out. He staggered back to his room and sat on the bed, fighting to keep his eyes from leaking. Failing that, he wiped at them with the heels of his hands. He reached under his bed and pulled out his hockey stick. Flimsy with age, the lip of the tape unraveled around the blade. He wiped his eyes again and got up to leave.

When he arrived at the playground, he found Robby huddled by the concrete drainage, rubbing his arms against the frost. His face lit up when Michael approached.

HI MICHAEL HOW YOU? ME BAD AGAIN. Robby tilted his head back and grinned. More bruises and pink abrasions were along his arms.

WHY THIS? ME STUBBORN. NOT SING IN CHRISTMAS FOR DOCTORS.

Who do this?

L–U–G–G–I–N.

Why? You just a kid.

THEY NOT CARE. IF LOOK AWAY WHEN J–I– M–M–Y N–I–C–O–L–E… He made several unknown name signs…. *LOOK AWAY MANY SLOW CHILDREN WHEELCHAIRS WHY THEY WILL….* He clasped his hand to his chest, "aww!", *LITTLE BOY WHO NOT VOICE.*

Michael handed him the hockey stick.

My goodbye gift.

Robby examined it. *FOR ME? THEY TAKE YOU AWAY?*

No. I am just going to go.

Robby's face became taut with hope. He dropped the stick and stepped closer.

TAKE ME WITH YOU. "chow" HARD LIVE HERE.

I can't. T–O–O dangerous.
He pried Robby off him.
NOT CARE. ME OUT SAME.
I am sorry. Can't.
DANGEROUS BETTER THAN LIFE HERE.
Robby's lips clenched over his teeth. He picked up the stick with both hands and threw it at him. Putt! It bounced off his chest.
OUT. YOU NOTHING. NOT MY FRIEND.
His pudgy fingers linked the last part a few moments before breaking.
Come on…
SHOO! YOU LOUSY SIGNS! ME TELL G–O! SHOO! SHOO!
Robby looked at the fence, his face bewildered and bottom lip trembling. Michael walked away. When he turned for one last look, Robby sat on the steps, holding onto it and rocking himself.
—You stupid, selfish ass. Leaving him behind with Sam's stupid disappointments.—

They made shadows along orange patches of sunlight upon Farrow Field. The Whysees were gray specks in the crowd, their eyes open and alert. Hands backlit by the browning sky moved. It was hard to talk, for one wrong word and unwanted eyes might fall on them. The silence among his friends stifled him. He started the conversation in voice.
"Las day. Sure will miss this."
—Oh, way to go. 'Last day.' Jeez.—
Through the sheer eyes of the mask, Michael watched Sam lurching with the pillowcase pulled over his head. The cloth clung to his features, just two dents and a hollow dip where his mouth is. In his makeshift wedding costume, he kept a hand on Paul's wheelchair for guidance. Paul rolled on, wearing a crushed fedora and a Q–Tip taped to a black pipe

cleaner between his clenched teeth. Jose jumped and wove in between, signing *ME WHO* while wearing a brown shirt, black pants, and green construction papers cut into triangles attached to both ears. A helpful ward had tied a plastic bowl to his right shoulder. Everyone took turns guessing as Jose kept shaking his head with a triumphant grin. Paul interpreted as others guessed. Nancy with paper triangles perched on her ears, pipe cleaners for whiskers, and soot on her nose guessed *L–E–P–R–E–C–H–A–U–N*. Sam, from beneath the pillowcase, guessed *V–D* then *S–T–D*. Michael laughed. Henry, who wrapped his blanket around himself for fur, floppy beagle ears cut from Jose's tattered bathrobe, and with plastic fangs in his mouth, guessed *MONKEY* after Michael showed him the sign for the monkey. Michael guessed *E–L–F* and Paul guessed *A–L–I–E–N*. Jose's head swung, his reply exaggerated, and signed, *G–R–O–G–U ME G–R–O–G–U!* Michael peeled his mask over his forehead to see better and rid himself of that stifling old rubber odor.

"Meow!" Nancy said, scratching at the air.

Michael noticed Gertie, who walked farther away, carrying a cardboard cutout with colorful circles scribbled on it. In her other bony hand, she carried a pencil with pink yarns tied to the tip. She flattened it from time to time with the cardboard cutout.

"You are an artist, right, Gertie?" Michael called.

Gertie snapped something back.

'Ooo you are so smart to know that.' she said. Paul signed.

"As lee I'm nos one hitting my heah with the cus ous," Michael called back. He turned to Paul. "Whas with her?"

Nancy spoke and Paul interpreted.

"Gertie, an artist again. She's all mad and all that because I told her, 'Try to be something else this year!' She's not talking to me anymore. Meow."

Sam, who now carried the pillowcase in his hand, scrutinized Henry. "Hey, did someone draw a circle around the eye?"

"Duh–duh–deaf girl did for me."

Sam whooped.

"Hear that? Henry got a girl to do something for him. Why you wanna out here, see Michael? No *chica* doing things for you?"

"Shus up."

"Sam! Don't announce to the world!" Paul hissed.

"Is Sam mad? Meow."

"Yeah, shus up Sam."

Sam cupped his ear.

"Wha' cha choo say, Mikey?"

"Sam, stop it." Paul said and signed.

"Oh yeah, well you—"

Sam did not have time to finish his last retort, for he bumped into Nancy's bulky form that grew still. Jose looked up and then looked back toward the grass. Michael turned around, resigned.

"Fancy meeting you all again," Nat said, stroking an invisible villain's mustache. "Whoor ha—ha—ha."

Others in T—shirts and some wearing masks surrounded them. The T—shirts had charcoals scrubbed on them for the grayish color, and the T—shirt that Nat wore had a dusty colored star cut out from an old newspaper pinned to it. One wearing a mask called Moron stepped behind Nat, and Michael noticed the pitiful string dangling from that ward's flabby arm. A larger T—shirt nearby with sleeves that bulged with hairy fat and muscles belonged to Richie. Four more unknowns showed in masks. One was a Deaf Demoniac, same as Michael's, two Morons, and one Blind with no sheer eyes, the wearer grasping the elbow of the one in the Moron mask. There were about seven in all.

"Let me guess, the queens of Handytown," Sam proclaimed, and he bowed toward them with a flourish, then did a curtsey.

—Look how tough Richie is signin' in his pretend Whysee shirt goin', *CAREFUL ME CRUSH YOU*, Sam goin' in his bridal sheet, stompin', and wavin' him 'Come on' at himself, Jose still askin' this time Richie *ME WHO?* and Nat,

112

with that star on his chest, demanding Paul to say what everyone's talkin' about. One more ridiculous thing I'm gonna just die laughin.'—

Michael already felt giddy when Richie, amid the posturing, looked at Jose, who still was signing *ME WHO?* The bulk of the blockheads, yes he did, guessed that Jose was *C–E–L–E–R–Y*. Sam caught Paul's sign and voice for 'celery' and said with fake bafflement, *"Ai!* What's that? His favorite vegetable to insert?"

The audacity became enough for Michael to bite the palm of his hand to keep hysterical laughter from tearing out of his throat. Richie, realizing that he was being made fun of, stepped forward. The one in Deaf Demoniac mask peeled it off, and it belonged to Kelly who signed to Richie, *NOT NOW!* Richie froze, his rocky face set in disappointment. Sam concentrated on Richie, making a circle with his hands, pointing to his behind, and making a wider circle with his hands again.

"That's you, Richie Bitchie. That's you." Sam made kissy noises at the blockheads. "Ooo, Nat and Eggy just looove their Richie Bitchie."

Richie grinned uncertainty, his eyes rummy with rage. He made it as if to plod forward when Kelly signed again *NO!* Meanwhile, Paul kept speaking to Sam aside. Sam repeated something, then gave up.

WHAT TELL? Richie demanded of Michael.

S–A–M, not me, said he beat you.

"No, he won't," Paul said and signed. "We are just going to go. You all will be busy being Whysees for all. Let's give each other a break."

With Paul's comment, the menacing atmosphere became dispassionate air out of a pricked balloon stem. Nat said something, his voice wavering, and walked away, heading toward Meadow House at the far corner of Farrow Field. Richie signed, *YOU SMALL "mo" ME NOT WASTE TIME* and followed Nat, who slouched, other blockheads trailing him. A heavy weariness fell upon Michael, a resentful fog that comes when a person has spent too much time in such troublesome company. As if sensing the mood (except for Sam, who kept chuckling), they continued subdued to Meadow House. Inside the entrance, Sam addressed a fourteen–year–old Whysee at the front desk in a light tone. The Whysee's mouth twisted, and his voice barked furious orders at everyone to move through the propped open double doors that led to the gymnasium.

"Whas Sam sae, Paul?" Michael asked.

"Yeah, Paul, he should know," Sam said, laughing.

He was pretending to offer you for H–E–R–S–H–E–Y bar, Paul signed.

"A real Hershey for poking yours!" Sam bellowed before Michael shoved him into the gymnasium.

The gym glowed purple haze from the lights above and the orange and black crepes hung limp. Michael could sniff the cloying sweat and the warmth of bodies. In one corner, Richie was signing to a deaf couple, one in a scarecrow costume and another in clown costume, to dance farther apart. The clown frowned through her smiley face make–up. The scarecrow nodded and moved away, eager to cooperate. Near the table with hands clasped behind his back, Nat guarded a sagging table with bowls of potato chips, cookies, jugs of juice, and paper cups. When a chubby boy with a vague smile came up to get more cookies and chips, Nat snapped something at the boy. The boy gave a weak smile and wandered away. Three others in marked shirts kept order near the dance floor.

Sam drifted away from Michael and Paul. Five minutes later, he was speaking to an unknown deaf girl, his lips forming and hands gesturing at each word.

Last time here, Michael signed to Paul.

Sorry give you a hard time.

I guess.

He miss you already. That why he is that way.

I just want out.

Jose came up to them just in time to conceal an uncomfortable pause.

ME DANCE WITH GIRL FINISH!

Michael looked at where Jose pointed. A small part of him was glad to see she was a scrawny girl in a blue dress, with a weak jowl of a chin, yellow papers pinned on her black hair, and her hand slipping to show her missing teeth. So, he gave Jose, whose smile was pleased and unsure, a thumb's up.

Dance with her again, Paul told Jose.

Jose responded with an "okay" gesture and returned to the dance floor, where he and the girl danced hard, their limbs flailing wild, and several feet away from each other. Sam came back, nursing his cheek.

"Got to learn more signs," he said. "All I know to tell her is this." He inserted a finger into his other hand that formed into either an oll korrect gesture to Sam or the hand shape for the letter F to Michael.

"Oh, you sae bang."

No dignity, Paul signed and spoke.

Sam answered, and Paul laughed.

"Whas he sae, Paul?"

He said, 'my D–I–N–O is more important than dignity.'

Michael laughed because it seemed dirty. Sam looked over his shoulder. "I got to get me some. Maybe a mute so I don't have to…" He made as to cover someone's mouth.

"How come?" Michael asked.

He almost get catch last year with a girl, Paul signed.

"Hol–Sam, how come you never tole me?"

"Too young, I guess."

"Thanks a los."

"Also, too girly."

"Shus up."

Sam clasped the pillowcase to his chest.

"Ooh, a blushing bride, like me."

"Go hell, okay?" Michael said. He turned, dismissing him.

Sam's grin faded.

"Okay," he said. He plucked up the sheet and wandered away.

Rough on him now, Paul signed.

Can't treat me like this. Just because I don't read good or talk good and not strong like him, he can't go around thinking I am no good.

He think good of you. He think you are good at hockey.

Michael looked toward the dance floor, his throat hurting. The wards shifted rather than danced, cuddling with each other. Their faces seemed serene, secure at being a part of a pair and not alone like him. There Nancy swayed, her generous bulk, a black soundless bell with a cat's face, leaning on a skinny dog that was Henry. Both were as if leapt from a child's imagination, dancing in the purple light with the trills of the melody and the low–toned bass turning all sad and sweet.

Don't know. I think me and him will play hockey outside B–A–R–R–I–O in winter. Now I see him softer, older, and afraid, and I am not there for him.

Paul's smile turned into a grimace. *We will be alright.*

Across the dance floor, Gertie and Nancy hugged, both weepy at how they made up on the most important night of the year. His stomach shriveled at the sight.

"You know, I don's wanna to stay an' pus up with, do this, don's do thas, beg, smile, go way, come here, reh of my life. I gos my one life and I wans to live is the way I wans."

Must be strong in you.

"An' I'm afrae. My asshole's all pucker."

Paul snickered behind his fist.

"An' someday when I laugh I don's wans to cover my mouth like you dis. I go to spregg my arms an' laugh laow. I wans to fall in a fiel of grass an' roll. There jus so many things I gos to do."

"I can do that." Sam came up, hands in pockets, his face serious for a change.

"Get any?" Michael caught Paul saying.

Sam's head hung, and he pouted. He showed them his empty hands.

"Someday," Michael said, to show no hard feelings.

Sam snorted. "My policy. I ain't leaving until I get at least a B.J." He signed the crude last part with the pumping of the fist near his mouth.

"How you get all girls?" Michael asked, the need to know bright in his mind.

Sam checked his fingernails. "Persistence. And my muscles and pretty boy looks don't hurt either."

"Don't forget your modesty," Paul added in voice and sign.

"See, I got every right to brag, but still keep my mouth shut. Right, Mikey?"

"Uh, yeah."

Sam slung his arm around Michael's neck in a half hug, and Michael's hearing aid squealed. "That's my boy!"

"Cus is ous man! I am nos a boy!"

"Oh, a girl then."

"Thanks a los, ass!"

Sam held up his hands in mock surrender. "Just kidding. Who am I gonna push around?"

"Nas. I wish the worse for him, anyway."

Sam smiled. He jerked his head toward the dance floor. "Yeah. Listen, I'm gonna see if I can get some, and then I'll stop by your room."

"Okay."

—Don't think will come back. If come back, would see the messed bed and home dull light twinkling in my room. I might get layin' down a little while. Then drift off to sleep. Then when wake, it's gonna be too late and will live another day here. No, better go now all way end of Handytown before I forget to be brave.—

"Know what, Sam? I have to keep going."

Sam's jaws tightened. His eyes got damp, then he gave a weak smile and a soft clumsy punch into Michael's chest, which made him stumble back. "Good luck, Michael."

"Yeah, I am going to need it."

The last touch from him was a gentle pat on his shoulder, and Sam sidled away to the center of the gymnasium.

He is something, Paul signed with envy and admiration.

"Place nos same withous him."

You. He is staying.

"Yeah."

Michael stood by Paul in awkward silence. He searched in his mind to dredge up something to say. He opened his mouth, and the makeshift cigarette holder in Paul's mouth bounced as he raised his head, listening.

"Can's believe we waste four years here."

We have each other.

"I guess bus goin' to en.' I shool be happy bus…"

Death of our friendship.

"Aw, come on. Gonna be 'see you laser nos goodbye.'" He paused. "For me, I hope. Whas time?"

7:30. Clock near middle wall of gym.

"Wonder how long takes Sam to ges a girl?"

Paul shrugged, then straightened in his wheelchair. *Look, there F–R–A–N–K dancing with that girl.*

Michael looked over at the crowd. A blind boy was dancing with a girl, the soft glow of lights shining on his unfocused eyes. His fine–fingered hands were on the hips of a brown–haired pretty girl who looked adoringly back at her partner.

Excited to have a boyfriend. Paul said. *Remember her from before?*

Yes, S–A–M almost get me with her. Under the dock. For my fifteenth birthday.

He remembered him and Sam under the dock and him shivering in the frigid air of early February. Her vacuous face had been expressionless when she spread her legs, and Michael could recall a dull thatch of hair between her thighs.

—Felt like having blue fire shootin' through veins. Thought she's, like, thirteen years old.

(Sam's jolly voice and something in Spanish, *'Felicidades mi major amigo!'* and his receding surprised face when you run. A stupid–assed fifteen–year–old ward, that's you. Right then next day, 'Sam, I didn't do her 'cause I didn't want to break no laws.'

'¡*Muy stupido!* She's sixteen, not thirteen! You could've gotten her.')

Yeah, I didn't get her then, and now here I am, might have to end my life not getting nothin.' Wish I been doin' her, though. Now she's eighteen and could've done her. Not that I am stayin' with her though.—

Michael, Paul signed, *you look mad at first, then your face become sad. What are you thinking about?*

"Nothing."

Paul nodded.

"Wonder how he coul see to ges in her," Michael added, not able to keep the peevish tone out of his voice.

S–O–N–A–R, I guess.

"With a hole like hers, it migh sen' echoes."

That's low, Paul signed. But he laughed.

"Too easy, I guess."

Not for you.

Paul pretended to look terrified. *No. Please no! Too much! Please let me go!*

"He tole you whas I sae long time ago, huh?"

Paul laughed and slapped his knee. Michael felt a rueful smile tugging his mouth.

"Yeah. I can't believe he try to ses me up with her on my fifteenth birthday for my presen."

A crazy but good intention.

"I almos wish I do her. I wooln's be afrae to die an unvirgin."

Paul's mouth pinched. *You better be smart out there.*

Michael felt unsure of how to answer. Paul waved his hand in a dismissive gesture.

"I guess I am kine of dumb."

Don't let people tell you that.

"I'm just deaf, whas do I know?"

Finish, O.K.?

"Fine."

119

Next time you put yourself down, I will just said, 'G—E—E, why not kill yourself?'

Michael pulled the back of his collar and let his head dangle, his chin on chest. He closed his eyes, stuck his tongue out in a parody of death.

I was just kidding. Just don't let no one talk down on you, O.K.?

"Yeah."

I mean it.

The Watchers did not think much of his cunning, so he was able to slip past them during shift changes.

—Seventh Street, right? Oh, who knows? Only me and the dark.—

By the fence along Virginia Avenue, Michael reached up and hoisted himself over it. His sneakers scrabbled and his foot caught between the rails. He lunged and clanged to the other side, his body smacking spreadeagle against the bars. He grunted with pain, and his feet straightened, then descended to the sidewalk.

—Seventh Street, where's that? Can't find numbers. Wait, remember Paul signin' something about green crosses with letters and numbers?

(Paul's face was earnest in the late afternoon light before the Halloween party. *You see it on every corner. The number on the poles in green... or black.*)

Where's... um... there. Virginia Avenue, kinda like you, Michael, ha. Yeah, funny, funny, funny. Where am I?—

On wobbling legs, he made his way on the sidewalk.

—Why so close to Gate? Be getting' caught easy. Safer to go back, don't know why. Guess easier to stay where, see tiny lines of pink lights from the streetlights of the Gate. Wonder why not turn on streetlights near the fence. Oh, right, might make it easier for me. Who would do that?—

The moonlight casted cracked sidewalks into milky smoke that showed the lost pitch black of the streets. His sneakers crunched on loose gravel. He stepped as if potholes on the streets were deep pits in the bluest darkness. A hand fell on his shoulder. Michael spun to see who.

"Ick or Eet?" a wavering voice said.

The glow of the flashlight showed a wrinkled white face. Lips smeared in red gave a broad smile, and the black triangles over her eyes rose. Her gnarled hands held a sack with crumpled papers, stale bread, and a blackened banana. Two other forms flanked her, the lady's chaperones. The old woman dressed as a tall clown with four–inch blocks under her blue sneakers and a candy cane colored wool jumpsuit. Another dark figure signed next to the old woman, her hands bronzed by the weak glow of the flashlight.

YOU OUT WHY?

Me twenty.

The hand gripped the old woman's flashlight and guided it to her face. The glow showed another woman's younger and angelic face.

B.S. BUT NOT MIND YOUR LIFE.

Thank. Where is Seventh Street?

She used the air as a map and made dots with her finger.

Can you just point?

The other form signed, then pointed. The flashlight's beam revealed a pleasant–looking male's face. Michael's eyes followed his finger.

Thank, he signed to them and jogged where the man had pointed. Out of gratitude, he waved at the bob of the light dwindling away.

—Darkest without that. Should've gotten one. Oh yeah, right from Nat? Good luck with that. No time to worry, gotta keep movin.'—

He stumbled into an unlit streetlight and clutched at his knee, his lips stretching into a stupefied grin of pain.

—Arrgh! You stupid! Way to go, Michael. Waaay to go. Knee bone all dented. Be careful and stop foolin.' Find the seventh streetlight. It could be nine forty by now!—

He rounded the outside corner of the fence to wade into the shrouded streets, further from the Gate. No warm pink glows guided him. No familiar marks showed him the way, but fear and sheer dumb luck. His hands scraped against the bricks, and a few times he clambered over entangling brushes and waist–high fences. Sometimes candles flickered from a few glassless windows. That was his world: the blue moonlight, squealing hearing aid, and the concrete below his feet. He made it to the next corner and peered at the street sign.

—Three more streets. Just go one way. If numbers less, then go opposite direction. No big deal.—

The mask on his head stuck to his sweaty forehead, so he took it off to carry it.

—All sticky. Yeah, course I am. I'm alone. Can't see. Which street? There's the five. On the right track here. Goin' make it. Seventh Street. No problem. Right up there.—

He stared at number 7 in white in the moonlight. The background of the sign looked black, though he knew it to be green.

—Yeah. Found it all right, but which 7th Street?—

He looked to his right. The darkness barred the sign of hulking walls of the houses, all floating in a void. Dots of pink lights told him how far he went, as if in a tunnel, he was going from the light instead of to it.

—Another pole. Can't read the sign. Where am I? Gonna be stuck wanderin' around you, stupid. What if all a lie? A con job. Fine, I'll go get Sam and we'll get them next year in Handytown. Yeah, just Sam and *loco* messed up Michael after the Postman. See their faces blubberin' for mercy, but we'll teach 'em. Kick their assess and take over.—

He neared the border of Handytown and noticed the crisscrossed outline of the fence that separated Handytown from the outside.

—Electric so stay the hell away, all right? Don't want Paul and Sam hearin' about me being scraped off at dawn. Not enough information. It's real late now. I'll try something one more time. Then give up and just go back. I will get up to the fence. If meet no one, then I tried.

('Hey Sam, I tried. There's no one there.')

Sam gonna be squealin' laughter and makin' wings with elbows.

At least I got farther out than he, so there.—

A purpose settled upon, Michael eased himself closer to the street that must lead to another fence two blocks away. Something scraped nearby. Michael tensed, ready to run. Another dark figure, a black shape of a head, and an arm gesturing.

—Think is that guy.—

Michael crept closer, whispering, "You him, huh? Hello, you him? Huh?"

—He's deaf, dumb ass.—

The hand lashed out and grabbed his shirt for the third time today, not counting the Whysees' handling. Someone grasped his hand and tugged him to stooping level. The touch became light and ticklish.

"Whas?"

The hand entangled in his shirt.

WAIT, the other hand under Michael's, signed. The hand lifted away. He felt and then sniffed the finger that pressed against his lips.

—Stinks, get away! How know the right person? Can't see red here.—

The formless face stayed still. A slick paper slid into the palm of Michael's hand and his fingers rubbed on the slick magnetic strip. He pocketed it. He made to stand, but the figure pulled him down again so hard the crumbled gravel bit into his knees.

"Wash it, asshole!" Michael hissed.

The form's hand mussed his hair. He struggled and felt a slap on his chest. The hand in his hair tilted back to position his head upward until he looked toward the fence. An upright figure strode two blocks away, the sure figure of a Whysee, not the hunched movements of a ward. They waited, hushed, while the form eclipsed the fence and passed, growing smaller until it disappeared around the broken building to the next street. Then the form prodded him toward the fence. A thin shaft of light winked from the streetlight across the street outside.

The dim light showed the face of a dark–skinned, hatchet–faced woman with gumball–colored beads in her locks. The woman carried a thick wool blanket over her arm and dragged a large wooden cupboard door under the other. She hunkered right below the barbwires and looked over her shoulder before throwing the blanket over the fence. Sparks crackled from beneath and his nostrils sensed smoke. He was about to touch the fence before she yanked him back.

MATTER CRAZY?

Think time to go now.

KNOW MUCH ESCAPE SAME YOU KNOW A.S.L.

Exasperated, she tapped the board and then slid it under the hung blanket, her movement deliberate.

STEP, she signed and linked her fingers.

He put his hand on her thick shoulder and lifted his foot to her palm. She grunted and felt her palms jackknifing him over it. His fingers brushed against the wires beneath the blanket. Then his hands cramped hard, as if his skin were chewing on his bones. Her palms beneath the soles of his sneakers pushed harder, and he pitched right over and landed on the other side, yelping with pain. The clean sidewalk rammed into his shoulder and hip bone. Stunned, he stood on shaky legs. He staggered a few steps and glanced at the woman, unsure. The woman's face twisted with frustration, and she pointed northeast. He hurried into the mesh of well–lit streetlights, smooth brick walls, and high–arched fences that walled up each yard. The streetlights shone brighter in the outside world making it easier for him to see. He crossed his arms to rub his scraped elbows and made his way through the neat, narrow houses.

—Hope don't look worse for wear. Might get caught. Wonder what do if get caught. Go for train. Will train take me all the way over? Maybe, but worth tryin.' Wonder if could find railroad. If find just follow track. But what if followin' in wrong direction? Stop cuttin' yourself down, idiot! Focus on what supposed to do. Follow straight line where she pointed. You're bound to come into it. It's hazy.—

Puffs of steam rose from the curbs in the damp air. A faint rumble grew.

—Maybe truck or something.—

In one alley, two forms of colorful clothing darted across and away. He moved past a two–story store and a four–story building. Parked cars shone beneath streetlights, and steel roller cages covered the entrances to small stores. A slow roar built in the distance. He could sense it, the uncertainty starting with the stiffness and the awkwardness in his joints. Footsteps patterned the street, and a male voice hooted from somewhere. He slowed and a husky man wearing a bulky apron with silvery tools jogged past him. The man shouted, his voice muffled from his own PhtoneSkin mask.

Michael shouted "Okay!" at the man's retreating form although he never knew what the man said.

A college aged Black woman in a pink tutu and wings ran up screeching. She scrunched her face and gesticulated, wild with her hands. He grinned, although he did not like how she mocked sign language. The young woman ran away. Next, a clown in a blue and gray college jacket wielded a metal baseball bat. The clown's mouth in his red painted smile curled into mirth.

"Gee Eee!" he screamed and waved the bat over his head.

"Yeah!" Michael shouted after the clown.

The clown bellowed and headed toward the Gate. Michael hesitated. The darkness and the streetlights reminded him of almost leaving Sam and Paul behind that morning in September. An image of poor Paul and Sam's fates passed through his mind.

—(Screams, eyes scrunched shut, hands trying to ward off blows.) Damn it, why such at a bad time?—

He froze where the road rose to a peak and saw from the concrete fences lining both sides that he was on a bridge. He peered to where the lanes slope below him. There, he saw dark colors milling around underneath the traffic light. Colors, hundreds of them, with screams from gaping hungry maws of mouths, rushed toward the Gate and to him. Hairs, a few bonnets, tiaras, hoods, a shady hat, fedoras, cones, red lips, and skin congealed masks streamed closer. Rage and purpose hardened their waxy, contorted faces. They streamed toward him even when one girl in a blue dress and saddle shoes stumbled, and the crowd trampled her into a broken bloody heap.

In despair, he felt his squeezing bladder void. His thighs burned from the heat of his urine in his dampened pants. He ran and something fluttered. The soaked ticket fell, and he glimpsed something slashed on the back and the words written in marker **V I D** and was not sure if the sloppiest of the letters was an **O** or a **Q**. He thought he might ask Paul about that. If Paul will speak with him after such a failure. The street flew beneath his feet, and by the time he neared the *barrio*, he could cut off most of the mob.

The tide of bodies swelled around him, the outside world surrounding him with bright masks, costumes, and make–ups. He surged, and a voice shouted approval behind him. At the Gate, the clown wandered around the *barrio*. Michael grabbed the chain–links, bracing for the pain. There was no jolt or cramp, just the lukewarm metal. He pulled himself up. Adrenaline drained from his sweating body. He climbed higher, and the fence folded under his weight. On the top, he felt a flutter in his belly.

—That's what you feel when you fall into dreams.—

He threw his leg over the fence. He stayed, resting and wondering if the mob would find him there, plastered to the top, a wet caterpillar. At last, he eased to the other side and landed, ankles stinging from the impact. In the sweetness of the clear night air, the mob rumbled. He scrambled toward the Gate, panting. Ghosty alleys blackened by the dark smears, he headed down Virginia Avenue, giggling from hysteria. The same man he saw earlier slouched against the window of one building. The clown and the ballet dancer sprinted from door to door, shouting in high, harried voices.

—Need see Sam. He should know what to do.—

His arms throbbing, he pulled himself up the iron fence and heaved himself over it. His legs felt as if bags filled with wet sand, and his ribs were coils of a heated electric stove. He forced his right leg up, and he winced as his testicles squashed between the tips and his left leg. A lightning pain ripped through the back of his right thigh, and he screamed as he toppled. The row houses and the street flipped, twisting into grass that rammed into his nose and elbow. His hurt elbow tingled hard, an iron hit by a sledgehammer, and the tingle reached his spasmodic hand. He groaned and propped himself to his feet, wetness streaming down his nostrils. He looked toward the booth. Around the outside corner of an old Victorian house, he saw a Whysee stealing away.

—Hurts, damn it. Hurts.—

He wiped at his nose, saw a faint smear of blood on his hand, and wiping it on his pants, he moved across the meadow of Farrow Field and the football field. Past the slope through the chain–link fence along the bleachers, he observed the ragged witch and a knight in tinfoil carrying a broom for a sword. A sleek girl in torn tights and wearing a top hat with a papered toothbrush mustache slinked after them, and the look of her body stirred his groin.

—She's dressed better than Nancy, that's for sure. Nice. Never saw her before, cute longish legs, delicate face, hard to see. Gray band on her arm, aw, not her again!—

His lust faded as the vapors from his breath, as Dimitri continued to the dorm. He staggered upward toward the slope to the bleachers and collapsed by one, air gushing in out of his starved lungs. With his head up, he searched hard for Paul, Nancy, or Sam. He hurried to one gate and lifted the latch, stumbled through, and plodded up the steps to the Hill Circle Road. He collapsed on the curb, feeling sweat running along his spine and the inside of his thighs burning from the drying urine. A breeze played with the top of his hair, and he grabbed for the missing mask.

—Must have fallen way back.—

The red tail of what he guessed to be a devil costume passed, and it was hard to see the paper cutout of horns on that person. The next one passed the figure with a spot painted around his eye. He noticed the red hair and the gangly walk.

—Henry!—

He heaved himself from the curb, fell backward, and struggled up again, and it was as if running through an invisible patch of quicksand. The paper ears flopped as Henry twisted around to hurry back to help. His long, sweaty hands grabbed Michael's flailing one and pulled him up to stand.

"Where's Sam and Paul!"

"Yuh–you–you–welcome buh–back."

"Where are they?"

Henry stuttered and pointed toward the cafeteria and the dorms.

"Ges yourself to the room. People are after us."

Henry pointed at Michael's pants.

"Duh-dih did you wu h - wu h -"

"Shus up an' jus ges going!"

Michael left without a reply and hurried to the dorm. He took the steps to the plaza two at a time, slipped and fell to his knees, his cursing hoarse. His right knee bruised, he now limping to his dorm. At the dorm, he yanked open the entrance door and floundered through it. Inside, several wards looked at him, most of them wearing those T–shirts streaked with black marks and curled gray paper bars taped to the sleeves. One deaf stared at Michael's crotch, and his eyes lit up.

BATHROOM HIMSELF BATHROOM HIMSELF!

"How nice of you to join us," Nat said, ignoring the signs. He strolled to the lobby, his hand gliding on the railing. The paper star still taped to his undershirt was now wrinkled. Eggy followed, clutching his Moron PhtoneSkin in his bony hand.

"I don's have time for this. I gos to see Sam."

Nat's reply was a headshake, his voice clucking.

"(Something) ran much," Eggy bawled out. He slapped the mask on his thigh.

The door to the first floor dorm rooms opened. Richie walked into the lobby and stood, his flabby arms crossed. Michael drew a deep breath, sighed, and talked and signed the best he could.

"There are people comin' over an' starsing a bbq in the village ousize. I came here to les you all know, we're gonna be deher than whasever if we keep having a long discussion abous manners an' other things. Thas may be very wonderful and generous of me to warn you stupis assess bus hey...." He spread his arms. "Thas the kine of a guy I am."

Richie's eyebrows lowered as his eyes, beneath his heavy forehead, became beadier. Nat giggled and descended the rest of the way. Eggy stayed behind on the second–floor lounge, leaning on the railing, and twirling his mask through the left eye dent. Nat bunched his cheeks as if touched and nodded, his expression thoughtful..

Nat then said something along the line of "That was sweet, but I'm not buying it." Then he shrugged. "You may think me to be stupid, but I'm not."

Richie moved closer, his thick fists knobbed.

"I don't have to think you're stupis, Nas. You prove thas all by yourself."

Someone tapped him. He turned around and braced for a blow, and Henry peered back.

"Muh–Michael, wuh–why you in huh–hurry?"

"Henry! Grae to see you. Ges over to Sam an' Paul. Tell 'em I'm here."

Henry smiled. "Thas puh–puh–pronounced get." A spittle hit Michael's face.

"Jus ges over there for Chris' sake!"

Michael wiped his face and his shirt as Henry ran off, brushing past Richie. Nat shouted at Richie, but Richie did not react. However, he approached Michael. In the background,

129

Nat shouted to Henry, who nodded, unaware of Nat's fury, and then headed for the hallway. Nat threw up his hands and ran to the door, but it had closed after Henry. Richie took a step, and he was facing Michael. He started with a gentle push. Then his hands rammed into his chest. The tile floor thumped against the pelvis as his buttocks slammed on it. He signaled for mercy with a pleading come on gesture. Richie gave a gleeful headshake and his bulky boot raised to stomp.

WET YOURSELF AGAIN? SCARE YOU?

—Wonder what the pain would be like? What feel like the breaking bones? Will pieces grind against each other inside my body? Whatever happens, don't cry! Will they find me like this? A passed out deaf with pee stain on his pants. Should've taken a leak before.—

The door to their rooms opened and Sam came out, still in his bridal costume. He had wrapped his costume around him like a huge towel, and his sheet rode up in front. A part of the sheet stuck out of his open fly, a tongue that wagged. Sam talked past him, scowling at Henry, who was behind him. His face lit up when he recognized Michael.

"Hey what happened? *¿No tienes bolas?* And did you just...?"

Sam glanced at Michael, his forehead wrinkled.

"Nees a little help."

Sam turned to Richie.

"Tsk–tsk, Richie, molesting my friend again?"

Richie turned and raised his fists at Sam. Sam gave Richie an irritated look, then his leg thrust up, knee ramming into the bigger ward's groin. Before Richie could hold himself, Sam grabbed him in a headlock and rammed him against the wall three times. Richie shuddered and slid down the wall, clutching his head.

—Too bad huh?—

"Sam," Henry said, and he said something to Sam.

Sam caught Nat, who had been creeping up to them, the flashlight raised and spoke, his tone calm, his words clear to Michael.

"Put that down before I see how far up your ass it goes."

Nat lowered the flashlight sulkily. "Wait until you light out and…"

Sam stepped toward Nat, and Michael tried to read his lips but could not.

—Don't know what he sayin', but if Sam lights out, and Nat did something, he better kill him before he wakes.—

Sam looked at his own crotch and pulled the sheet out of his pants. He winced when it snagged on something before falling out. With a sheepish smile, he turned to adjust himself. He faced Michael.

"Okay, what's going on?"

"There this crows an' perfes people coming over with clubs, pipes, an' stuff an' then–then." Unable to help himself, he started babbling.

"Wait, slow down. Come with me." Sam slapped Michael on the shoulder before they headed to Paul and Sam's room.

"Get out of my way," Sam said as he shoved aside Eggy, who tried to block them.

The closing door cut off the view of Eggy sitting on the floor, fighting back tears, his legs splayed. In the hallway, there was Paul, already wheeling toward them.

Michael, he signed. *You are suppose to be gone and now I must–*

"No time for catch up," Sam said. He looked at Michael's crotch, puzzled. "Did you just–…"

Michael started signing right away. *People outside coming all piss off over something. They get in the B–A–R–R–I–O, they are coming for us.*

The door to his friends' room opened, and a girl poked her head out. Smatter of pimples across her face caused her to look unclean. She signed, *WHEN SEE YOU AGAIN?* Sam nodded at her and gave her thumb's up and waved her away. She smiled and left with *I–love–you* acronym hand sign.

"Did she say that?" Sam asked.

Paul signed and said, "She said I love you."

"If she does, she would've done something with me."

Sam groaned and clasped a hand to his forehead. He wheeled around and hit the wall with his fist. What he said afterward, Michael didn't know.

"Look is nos importans."

"Nerve of that girl," Paul said and signed, "Wanting to talk to you after you tried getting her with you."

"Yeah, maybe if you had left, that would be great," Sam snapped. He glared, his lips pooched at the injustice of it.

"At least you have good taste."

"Lissen—"

"I didn't even ask her name."

Paul spoke to Sam in a warning tone, and Sam chuckled and held out his hands, palms down to indicate children heights. "I could see that. Little *nino* running around. That'll be the day."

"Look, you asses, I came to tell you people coming to hurs us!"

Paul reared his head back.

"Oh right," Sam said. "He ran back here because he said people after us. He's all jazzed up about it." All that said with a meaningful glance at Michael's pants.

"Sam, shus up! Is jus sweh from running. Is true, people affer us!"

If you get scare, you don't need to hide it, but I don't think I should talk to you anymore.

"I'm nos! Is—"

Michael pictured them already in there.

—(Clean hands enveloped around the bars, bright colorful clothes rustling and waxy smooth faces contorting in fury.)

They're running on the field by now.—

Michael took a sharp breath. "They're coming. Righ behin' me. If you don's believe me, then see for yourself."

Sam's mouth closed. He thrust up a hand.

"Shh."

132

"Whas?"

"I hear yelling. Paul, you too?"

"Wait… yeah."

Paul started rolling himself through the hall. Sam's face grew serious, and Michael followed them out into the lobby. Richie was sitting on the steps, his hands pressed to his head. Nat stood by him, demanding something. Nat looked at Michael, and his voice became more strident. Eggy shrank away and fled up the steps to the second–floor as they passed. Paul stopped at the glass windows along the lobby and squinted. Sam and Michael stepped outside and stood shivering in the cool night air. Sam shaded his eyes. Michael looked at Paul through the glass.

See anything? Paul signed through the window.

"See anything, Sam?"

Sam looked. "People in costumes, they're yelling and laughing."

He took a step forward, but Michael snagged the tail of his shirt and pulled him back.

"Wae, don's les 'em see you."

Blue lights flashed beyond the bridge by the Bline Memorial Building. They disappeared around the corner.

"They didn't even stop to warn us."

"Maybe Paul knows whas to do. Is cole ous. Les go back in."

Sam hurried back into the lobby with Michael, his eyes strained with worry.

"What's out there?" Paul asked and signed.

"Ten o'clock bedtime! Ten o'clock!" Eggy shouted.

Nat pointed his flashlight at Michael. "You. Go to bed. Ten o'clock."

"We don's have time for this."

Richie got off the steps. *B–E–D.*

Forget it, Michael signed.

Richie lurched toward Michael. Sam passed Michael with a pleasant smile, then stepped closer to him. Richie went back and sat on the steps.

"It's the rules!" Nat shouted. "Bedtime for all!"

"Then good night," Paul said and signed.

"Can't do that!" Eggy shouted.

Several of the deaf followers took up the cry in signs. *CAN'T DO THAT. CAN'T DO THAT.*

Should we? Paul asked. *People might get hurt.*

Sam shook his head like a wet dog. "No. We can't just wait for them to come for us."

"To beds! To the beds!" Eggy chanted from above them. He pounded on the sheet of tin below the railing that clanged throughout the lobby. "To the beds!"

They maybe not find where we are. We can block the door and glass of the lobby, Paul mused.

"What he said?" Sam demanded.

"We shool stay in. You think?"

"No way, man!"

"Go to bed." Nat had joined Eggy upstairs and pounded on the tin next to him with his flashlight. The next pound snuffed out the dim glow of the bulb.

Sam glanced at the blockheads.

"Shut up before I shove that light down your throat."

Nat replied, which made Sam growl and stomp toward the steps to Nat and Eggy. Michael grabbed his tensing shoulder.

"Nos now, please."

Nat stood stock still, Adam's apple bobbing. Eggy had his hands raised as if warding off blows. The Moron PhtoneSkin mask had dropped from his hand. It now lay limp on the tiles below them, the mashed rubber face thin and hollow.

"Please nos now, no time, nos now."

The muscles of Sam's shoulder loosened beneath Michael's hand. Sam snorted and turned toward the windows.

"Someone's screaming out there now."

They quieted. From the hearings' reactions, Michael guessed the sound hollowed from the distance. Sirens squalled, and they watched the blue flashes on another security car disappearing.

"You think they're going to stop at the *barrio?*"

"Don's think so."

We must stay in. Paul's hands shook as he signed.

"I hope they don's go to children's dorm."

"Oh, I didn't think of that. Paul, the playground's right on the edge of the Gate." Sam pinched the air a foot from Paul's face. "They're close."

Paul looked at Sam, then he started talking and signing. "Pull the wake alarm. You know where. Then meet us outside."

Sam clapped Paul's shoulder and left the lobby through the door to their rooms. Soon the lobby washed in flashing lights. Sam hurried back, grinning at the din he had made.

"Why nobody's coming?" Michael asked.

Sam laughed. "Oh, they thought it was morning. They thought it was morning." He pointed.

Michael saw through the window the other docile wards filing outside the dorm. They had taken the exit door. Paul turned the wheelchair and rolled himself to the lobby door. Sam opened the door for him, and Michael followed them. The crowd milled toward the cafeteria before few looked about themselves and stopped in their tracks as they realized it was still dark.

After Michael and Sam helped Paul on the steps to the plaza, he wheeled himself to the front, waving his arm for attention. He shouted and signed at the same time for everybody. With the signs he had learnt from Michael, somehow, he got through to them.

"Everybody over here. Outside people are angry with us. They might come over and hurt us. I need people to line up in the field where there are benches. Any help?"

The others signed to each other, their faces wary. A chubby boy with a scraggy beard stepped forward. Michael recognized him as one ward who had helped carry him to the Health Center.

MUST. *WE NEED SLEEP. WHY? WORK TOMORROW*

There will be nothing to wake up to tomorrow if we don't do something.

A taller boy waved, and Paul pointed at him.

"Damn!" Sam whispered. "*Justo a tiempo. En afliccions'* standard time?"

Michael looked through the iron bars and saw outsiders running around.

"They don's see us, yeh."

The taller boy was signing, *WHYSEES PROTECT US WILL.*

Most cackled at that. Other hands moved, opinions, other questions. Paul held up his arms and waited for the laughter and yelping to settle. Sam moved, seeking the hearings, and talking urgently to each. A boy with withered hands and limbs for arms held them up, shaking his head. The other showed Sam the braces on his legs. A drooling boy simpered. Another figure stepped in from the crowd. The hairy breasts showed through the teenager's T–shirt.

Kasy joined Paul in signing and shouting.

"The Whysees won't. We know that. We have to do it ourselves or they will hurt us all," Kasy signed and shouted.

The first deaf ward calmed and Michael, gratified, saw him nodding. The deaf ward signed to the taller boy and then he scooted. Another ward, a young one, ran up the female dorm and around it.

"Hey! Bedtime!" Nat shouted from the entrance. He banged his flashlight against the door. "Bedtime!"

"Bedtime!" Eggy echoed, standing behind Nat.

Richie walked past Nat and tried to glare. But the big teenager's eyes slid halfway closed as if trying to wake up from a nightmare. Then he signed, his face blank.

B–E–D NOW FOR B–E–D.

"Don't listen to them!" Paul signed and shouted.

Nat started toward Paul. Sam stepped near Paul and crossed his arms, his brow lowered. Nat stopped and raised his flashlight, speaking to the hearings, his voice hard. Two wards brushed past Nat and back to their dorm. From the female dorm, the alarms flashed. Female wards poured out and then from two other dorms, more wards including boys. When Nancy showed, she squealed and ran over to hug Henry. Holding hands, they walked over to the front of the multitude, where Paul waited. Sam shook his head in disbelief.

"Just like a high school rally."

Paul signed to Kasy. *Tell them what happening. Don't let anyone force or pressure other to fight. I only want volunteer.*

Kasy nodded and waded into the crowd, telling others in sign language what was going on there. The alarms from the dorms kept flashing, lighting the faces of the wards crowded on the plaza. Most of them looked to the safety of the dorms. Only a few edged there. Most faces hardened and several smiled in anticipation.

"Should girls fight too?" Sam said.

"Why, you scared they might heet you too?" Paul asked in voice and sign.

Sam looked offended, then rocked his head back, chuckling. "Yeah, that came to mind."

"Better ges moving."

Sam started for the field before pausing.

"They carrying?"

"Whas?"

"Weapons. They have weapons?" Sam's hand made as if holding a pistol.

Michael shrugged. "Mostly tools, bats, knives, buh no guns, I think."

Two wards walked up to Michael and Sam. The male has the familiar slanted eyes of a person with Down's Syndrome. His body was more muscular than Sam's was, and he beamed beneath his shaggy hair. A blonde girl stood with him, and she seemed elegant except for a cloudy look in her blue eyes. Her fine arm curled around the other's thicker one, delicate as a grasshopper's leg. She asked something in a lilting voice, and Sam shrugged. With a broad grin, the boy reached beneath Sam's armpits and picked him up as if picking up a jacket. Then he planted him back on solid ground after Sam's nod.

"Whas happen? You stole his girlfrien'?"

"He wanted to stand with us. He could risk it."

"Whas make you sae thas?"

"I don't want him to heet me, all right?"

Sam started away, not toward the field yet, but toward the stairs that led to the underground lot. Paul, who was busy signing, did not notice. Several deaf followed Sam, Michael too.

"Where are you going?"

Sam's bloodshot eyes were bright, and he cracked his knuckles.

"The *utiliti* building. I think some there we can bust them like shovels and hammers."

"I'll go."

"You sure? People gonna get hurt. Me too."

"Sorry, you're stuck with me!"

Michael felt the nervous twitches in his stomach. The veins in his arms and legs thrummed, urging him to run. After all, the piss had dried in his pants.

—Gonna be more ready. Wonder if could tear a person apart with my hands. Strong enough to.—

Sam looked straight at Michael and chuckled as they jogged to the utility building. They stopped at the door. Sam pulled at the handle. He let go and searched about it.

"Whas you sill looking for?"

"Flat metal to pry the hinges."

He scratched his neck. His eyes widened as he stared back at the parking lot.

"Stay, Michael." Sam took off, leaving him.

HE KNOW DOING THINK? The chubby boy asked.

I guess. He tell me one time he learn too much living near Hunt— T–O–N Park A–V–E in Philadelphia when a kid.

The boy who asked gave back a quizzical glance as they waited in discomfort. Sam came back, a piece of chrome glinting in his hand.

"Where you ges thas?"

Sam grunted as he stood on his toes and reached up to pry the top hinge.

"Chrome from a fancy nice car. Used to be. Poor bastard gonna be pissed."

His hands tightened on the bar and scraped against the screw at the top. The bar screeched and came off bent. Michael grinded his teeth at the thought of metal cutting metal.

SHORT WAIT? The boy signed, his lips curved into a questioning frown. His wide form was hard to ignore.

Michael poked Sam's back. "How long, huh?"

Sam checked the bent bar. "Dunno."

The other boy stamped his foot in frustration. *HURRY!*

"Please hurry," Michael said.

Sam gave him an irritated look and held up the bar.

—Goin' be tired next day. Hope we won't have to wheel the bricks to dock. Nothing but crumbly bricks hauled all over... wait.—

"Hey, Sam, wae a secon'."

Sam sighed. "What?" he asked between his teeth.

"The bricks. Up ah the building. The loose bricks."

Sam dropped the bent bar onto the gravel. "Jesus, you're a genius. Tell the others."

Michael, body swelling with pride, told his idea. *We can use B–R–I–C–K–S, so we don't have to come near them. Stand on high hill and throw at them.* He motioned as if throwing a brick.

Their faces lit up, and one clasped Michael's back.

"All right, *vamos* the ruins."

They stopped at the plaza to tell more wards of the plan. There, Kelly jumped enraged, signing at the girls who won't go back. Her arms jiggled as a monkey's would, and most ignored her as they crowded around Paul.

"Girls too?" Sam said in disgust.

Paul signed, *only volunteer, just volunteer.* He turned around in his wheelchair. *We get more.*

"Buh they're girls."

We need all the help we can get.

MY BUSINESS NOT YOUR, one girl signed. Her lip curled. She still was attractive, despite her cleft upper lip.

Fine, Michael signed, rolling his eyes at Sam.

"Are there more?"

Paul gave a negative headshake. He used voice and signs. *Most left when Dimitri come out and stare them down. She C–R–E–E–P–Y. She got most back into the girls' dorm.*

"But I said no!" Nancy shouted from the crowd. Henry tried to snuggle into her bulk for warmth.

"Man, your roomie getting some," Sam said. "Unlike a deaf we know."

"Shus up, Sam."

Paul came up to them again. "Where are the tools?"

Sam talked fast to Paul and explained what Michael had said earlier.

Paul nodded. *Alright. Take the road to the other side and around. Don't let them see you all until everyone get a brick in hand. When they start across the field, let them have it.*

A few minutes later, the wards started moving in groups. Kasy's group started striding the road to the other side of the Gate. The heavy set boy's group was next, hurrying around the Bline Memorial building.

"Michael, you lead this group," Paul called.

Michael flipped off a salute and, not waiting for others, he ran to the wreckage with a burst of energy. There, those who arrived early were stepping about the ruins, picking their bricks, and weighing them in their hands. Sam, with his group, had several under his arm, and he tossed one in the air and caught it as he peered through the hole in one wall left standing.

"Look, they don't even know what they are doing."

Michael peered through the same hole and scrutinized the outsiders. They have not reached the empty football field.

Patrick T. Kilgallon

Forms ran amok, calling out to each other along the fence far away. The fence swirled with red, orange, blue, and green, and the bright colors sodden with brown, black, and pink. The masks along the fences made their faces into alien beasts, and their squabbling roar made them even less than human. Slashes of light fell upon the familiar elderly woman crawling on the sidewalk on the other side. Her clown make–up ran, red paint drooling over her mouth as her face turned into an exaggerated parody of sadness. Two costumed figures darted from the crowd and capered around the woman. She rolled into the gutter before Michael realized the two figures had been kicking her. When she tottered to her feet, she had one pigtail left, and the other one looked like torn wisps of cotton. Other residents caught outside fled from the costumed figures. Sam spoke, and Michael turned to read his lips.

"I said, 'They don't look so big and tough.'"

Sam waved his arm in a circle, motioning everybody to get out to the bleachers.

"Ready to get them back?" Sam said with a maniacal grin.

"Yeah, I was born raely. Here I feel raely, all righ."

Sam whooped and ran, holding a brick aloft and four more cradled in his other arm. Michael screamed and ran after, his arm cocked back. When he sprinted across Farrow Field, a sense of disquiet grew. Not like the hissing of steam before the boiler explodes. More like a simple turn of a valve shutting off the steam. The roar lowered to a rumble. Costumed people pointed at them.

"Come on, want some?" Sam hollered, brandishing his brick.

A man in carpenter costume wandered away from others along the fence toward the children's playground. The remaining outsiders looked at Michael, Sam, and the others as they neared with curiosity and amusement. Masks peeled over their faces. Michael peered through the fence, seeing smiles of wonder. Sam stood, his angry grin fading.

"You come over to ges us?" Michael screamed.

Someone from the other side giggled.

"You afraid?" Sam taunted.

One man in a clown costume held up his cartoony white gloves and backed away, his face composed in exaggerated fear. Another snickered.

"Why they not coming for us?" Sam whispered.

People on the other side tapped on the fence, their faces intent. One laughed when a ward approached with a brick. Another outsider waved his hands about, mocking their signs.

"Wubba althaliaaa!"

"Yakaka oooga."

"Braggggh! Braaaaagggggaahhhh!"

—What's goin' on here? Not takin' us. Cuttin' us down, then laughin' about it. Expectin' us to laugh with them.—

A couple of outsiders jumped back when Michael heaved his brick at the fence. The brick arced but only thumped somewhere in the morning darkness. The Black ballet dancer wagged her finger at him. Another thought streaked by in his mind.

—You came back here for nothing, you stupid stupid—

"They're making it a big joke. What do we do now?" Sam said, his voice defeated.

Michael looked up Virginia Avenue. He saw stubby figures clustered in the children's playground. Two adult forms moved to the border of the Gate Institute and had caught something between them. Back on Farrow Field, the wards let bricks drop from their hands. A few made threating gestures. The mob thinned and quieted as if party ended.

"Sam, I gos to go to the children's wars. You come?"

Sam's unsure face looked back at him.

"I don's think they're affer us anymore. They think we're a big joke."

"¡Calabaza, calabaza, cada uno para su casa!" Sam called out to the outsiders.

142

The night rotted away. Sam let his own brick plop to the grass. Thump. Then his left hand opened to let others fall to the grass, and Michael hopped away from an erratic brick. Sam's face contorted into bitterness as he spoke.

"They are not taking us seriously. Causin' trouble and then expecting us to laugh it off."

—Whysees coming from the bleachers. Too sluggish to move. (A soft feeling of falling in tummy. Spots floated.) Blue light? Am I wakin'?—

They walked away, ignoring Whysees' cries of commands from the bleachers.

Sam squinted. "I could see them and they're grabbing at the kid. I better make sure they're okay. No."

"Sam—"

"Let 'im alone!" Sam tore toward the playground.

Michael ran after him, the humps of the grasses seeming to flatten with speed. In the playground near the fence, he saw a short and skinny figure wrenching himself side to side as two bulky large figures held his thin arms.

"Robby!"

Sam was climbing over the waist–high fence between the playground and Farrow Field. Before they could get there, Sam's head cocked, his face quizzical. He toppled to the ground, convulsing. Michael hit the waist–high fence running and scrambled over it, his shirt catching on the link. His legs started lagging as he staggered toward Robby, who kept trying to heave himself out of the costumed men's grasps. Rough hands squirmed between the bars as they held him captive. A hockey stick lay nearby. The milky moonlight shimmered upon the tears of pain that squeezed out of Robby's eyes. The pale light also glinted upon the hacksaw that the man in the carpenter costume produced from his apron. Tiny steel teeth dimpled Robby's right wrist.

—Out the children's playground, in come harsh blue lights fallin' and de deh bah eh–eh–bah–bah ground comin.'—

143

After a while, his shoulder was shaken. Then his face stung. His eyelids flew wide open. The blonde Whysee's face, breathing cinnamon, came close, his hand upraised, and the expression caught between irritation and exhilaration. He felt the breeze in his hair as the Whysee straightened and made impatient rising motions. Michael staggered to his feet. Past a paramedic in white slacks and a blue windbreaker with a yellow cross stitched on the back, he saw what remained of Robby. Similar to two fat spiders, one nested on the ground between the bars and the other in the damp grass below, glossy in the moonlight.

"Robby?"

The Whysee snapped something.

"The boy!" Michael hollered.

Taken aback, the blonde Watcher pointed toward the Health Center. Then he spoke fast while making sweeping motions. Michael's response was to point at his ear and shrug. The Whysee replied with a headshake and reached out to grab his elbow. As Michael was marched toward the gate out of the children's playground, he saw Sam ahead in a heated discussion with the leader. He wrenched his elbow out of the Whysee's grip, ducked a swipe at his neck, and hurried over to them.

"I saw everything. I can help you ges them."

The leader turned toward him. His naked head and his worn eyes made him look vulnerable in the fading darkness. Sam rubbed his own head.

"Forget it, Michael. They're not doing anything."

"An' they gos carpender costume an' one has um this magic man costume with coney has stars on robe an'…"

The leader gave the blonde one, who had caught up a blank look. The blonde boy spoke in an apologetic tone, his eyes flashing accusingly at Michael.

—Just like Nat both.—

"Will you ges them?"

The leader's shoulder lifted in a shrug.

"Oh, come on! They cus off his hands!"

The blonde Watcher sighed hard, and the leader fished out his notebook from his pocket. That was when Sam said something in a taunting voice. The leader glanced up at him from his notebook and queried him. Sam retorted, and the blonde one gave an imploring gaze at the sky before pulling the latch up on it. The gate swung open.

"Whas you all talking abous?"

Sam, ignoring him, made a comment in an innocent voice. The leader's eyes bulged in shock, and he clenched his fist, roaring something at him. Michael left before the leader's furious face could fix upon him. Sam took his time, even lifting his bedsheet. Humming a cheerful tune, he leisurely strolled past both Whysees and walked through the opened gate. Michael slowed so Sam could catch up to him.

"They doin' something for him, righ?"

Sam's reply was a bitter faced hard headshake.

"Lying Whysees, huh?" Michael added, once they were out of their earshot.

Michael kept talking on the way back. The Adam's apple below Sam's chin kept ticking and his sleepy left eyelid still twitched.

"We gonna do something ahous this, huh, Sam? We gonna ges the people who dis this to Robby? You mas ah the Whysees? Whas dis you sae to make leader ges mas? You okay, Sam? Can you sae something?"

Their dorm loomed dreary before them as they walked up the steps to the plaza. They reached the door.

"Sam? Maybe we can fine the guys thas gos Robby? Can we visis Robby in the Center?"

Sam whirled, grabbed him by the collar, and slammed him against the door.

"Michael! Shut up with your funny talk! I don't know, okay? There's not a thing we can do!" He bit his lower lip, turned, and yanked the door open.

Stung as he was at Sam's reaction, Michael followed. Brief pictures, a quiet cry, and thoughts ran through his mind.

—Why Sam gotta be that way? Robby's my friend too! (Two thin arms stretching against the bars of the fence. The man in the carpenter costume giggles.) Jesus, so helpless. (His head comes up close to the carpenter's waist. Streetlight falls on a glint descending between the bars, metal teeth. A clink against the iron bars. Flesh folds in with the pressure. Robby thrashes, his eyes widening. A red scratch first, then skin peel. Faces of the men contort not in malice but in curious concentration, brows furrowing low.) Robby, sorry, sorry, can't save you, sorry, damn it. (A raspy wobbling scream before dullness caves in head.) Whysees! Whysee! Whysee! Why see Robby scream! Just a little kid, that's all! Just a little kid! Didn't get those perfect people for that! Laughin' at us! Not take a boy's pain seriously! Just wanna get over that fence, sink my fingernails into your smooth faces, just sink teeth in and tear you apart. You don't fuckin' stand there while I rip you all apart, so come on, you cockeater! Cockeaters!—

Michael wiped his eyes with his forearm and watched Sam stagger toward the door to the hallway and lean against it, knees buckling. The opening door made Sam stumble.

"Oh man," Sam mumbled, his bloody lower lip puckering. He leaned against the wall.

Paul came into the lobby and signed, *Wrong?*

"He's gonna be okay." Michael said. "Ambulance guys are helping him."

Sam nodded, his forehead pressed against the wall. The hair, wet from sweat and tears, spread and left a patch of wet spot on it.

—Looks like bits of black feathers. Poor Sam. Gave his heart to the kid. Whysees gonna better watch out. We gonna figure out something.—

Michael, what is going on here? Paul asked.

A yodel sounded, bouncing off the tin around the railings from above them. Sam looked up, eyes bloodshot, and Nat's head stuck over the railing, running his mouth at them.

—Doesn't he know? They hurt one of us! They go all the way from who knows where and cut off a kid's hands.

146

Robby better be okay, just better. Damn it, why they do that? Nat callin' down, Nat just botherin', botherin.' Should tell him what happened? (Nat's honking laughter. 'Cut his hands off? Why, how could he communicate? Haw HAW!') Leave it!—

Michael looked at Sam's lips moving and heard his hoarse voice through the hearing aid.

"Paul, there's this kid. He got hurt. Real bad. And I got out of it and can't help."

"Sam, you know nos your faul."

"It is. I should've pulled him away instead of trying for the people outside."

Nat started talking above them.

"Bedtime!" Nat ordered. "Bedtime for all!" Bang. "Bedtime!" Bang.

Sam raised his head toward Nat, who kept hammering his flashlight against the railing on the second–floor.

"Bedtime!" Eggy echoed in tune with Nat, hammering the railing.

Nat started stamping the steps down to the lobby. Sam had a grim smile as he stomped up the stairs. Nat kept yelling, although his voice raised several trebles as Sam closed in them.

"Paul, whas they saying?"

Yelling thing.

The door to the rooms on second–floor flew open and Richie came out, his coarse hair sticking up like an aborigine. He lumbered toward Sam.

—Didn't we do this before? A run, wild yell: owieee! But the stairs so much higher and longer now all the way to the fourth floor.—

Sam started pushing Nat along the railing. Richie clumped in behind Sam with his fist raised.

"Sam, look–"

Richie's fist clubbed Sam across the shoulder, forcing a lurch toward Nat. Nat grabbed a chance to raise his flashlight. He did with a triumphant screech: "Whaaack!" Eggy whooped when the flashlight clonked on top of Sam's head. Michael ran up the stairs again.

147

—Dirty coward! Stupid, dirty coward!—

His feet flew up the steps. He grabbed Nat around the waist. A crazy dance. Nat's elbow jolted into one eye, the eyeball yielding to the bone of Nat's elbow. He saw red stars shining. Through a burning eye, he glimpsed Sam slamming his elbow into Richie's face; the blood smeared on his arm. On Eggy's floppy face, his lips peeled back into laughter. From below came a sharp shout. It turned noiseless except for Eggy's voice that burst clear and through, despite Michael's numbed state.

"Oooooh, yoooorgh in trouble now!"

With the heel of his hand on his blurry eye, Michael looked down and noticed well–shaped torsos, in gray shirts, four of them. His eyes filled in the faces. Two were unfamiliar. The other two, Michael knew.

—Remember puzzled face looking from above that day in September…. and just a while ago? (Then the other's blonde–haired boy's cinnamon–breathed lips forming the words 'Monkey House?' in the morning's hue before and his glare just an hour ago.) Ohhhh, now you're concerned.—

The leader gave Sam an order. Sam let go of Richie, who staggered to his feet, his hands leaking blood from covering his snuffling, bent nose.

"Time for beh, huh?" Michael said, standing on the staircase. He gazed one floor below, where Paul waited.

The fluorescent lights far above reflected on Paul's glasses. Michael looked over his shoulder at Sam, who tried straightening, but his body listed toward the railing as he fought for balance. He murmured, his dark eyes squeezing back tears. Michael read his lips.

"Come on, you big queer," his lips said, "come and make me."

The leader's face tightened. Richie moved away, his eyes wide, the blood dripping tiny splatters on the tiles through his cupped hands. The blonde Watcher seemed reluctant as he touched the leader's shoulder. The leader shrugged the hand off and started for Sam.

"Sam, you're going too far," Michael called, and he hurried to the platform where Sam stood, his chin raised.

"Shut up, Michael."

Sam bunched his fists and backed away. The leader stopped halfway up the staircase. His voice started off calm, hands raised. Sam kept his fists up to him. He grinned through tears, saying something.

"Little boy… Robby… stop this… didn't…"

On the move a few steps higher, the leader passed Michael, the syntenic wool cotton of his sleeve brushing Michael's shoulder. Nat screeched, and Sam backhanded him without a glance. Nat stumbled and dropped his flashlight.

"Sam, damn is!"

The leader rushed Sam, his face set. Sam's fist swung and connected with his jaw. The Whysee leader fell back three steps on Michael, and both slammed against the staircase railing. The lobby rushed and Michael saw Nat running along the railing to the separate side of the lounge and stopping with a sickish smile. Sam stood still.

"Sorry, Michael. Just stay out of our way, huh?"

Michael saw the aggrieved look that the leader threw over his shoulder. The load lightened as the leader scrambled up to his feet and charged Sam. Sam backpedaled up the second flight of stairs, giggling madly. Below, the blonde Whysee's boots pounded the steps, his well–shaped hands trailing the rails while he hurtled, shouting.

Paul screamed from the first floor, his face small, and his words clear to those fighting.

"Sam, stop it, you idiot!"

Sam collided with the leader, fell sideway, both flailing, and disappeared past the next flight of steps. Beyond the steel underside, there was a crash and a grunt of pain. Someone seized his shirt and the blonde Whysee's other hand grabbed Michael by the elbow, his head shaking firmly.

"Lemme go!"

Michael ripped away and the blonde Whysee stepped back, his mouth agape.

—Gone bad. Got to do something. Time draining, gotta have time get goin.'—

Michael stopped to catch his whooping breaths, leaning over the railing far enough to see speckles and aluminum–colored grids on the floor of the lobby. He ran up the next flight of stairs, hoarse and dizzy. When he reached the fourth–floor staircase, the leader had the better of the fight.

There was a scratch alongside his cheek, but the leader held Sam on the steps with his right hand, and his left fist hammered blows on him. Sam scrambled back, his forearm warding off the heaviest of the blows. His heel shot, a piston and thumped under the leader's belly. The leader sagged to clutch at his crotch. As if in a silent agreement, they crept up the stairs to the upper floor, using the railing to haul themselves to their feet. They faced each other, breathing hard.

—We will be friends, all will be better tomorrow, better work, and more food, better punishin' if we did wrong.—

Sam's mouth moved in a whisper. The leader stepped closer, his voice dull.

—If can hear right, will know what they said. But if hear right, wouldn't be standin' here watchin' this.—

The blonde one came up to where Michael stood. Both waited to find out what and what will pass from now on. Sam shoved the leader with three fingers. The leader, a snarl on his face, threw his arms around Sam's waist and lifted him above the railing over his shoulder. Sam's face became aware, his head dipping toward the lobby four stories below him.

"Wait—"

His hands scrabbled at the rail. Paul's voice screamed again.

"Oh no, Sam!"

Sam teetered before he dropped the wisps of his sheet and the last of legs blurring past everything. The sound was a sledgehammer striking a cinder block. Silence resounded but for the sound of Paul's hysterical weeping.

Michael's knees hurt when he raced from the third floor to the lobby and slammed them on the tile, oily with

Sam's blood. The pupil of Sam's left eye had shrunken to pin size. The right pupil swallowed the thin rim of his mud–colored retina. Blood continued to spread, a rivulet soaking the knees of Michael's pants. His throat thickening from the pain, Michael could not stop his eyes from leaking clear star–shaped splatters on Sam's costume. He looked behind at Paul, who buried his quivering face with his hands, his shoulders shaking, helpless. High above, the leader's face could be seen, his eyes lead pencils points from the distance. Old pictures of Sam flipped through his head, the stills, and others in movements.

—(Sam's face, chubby with baby fat, studying him when Mom's gone and there's nothing to be done about it. He tries to make everything all right. As a fifteen–year–old, his shocked face and the retreating figure of the girl who Sam had talked into being your birthday gift. Sam's face is older when he hurtles up the concrete steps and pulls Richie off the sobbing girl, Nancy. All the gleeful sneers whenever Sam is right and all the sheepish smiles whenever he is wrong. One time, through the half–closed door in passing, Sam sits on his bed talking, his hand fingerspelling the alphabet 'AYE…. BEEE…. Ceee…'

His black eyes turn to light brown during talks of playing hockey in the streets of the *barrio* outside them. His grins when helping with the wheelbarrow, his goofy smirk when Nancy shows interest in you, both never forgotten. Sam, his face tight when he fights the leader and at last, his stupefied face as he topples over and drops.)

My heart breakin' so bad. Hurts. Too blurry.—

"Mmmmmmm."

In the teary blur, Sam moved his head. Blood still trickled his nose. He struggled to speak, but a red bubble swelled on his lips. Michael saw himself in it, a wide–eyed face with mussed hair in the red crystal globe, and then his haggard face burst into a mystic red. The floor beneath became more wet as the oily blood widened from beneath Sam's head. His mouth moved, and he murmured something dreamily. Throat burning, Michael looked at Paul again.

"Is okay, he's okay."

Michael gripped Sam's groping hand.

—Not care if look like a queer, don't care anymore.—

"Mmmm?"

His few sounds were mutters. Michael felt a damp hand squeezing his shoulder.

—(No more him sitting across from you in the cafeteria. No stronger tan hands that grab the handle of the wheelbarrow when it's ready to fall.) Me too weak. (Where there's harsh laughter, there's emptiness. Only a second, a long stay, all this happens.) Should move hands together. Too late you...—

"Please Sam... nos now..."

Sam said, "me–se–de–ce."

Paul faltered before he sagged in his wheelchair, uncertain what to sign. Sam tried one last crooked smile, but it came out as a grimace. The left eyelid slid, a grotesque wink, his breaths smelling of zinc and fear, slowed, the sound softer and quieter, the pupil of his right eye contracted, so it was the actual old Sam who looked with one eye still open, the chest stopped its rise and fall, all the shine in its right eye dwindled, and the body became still.

The leader

—Killer.—

descended the rest of the way, his legs silted. He shifted his head toward the speaker mic on his shoulder. He said something and the slim radio at his belt crackled. At one point, the leader's knees buckled. His other hand scrabbled at the rail for balance.

—Fall! Fall! Fall! Fall! Fall and break your goddamn neck!—

The leader managed his balance and murmured an inaudible reply to the clipped speaker mic.

—(This is you at eleven. Peter comes over with the walkie–talkie. Few minutes he is on the other side of your house. Mom is in the living room drafting another book of scary poems for children, and Dad's at work at the

152

supermarket. Your friend's voice, the statement always expected from a hearing, through the speaker, 'Michael, can you hear me? Huh? Can you hear me? Um, over.' even though you had pressed the clip and said, 'Yes, loud and clear, uh, over.' At last, his voice says something different.

'Hello, you copy, Mikey? I saw a big wolf!'

'What!' you bellow and tear around the house.

In your head, you imagine a hunched furry form menacing Peter. Or a coyote. Or Mr. Arnold's growling black dog, Luger. Peter waits in the backyard, looking toward the next yard.

'Where's the wolf!'

'What wolf?' Peter asks. 'I said I saw a pool over there.'

A pudgy boy that Peter and you mock shows up and pedals over to you both. Peter's hand darts in to snatch the walkie–talkie that's supposed to be for you out of your hand and drops it in the boy's basket. Then he dashes away, speaking in his walkie–talkie, the other boy answering, both shrinking with distance. Peter is gone for today.)—

Old resentments smoldered against his childhood friend pushed Michael's stifled rage to a reckless point. The blonde Watcher followed the leader downstairs to the lobby. They stood regarding the body, their faces still. The leader sighed. Michael spotted the pink and reddened spots where Sam's knuckles had landed, like bizarrely placed rouges and the trapped gaze in his eyes.

"I–" the leader said. He stopped speaking and held out his hands, helpless.

Paul turned his damp face away from him. Michael pointed.

"You."

The leader's eyes fixed on him, and he tried to speak, but Michael cut him off, interrupting.

"Oh, you perfec this, you perfecs thas, bus you all nothing like Sam."

The leader blinked. Michael felt a tug at his shirttail. It was Paul. The leader gave an order and pointed to one door to the hallways. In various parts of the lobby, doors clanked open and shut among blurs of hurried movements. Only Michael and Paul remained.

"Get back to your rooms," the leader's lips said.

The blonde Whysee next to him seemed numb to the confrontation, for he kept gulping.

"I knew you won's unnerstan'."

The blonde Watcher whispered something to the leader, but the leader shrugged.

Michael pronounced each word. "You not perfect." He sniffled and wiped his nose with his forearm.

The leader spoke with a hard voice, ordering him.

"Fuck you," Michael replied, although he was not even sure what the leader said.

The leader took a deep breath and spoke slow. "I am losing patience with you."

"You los patience long time ago."

"Maybe you should stop talking like a freak."

The blonde Watcher said something terse, and the leader turned to answer. From the way the blonde Whysee backed a step, his face placid and his hands raised, the glare from the leader must have been baleful.

Michael looked at Sam's body. Then he clenched his fist, stepped wildly toward the leader, and swung hard. His knuckles collided against the leader's nose, and the leader glared over his cupped hands. Michael stared back, satisfied, but something hard rammed up his groin. It was the leader's knee. Michael's body folded with a woomf! Dull, sickening pain spread from his guts, weakening his legs. He reeled before crashing to the floor, crouching a human crab. Michael gagged and clutched his stomach. The corners of his eyes caught the leader being prevented from attacking again by the blonde Watcher, who had placed his hand on the leader's shoulder to break his stride. The youngest of the unfamiliar Whysees gave a shout when the lobby door swung open. Two more Whysees entered, one a Black person and the other Caucasian.

"He push him," Michael called to them. "Thas the boss. He dis is. He killeh Sam."

They conferred with the leader and the blonde one, ignoring him. The leader gave a dismissive shrug and left, brushing past Michael, who shouted.

"Where are you going?"

The leader muttered about the way things are and was gone. Everything froze when the door shut. White spots danced in Michael's vision and his stomach rumbled.

—Haven't eaten since Halloween, back when Sam, oh, Jesus, was alive.—

Rough hands dug under his armpits and hauled him to his feet. Paul cried out, his face miserable and signed, *They are taking you to the house! The house!*

Michael saw the younger blonde Whysee freeze, his arms dangling, and then ran outside past Michael and the other two Whysees. As the glass door closed, the cool air shut off from them. His stomach jiggled, dry terrors skittering his spine.

"Please, nos the house, nos the Monkey House, all righ?" Michael said calmly. "I am sorry I his him, buh I gos angry. Nos the house, all righ?"

The other Whysees did not spare him a glance. The holds tightened and pulled him from the broken body.

"Listen, please, please, I'll be quies, please nos. Nos the House." He struggled, but his arms locked.

—Weak, stupid, mumbling pleas but bad things there. (Paul signs long ago during lunch hour about seeing a fingernail poking out between the bars of one cell. *So big, like a rotten banana peel.*)—

Then he bucked his body, legs scrambling to stay on the floor. His splattered sneakers flicked dark, gild spots everywhere, and he cried out.

"No House! Please! Gos no! No! No! No! Nononono!"

His legs still pedaling, solid arms dragged him past Paul, who tried to reach him. Michael pulled his right arm out of the Black Whysee's grip and grabbed the edge of the doorframe. Eggy's voice yodeled from above them. The

Caucasian Whysee pulled out a leather coiled cord, and a black blur cracked on Michael's hand. White pain writhed through his constricted arm. He felt his hand get numb fast, then spread to his elbow with brutal pain. He shrieked, letting go. Cool air greeted his throbbing hand while he was being carried out by the Watchers. He struggled harder, but his sneakers kept skidding on the plaza. Female faces pressed against the glass of the Knell Dorm, and one girl's mouth dropped open.

"Nancy! Tell 'em nos to take me to the House!"

Her face reared back. Through the window, he saw her running to the front door, but Kelly and several girls surrounded her bulky form. Michael fell to his knees on the sloping roadway. The Black Whysee stopped, waiting. He bent his head close. His lips moved, halting at each word. "Come.... it's.... not.... that.... bad..."

The Caucasian Whysee blocked the other's head. His mouth became a ragged hole and when he moved, Michael felt a heavy blow on his back. He staggered to his feet. They moved him farther to the school building where the Whysees go to classes.

"Please, nos the house," Michael begged, crying.

The Black Whysee stopped to give him a slow shake of his head, and they kept walking him further. At last, the Monkey House waited, the brown bricks housing the worst of the wards. Michael remembered ominous music from the ancient, downloaded horror movies collection that his father had that he had watched as a child.

—Name of movie collection, what is the name… oh yeah, *Creature Features.*—

Michael chuckled at himself for remembering. His belly cramped as he neared the door to the Monkey House. The Black Whysee punched in the access code and the door clicked. Michael heard a grunt from the first Whysee as he pulled it open. Hard hands let go and Michael thought,

—Run! Where?—

156

In the bleak hollowness of Monkey House, a slouching figure stirred in one cell. A hand grabbed Michael's neck, and a thick brown hand dug into his right armpit.

—Here I go now!—

He opened his mouth for one good yelp before he was taken inside by the Whysees. His heels scuffed the floor. Chains dragged as things rustled in the dank air. The Whysees' hands became slippery with sweat as they jammed into Michael's armpits and neck. A face lolled against the bars in one cell, with sleepy eyes and drooling mouth. The head seemed out of proportion to the body.

—It is backward. Oh God, oh, Jesus, oh, Jesus.—

The face drooled over the ridges of a naked back, and the head turned. There was another face looking back. The mouth on the second face blubbered something. Someone hollered and laughter screeched from far away. A sobbing sound and a loud, rasping noise came from the other side. On that side, heavy flesh filled the small cell. The dweller's hand, about three feet big, squashed against the bars. Above, the giant's face strained in pain. The body stooped a mournful gorilla. Something fluttered in the next cell. A leathery wing flapped and between it was a brown face of a boy. The boy grunted, excrement dribbling on the floor. Michael could smell its wet fur. A few cells down, a heavy face squatted upon a neck like an industrial can and the form loped to the bars. The enormous head's rubbery lips called.

"Deaf boy! Me. Morning lights! Me. Morning lights!"

In the next–to–last cell, a boy dragged his unfinished brother welded into his backside and head. The creature trudged around, one head bouncing while the other bent at a grotesque angle. Michael squeezed his eyes shut. He breathed in the sick sweetness of feces and copper. The floor knocked against his sneakers. His arms shook from the force of the hands on them. Steel slid and hands moved him forward. His hands were crammed into steel bands, the skin pinching from the snaps of the brackets. Metal slid again and there was a hopeless clang. The hurried footfalls became quieter and quieter.

—Close your eyes. (Dust scum under eyelids and an itch in the nostrils.) Ke–chew!—

On the concrete slab, he sneezed and tried rubbing his eyes, but the chains dragged his weary arms to the floor.

—Lost in dark can't sleep with heartbeats tickin' in me. Somethin' whistlin' but can't move to fix hearing aid.—

He opened his eyes again. In the cell next to him, a figure was wedged against the bars.

—(*WORK UNDER ME OR DIE!*) One lone sign with a flip of his hand.—

"Postman, I didn's ges ous. Mister Postman?"

He slid over until the chains stretched. He made it to the bars between his and the next cell and looked closer at the Postman.

—Shouldn't bother.—

The Postman's hearing aid dangled from its own ear, whistling. The cap had been twisted and pulled back and a neat hole showed on the boiled part of its forehead, the edge caked with rust of clotted blood. Michael turned and leaned against the coarse wall and tried to think of nothing. He lifted his arm one last time to turn off the hearing aid, trying not to listen to the hums in his brain.

—HmmmShmmmup! Hmmmmmmjustmmshutmm mmmupmmstopmmmmmmmmmmmmmmmmmmmmmmmmmm goin' HmmmMMMMmmmmmmmHmmmmmummm shut up can't think... don't look don't listen. Keep your eyes shut. HMMMmmmmm. Oh, Jesus please... Sam help.—

For an hour or day, he did not know, he slumbered, crying out when a breeze ruffled him and one time when a mouse scampered across his legs. Time melted along with the darkness. His head filled with pictures of past life.

—(The steel bars and long spaces between rows of cells are so still in the morning. They shimmer as if waking from a lone dream. The concrete walls and the bars run together into a blue wall with Dad's *Star Wars* preserved poster of Darth Vader, Yoda, Chewbacca, and Han Solo with Pete Rose's face. Another poster was the Flyers emblem and the team's picture on it. The concrete floor turns into the wrinkles and valleys of the unkempt blanket. Awake in bed at home, just a seven–year– old boy who left his nightmare. Just a dream, a whooping sigh of relief and wiping away a tear from your eye. Your recent birthday gift leans against the chair and desk, new and white with a red band around the top, the blade smooth and sturdy, hidden beneath the curtain of the window.

You swing your legs from under the blankets and stand up, rubbing your eyes. Then you are in the hall with pictures of flowers on the wallpaper. Round the edge of the hallway, sunlight through a window reflects floating microbes and dust) that is what they are, Dad made me look up the word. (It is a walk and turn to Mom and Dad's bedroom. There, Dad's hair sticks up from beneath the blanket and Mom's face and shoulder above the blanket on her side of the bed. Today is… Today is…. Sunday and let's get Dad! A run in the room and a clamber on the giant bed, and you made Mom's body shift and her bleary eyes open. Dad turns on his back and opens his. He pounces.

'Warrrgh!' *Wake me, you!*

Dad's hands air pound uh–oh you for waking them up, and you bat your hands at Dad until Mom gets up in her fluffy pink nightgown, giving you and Dad a dirty look. There is breakfast in the kitchen.

Mom, Gray Man come, take you, me and put us behind fence.

That awful! D–I–D you save your Mom?

D–I–D the Gray Man said, 'Belagghh! That kid stink. Better leave him and just take Mom?' Dad smirks as he signs that.

Dad! Not funny!

Laughter comes from Dad as he hovers over his own plate.

The butter scent of French toast, the slow syrup on the tongue, and a glass of grape juice, the sweet cool liquid trickling the throat. That's how purple tastes, glorious morning flavors.

After breakfast, oh, yeah, maybe a walk to the park where baseball fields and woods wait nearby. In the woods, you might tell Mom about a dream of being taken by the Gray Man being deaf in a perfect world the way you told your dream of being trapped in a scary amusement park with monsters. Back at the house, Mom gets the yellow sheets of paper and writes more. You will help Mom with her story and tell her about the Fat Girl, the Gray Man, and the Shaking Boy that you love but not the way a girl or a sissy would, but a close friend, and a smart boy stuck in wheelchair who wears glasses. You will tell her about the boys in gray shirts and pants and ask Mom if they could die the grossest disgustingest deaths imagined and then Mom will laugh, and the door opens....)—

Another long time passed. The sunlight blinked to dreary darkness. Footfalls came and two gray uniforms moved closer in the dark. The cell door clattered as it rolled, a heavy squeal, and two Whysees stepped in the cell. The steel clamps unbuckled as they freed Michael's wrists.

—(Hands are light and airy.) Is that how Robby feels?—

One grinned at him and said something cheerful. Hands reached and pulled him up to stand. They walked him past the cells and to the entrance. They allowed him to reach up and click on the hearing aid. Fresh moans. Wails. They allowed him to click it off again. The two Whysees behind him walked him, their eyes set straight. Neither touched him but for a light grip on his elbow when he stumbled after seeing the giant middle toe squished against the cell door, big as an orange. Outside, he blinked as one Whysee remained to close the door while the other walked him back. When the dorm approached his vision, Michael rubbed his eyes. For a moment, he wanted to cry. The Whysee nodded and walked away, leaving him to stand and wait for the others whom he had thought lived and moved only in a dream. The lights on the windows buzzed and flashed. He clicked on the hearing aid and heard the bell ringing.

Wards poured out of the exit door, the huge older boy doing the last steps of his morning march. Nat came out with his face subdued, not jostling the others with his flashlight. Others looked as they had every morning for years with tired faces coming out, sluggish movements, and trudging feet. He searched for that haughty face among them. But only Paul wheeled out, his bloodshot eyes hollow and worn, his lower eyelids puffy beneath his glasses. Paul's head turned toward Michael, and he faltered on the step that led to the ground. Then he signed to one ward for help, the heavyset boy from last night. The heavy-set boy's eyes dipped toward the ground as he joined the streaming crowd to the cafeteria.

Michael hurried over and grabbed the handles of the wheelchair. Paul raised his eyes to him, the lips pulling down his face as he collapsed in his wheelchair. His fine haired hands held on the wheels to balance in his grief. He struggled until his wobbling hands steadied the wheelchair. Nat, farther away, glanced at Michael, his eyes widening in recognition. Then he walked away without protesting. The teenaged girls from the Knell Dorm streamed out of the building. Nancy parted from the crowd, and she trotted over to Michael and Paul. Her hands took hold of one armrest, and the wheelchair became easier to shift with her help. The door opened. The hockey stick slid from Henry's grasp and ended up cradled in Paul's arms. Henry helped lift Paul from the step to the ground. Another body came over and joined them. Looking back with bloodshot eyes, Jose smiled. There was a hitching noise from Paul as his own smile trembled. More Whysees came in sweat suits, checking them. They all headed toward the field for a roll call.

After the roll call, Michael got the stick from Paul and stashed it to beneath his bed before his shift. Grateful, Michael resolved to be friendlier to Henry, Nancy, Jose, and even Gertie.

Finished with his shift, Michael spied Paul working his way around the ramp. His eyes burned and were raw from hands rubbing away tears. His ankle still had a twinge from the time Sam and others brought him to the Health Center. When Paul's wheelchair edged into the plaza, Michael raised a hand in greeting. Timid and not used to having Paul to himself, he realized he won't have to worry about stealing medication again. That stricken him enough to wait to give himself time to erase the overwhelming relief that might have shown on his face.

—Poor Sam, lucky me, no more die lay tin. Just want to fall to the brick platform, bury the face, and cry for all you and Paul have lost. But here you are goin'—

"Hey, um, Paul?"

Paul looked up, flatness in his eyes that brought the image of

—(poached egg yolks.)—

They were still red, and he must have lain the entire night weeping, a luxury that Michael envied since Paul had the room for himself. Strange to think, for if Paul did not have the luxury, then there was no reason to cry. Paul's glazed eyes looked up, wary, and he whispered something, his voice numb.

"Nos unnerstaning you there, Paul. Whas saying?" Michael cupped his ear for effect.

Why you smile?

"Just thinking funny thoughs."

Paul nodded. His lips stayed pressed.

They kept moving until they were back at their dorm. Michael pulled the door open for Paul. Inside, Michael glanced at the floor where Sam died, now only an auburn smear. They moved through the hallway to Paul's room. Paul, on the way, whispered something.

"Whas thas?"

Not clean him right.

A tightness in his chest told Michael to use signs only. *They going come back and ask question from me?*

Paul's response was a bitter headshake as he turned the doorknob and entered his room. He opened the door wider for Michael, who followed, still signing.

They will come in my room and ask me who do this and I will tell them I see them. His teeth clenched, and he felt his stomach almost eating itself.

Paul's eyes rolled upward in impatience, and he signed, *They do nothing. They will said nothing happen here.*

"Whaddya mean, Paul? They threw him down 'ner! They cus Robby! They hur me! And you know whas they call dis thin' to Sam? You know what they call dis?"

Michael took a deep breath, remembering the word from Dad's old books, each with a silhouette of a fat man on the spine. He said the word aloud.

"Munder."

Paul tilted his head at him, his face perplexed. Then realization struck his face, and his mouth tugged into a sickly grin. He laughed sharply.

"Nos think funny!"

Paul snorted and covered his mouth. He signed, his face pinched, trying to be serious. *You are right. What was that again?* He snickered.

"No! You know whas I sae."

Paul laughed harder. Tears trickled his cheeks and beaded his glasses. He rolled his eyes at the ceiling.

"Sam, I wish you were still here to hear this. Michael said they mundered you," Paul shouted and signed, even fingerspelling the word the way Michael said it.

"Quis is Paul! Jus quis! You cry when Sam die. I real hate when Sam do this to me! So, don's do this to me foo!"

—'Sop is! Sop is!' Sam echoes. 'You cri–eh! I die–eh! Fock you foo!'—

Michael signed, for his throat had become incoherent with rage, his speech strangled. *Stop this P–A–U–L. Why you making fun of me? You cry like a baby last night and I don't. I don't cry*

163

a bit when they take me to that house. He is gone. I hurt. You hurt and you laugh at me! Stop this just stop all this. Stop it. Why you acting like this is nothing!

Because we nothing. Paul signed. *We nothing to them! Nothing going to happen and we going to nothing! We meat to them! No one going to get us out! No one going to punish Whysee! They are going to...* Paul pumped hands with an imaginary person in a double handshake... *Good work, boy! Good.... work.... boy.*

"Oh yeah? You talk like Whysees. You lie like them. You talk dirty."

Michael pressed the heels of his hands to his damp eyes. They were face to face, both screaming and signing hard. Paul kept shouting, something about how sick the whole thing is. Then he ran out of steam. They both remained in depressed silence. Michael stepped backward until the back of his knees brushed against Sam's bed and he plopped on it, his strength gone.

Yes, right, he signed. *I talk funny. You talk dirty.*

Paul nodded. *I am sick for telling the truth.*

Michael took a deeper breath. *I talk funny. But I hurt no one like Whysee. I am better than that.*

You can think all you want. They don't. Just the way thing are.

I hate them. I wish they get dead.

Me too. Paul signed with a sardonic smirk. *But for them, we will have to wait a very long time. Us, they won't have to.*

The next few days, blue lights still came to wake him. He still made bleary movements with the others and plodded outside into the dull morning with others. Sometimes it rained. One time, Michael struggled with the slippery handles of the wheelbarrow, too slow. Raindrops dripped off the brim of the blonde Whysee's hat as he brayed, his body tucked away in a gray raincoat. Michael grabbed the brick from the wheelbarrow and slammed it hard to the ground, scattering it. It satisfied him to see the Whysee flinch.

"Nos my faul Sam's gone! Your leeser mae him gone! Nos me! You wanna more work. Try nos killin' wards from now on!"

His breaths harsh, Michael lifted the wheelbarrow and found it heavy, so he reached in with both hands, tossed out more bricks, and let them drop by the rigid Whysee. He stopped and stared at him.

The Whysee lifted his hands defensively, saying something to justify the murder. He continued in a feeble, incomprehensible rant. His protest ended with him crying out, "Don't know nothing. You deaf… Just go around, blarh! urgh! We didn't know nothing!"

Michael dismissed him with a firm headshake, lifted the handles of the wheelbarrow, and shoved it past the Whysee. From side of his view, he noticed one of the soaked wards staring. A clawed hand swept across that ward's face as he told the others in sign language, *WHEW! PISSED OFF FINISH.*

So, life moved at its pace. He should be older inside and even stronger. He could not sense the changes inside him. Even if he fought to keep from crying at night, it would not bring Sam. There was no healing, only that his grief became less strident from time to time.

The Message On the Terminal Billboard

Stillness

That day after lunch (without Sam of course), he headed to the Billboard, looking forward to future encounters with Whysees if they dare to complain. It was as if he was blameless for less work done.

—That's right. Gonna do it my way. Not the Whysee way. If they do not like it well then, they could just…—

"Thas righ," he began muttering. "They can go fu… whuh?"

Michael noticed a chubby deaf girl staring at the terminal billboard in wonder. Behind, someone giggled and stopped. More wards stopped to crane their heads up to the board.

—Wonder if a power failure just now. But just left lunch and light on the ceiling flashed. I saw that.—

The bread burned his stomach. He tried to burp, but a spittle bubbled up his throat. The chubby girl still gazed at the board.

NUMBERS GONE WHOOSH, she signed.

What you think? Michael asked.

—Pretty cute. Almost like a chipmunk.—

A boy with a hooked nose walked up and put his arm around the girl's waist.

NUMBERS WHOOSH, the hooked nosed ward signed.

—Uh… I believe we estab–stabl… I believe we already talked about that.—

167

A ward cheered, and nervous laughter arose. A deaf Black boy with a sloping forehead smiled and did a funny jig. Silence rewarded him. Michael turned and observed the faces. One deaf girl in the wheelchair had her hands pressed to her face, the expression a mixture of joy and relief. A tall boy with squinty eyes gave a toothless smile. Jose had his fist hesitating below his chin, unsure whether to cheer or lower it in disappointment. Paul came up the ramp and wheeled himself toward them. He rested his chin on the palm of his hand.

"Iszi suppose to be goor Paul? Is this goin' be goor?"

—Can't stop this bad feeling.—

A short boy walked past to the dorms, a vague smile crawling across his face. Pear–shaped twin girls and dullness in their features leaned toward each other, giggling and whispering. Nancy stood nearby, her arm around Henry.

—(Henry looks so mature with his freckled, bony arm around Nancy's trunk.) He's all better now got a girl.—

Jose ran around the crowd, his arms up in a touchdown gesture. He skidded to a stop and signed joyfully, *NO WORK NO WORK!*

HAPPY? The girl asked.

Michael shrugged.

The teenaged boy with a hooked nose pulled his girl closer. Paul rolled his wheelchair back and lifted his face to the board.

"Whas?"

—What Sam would say? Good old Sam. Could hardly see what he looks like now. What's left of him, dirt on the margin of the football field. What if he comes up from there? (The body digging its way out, going in the Davenport Dorm and working its way upstairs, killing each Whysee it caught at his leisure until it reaches the killer's suite.)

That would be neat. Then he would come to my room and I would coolly go….

'Hey Sam, might be hard to get vaginas like that.'

'Still more than you would ever get.'

What? Oh yeah? Funny Sam. That's just funny! The asshole would say that.

Then Sam laughs and calls me *loco* for thinking that and—

Michael, what are you smiling at?

"Whas? Oh, jus thinking abou no work."

Paul's lips pursed and as if to himself, he signed, *free time.*

Someone skittered and butted in the group. Her eyes glittered through her thick glasses like two brown beans. It was Gertie, of course. She squabbled. Paul answered as Gertie kept talking. Michael became lost in his thoughts. He reviewed his feelings.

—Lunch then rested until blue light on ceiling goes off. Came out not wanting to do hard labor and gone toward the Billboard. Then the Billboard's all blank, white gray with green ghosts of numbers.—

Someone cheered, and two joined in with them. The late afternoon sky darkened. When Michael peered at the billboard again, it was as if looking through a photograph negative. He raised his head and saw the soft spot of sun hidden behind a drifting cloud. Someone else hooted. He stared at Paul.

"Is suppose to be goos?"

Paul cupped over his eyes as he stared at Michael, the sunlight glittering from his lens.

I am not sure, he finally signed.

Michael looked at Gertie. She reached inside the pocket of her scruffy wool coat and pulled out a wrinkled sheet of cardboard. She held up the picture of the flower face to herself, and he saw the brutal outline of Sam's thumb that had served as a leaf in her picture.

—Can't forget you anywhere.—

The Billboard, center of waking moments, had nothing to show. They still gazed at it with uncertain smiles and a few shrugged. Michael, seeing the dying newborns, his best friend gone, knew that there will be no shelter from the descending nothingness that will envelop them all. It will come, slow but inevitable, an invisible tsunami wave that will turn all things seen and known into an oceanic void. He had lived through this, been there before, and was only revisiting this in the depths of his consciousness. To the great empty, many will go. A breeze and it seemed as if invisible fingers plucked the drawing from Gertie's hands. Before she could squawk and rescue it, the drawing wove to the plaza. It landed on the brick pathway, the blank part facing the sky.

Part Two: The Dying Daylight

HURRY UP PLEASE IT'S TIME
HURRY UP PLEASE IT'S TIME

—T. S. Eliot, The Waste Land

A Visit From Past

In early November, biting cold raked the plaza and all: dorms, sidewalks, fields, and courtyards. A harsh wind blew the last few withered leaves off the naked trees by the dozen. No snow has come yet. The grasses and trees only grew crisp from the frost. Flu followed, germs spreading among the wards, weakened by lack of square meals and warmth. Many had grown too tired to step outside and clear their lungs, and sinuses of mucus, too weary to open a window to hawk and spit. Phlegm ran on walls and stained carpets in the hallways. The sickness had spread to all, and even the unlucky Whysees that walked too close, their noses snuffling and red.

It was decided that the wards must fend for themselves. With noses and mouths covered in masks, and hands gloved in latex, the Whysees passed out mops for the bathrooms, sponges for the walls, and dozens of buckets. They, with shouts and pinwheels of furious gestures, assigned several wards to each dorm and their shifts rotated each day. If there was any contact between the Whysees and the wards, it was from a thrown rock or any other handy object within reach.

Michael Poole squeezed the dirty soapy water out of the sponge into the bucket. He turned his head aside to cough. The back of his throat burned and tickled. With his lungs burning, his coughs bellowed down the hall as the soapy water ran over his goose bumped arm.

—Was I that loud? Gotta getcha back to work, scrap the smeared wall, my hands go up and down, up and down. Uggh. Jose not workin.' Just sitting on his ass next to his bucket, wiping his slimy nose on his arm. Do some work all right?—

Jose's mouth pooched out. His legs stretched out, and he kept clicking his sneakered feet between fits of coughing and wiping his nose. Bop bop bop bop. Michael wiped his forehead with his forearm and stood. He waved his hand at Jose, whose hand was wiping at his right nostril. Bop bop.

Do a little, he signed to Jose.

Fingers in his beaming mouth, Jose shook his head. Bop. Bop. Bop.

I can't finish by myself.

Nat came into the hall, a purple shiner beneath his left eye. He stopped, his face red, tears running down his cheeks. Bop bop... Jose's head snapped up at him, his eyes widening. Nat stepped closer to Jose, screaming.

"Nas, he's deaf, he don's know whas you're sayin'."

Nat whirled to Michael and pointed the battered flashlight at him. "Tell him to get up and work. Tell him!"

J–O–S–E, you get up and work.

Jose stared at the floor and shook his head. Nat jumped and screeched. He kicked the bucket. Dirty foam ran over the carpet. He turned to Jose, who shrank. Michael raised his hands.

"Nas, take is easy. Calm down, all righ?"

Nat clenched his fists. "No! If you don't do what I say, I will report you! Now do it!"

HATE YOU! Jose signed.

He almost dodged Nat, who swung his flashlight at him. It clunked against the back of Jose's head, and he stumbled into the wall. His mouth opened to scream, but it only came out with a rasp. He then fled to his room, his mouth in a silent squall. His hand fumbled for the knob, and he shoved the door open. Then it slammed after him. Michael stepped toward Nat, who turned along with the flashlight. There was a thud as if his skull had caved, and fog crept in his vision.

—Oh hum. Another one of Nat's fit.—

176

The thought was like ice, soothing the inside of his skull. Michael grunted as his clawed hands gripped Nat by the throat, and he rammed his knee up into him. Hard. He felt the other's body sag. It felt good, the way the flesh on Nat's throat folded to his squeezing hands.

"Thas for las September!"

He shook the blockhead by the neck, making Nat's head bounce, and shoved him hard. Nat flailed his arms against the door and crashed face forward into it. He huddled on the floor, his eyes weak and tired.

Michael pointed at him.

"Just sop this shit, jus sop is all. Why you on everyone's case?"

Before he finished, he bent with a coughing fit, his throat scabbed and burning. He stumbled back and leaned on the wall as he covered his mouth, coughing. He checked on Nat.

—Is that what too mean does? Take away more than good thoughts of others? Better be good if that is what bad is. The big ol' bad blockhead, his arms up.—

Nat covered his face, his shoulders shaking. The head of the block wiped his nose and started weeping. Helpless mewing sounds repeated in Michael's hearing aid as he leaned over and picked up the sponge. He resumed cleaning. Behind him, Nat got up and hurtled toward the door. There was a thump, then a slam. Michael kept working.

After he finished, he walked to the lobby. By the stairs, he put the filthy sponges in the trash bag. A short Whysee, the one who had yelled at him in September, sat on the steps. He raised his head, his eyes still fixed on the tile floor.

—Where Sam fell. Blood drainin' away. Shut up, stop thinkin' stuff like that! Nothing can be done. Nothing.—

The eyes of the Whysee were red, and he kept sniffling. He lowered his head again to examine his palms. Close to the short Whysee, he could see that the callused fingers, and a thin red mark jagged his wrists. Michael approached and saw the Whysee' Adam's apple bob over the gray collar.

177

"Wans me take trash ous, righ?"

The Whysee's hand flapped toward the door. His lips contorted.

"Don't go away now, you hear?"

"Okay," Michael answered, wondering if the Whysee had heard about his attempt to escape.

—All Whysees keep your eyes on Michael Poole, he's a cunning one. ('Don't mess with him, Sam said he's *loco*.') *Loco* Michael, that's me.—

He lugged the trash bag to the door and pushed it open with his back. He struggled as the door pinched the fat part of the bag, making him squish against it.

—Smells of rubbers. Thin plastic keepin' my arms away from hundred pounds of used rags and sponges smeared with gray and yellow glazes. Oh, darlin', press me tighter. Tighter! Ugh.—

The door swung wider. His face stony, the leader held it for him. The leader spoke, but Michael did not understand. Then the leader grabbed the bag with a grunt and tossed it outside. Michael had seen some wards with bruises from the leader's rebukes, including Nat. He hurried out past the leader. The door swung shut, and through the glass he saw him walking in and talking to the short Whysee. Outside, he turned from the two conferring Whysees.

—Nope, none of my business.—

He bent and wrapped his arms around the bulk, a leak of sheen slicking against the insides of his arms.

"Ugh," he said to himself, his arms sinking into the moist plastic.

He checked the distance and took the stairs through the underground parking lot. The bottom squished on the last step, and a few rags flopped out against his chin. He smelled sweat and dank breaths from them and groaned. His stomach clenched, and he might have retched if there had been food inside him. From the small portion of soup and bread served now, he doubted that He dragged it and spotted a dumpster near the utility building where Sam had tried to find weapons

178

to fight the outsiders. He took it over and set it down by it. The metal lid squealed as he swung it open, and moldy smells from emptied boxes of microwaveable pizza and pasta assaulted his nostrils. He bent and hugged the bag to his chest before heaving it over and into the dumpster, enjoying the clanging sound. He stopped as he headed back, for he noticed someone standing in the gloom, waiting.

It was a man wearing a white shirt and black slacks. He could read the name HANK stitched in red on the breast of the shirt. Familiar blue eyes with wrinkles around them seemed weak and full of fear. His graying hair was short, but Michael remembered him as having straight blonde hair. Michael's own curly black hair came from his mother.

—(*'Michael, it is not just her fault. It just happen. It nobody fault.'*)—

The stranger looked around, his smile hesitant.

Remember me?

The gloom failed to hide the mirth in his eyes. Michael's heart threatened to burst hard enough to make him want to fall to his knees. But he looked around for prying eyes.

Yes. You are my Dad.

You grow.

What are you doing here?

I come to get you out. Everything bad here.

It alway like this. After you let me and Mom end up here.

—Should sign it casual, nice and cool...—

He could not keep his hands from chopping the air, and the corners of his lips pulled into a jerky frown.

Dad drew his head back. His uncertain eyes flicked to the side before fixing on Michael. *We don't have time for this.*

—Just say, 'Hey…. Fuck you.' Flip him off nice and cool. Jesus! Hurts. My throat!—

His body racked over in a coughing fit, and he felt the weight of Dad's hand patting him on the back. His legs buckled as his father held him up and continued to pat him. He waved away his father's grasp, and the wrinkled hands fell away. His chest loosened, and he stood upright again.

Thank.

Need medicine? I will get them for you. Dad's face was all concerned.

I am O.K. Too much risk.

Dad's face became stern. *Not O.K. Meet me here tonight after dinner. I get off work at five thirty.*

Fine.

Promise?

Yes. Go before anyone see us.

Dad gave a lazy salute and strolled away, checking the lot as his footfalls gave way.

—Ghost from long ago. Must be dreaming. Did not know Dad was close. So close.—

After dinner, Michael came back. The darkness hid him as he waited under the steps again. A few Whysees passed chattering, and he wedged himself farther beneath the stairway as one stopped to tuck in his shirt before moving on past him. He breathed as soon as they turned the concrete wall and disappeared. Soon Dad hurried back, a brown bag in hand. He jumped, his eyes panicky, when Michael stepped from beneath the stairs.

Think catch.

Just me.

The bag rustled too loud as Dad placed it in his hands. Michael peered inside and saw a box, a package of salty peanut butter crackers, and a carton of orange juice peeking invitingly up at him.

"Foo?" Michael asked, and anguish rippled across Dad's face before he nodded.

"Can I ee now?" Michael asked. The scents of flour, salt, and nuts were strong in his nostrils.

Sure. I will tell you while you eat.

Michael tore into the package and fished out a piece of peanut butter cracker. He sniffed wheat, peanut butter, and tasted the nut oil when he took a bite.

I got this friend, a Black guy, L–O–U–I–S. Little… Dad held out his hands around his waist to show chubbiness. *You get to…*

His father's signs trailed as Michael finished the crackers and nodded while opening the carton of orange juice. He threw his head back to pour it in his throat. Everything got sharper in focus, and the leaden sensation in the pit of his stomach loosened its hold. He drank the rest as Dad continued.

Finish? O.K. You get to come over to the big house near the side.

His father pointed southwest.

Monkey House?

Yes. Hold on one week. Then next week, see that Black guy there little…

"Fas?"

Right. Be there nine thirty. He will wait for you. You uncomfortable for a while but do what he said. I will wait at the train station parking lot. That where the train are, little store, where you know that place.

Me and Mom go from P…. I forgot the… P.

Philadelphia.

Yes, I remember the train there.

I am sorry.

It was long time ago.

They became silent as the light from the outside grew dim and the concrete roof and walls took on that hard color.

—A real long time. Why wait so long? Why wait until I learned to care for everyone? Why wait until Mom's gone?—

One week, seven day. His father reminded.

Where?

Middle of country. It dangerous, many religion group conflict with federal law. Less Watcher but more police and soldier against us.

How get there?

Get to lie a lot. Pretend you hear.

Like last time?

Dad winced as if stung but answered. *You older now. They won't go deep like hearing test at the hearing center you and Mom fail. They check people paper, and we can figure out on the way.*

What we going to do there? Michael felt the sore need to wail.

We need to get there first. I need to go. Take the pill one each four hour. Can you read?

Bit. My friend made me many time. The boy in glasses and wheelchair help me learn better.

That is good.

Dad?

Yes?

I wish you D–I–D not have to sell your car. I see it in the lot a few time.

His father had a sad smile, his face full of regret. *My car. I want you to drive around when you are old enough. I look past forward to your grade in school and girlfriend you will get in high school.*

Me too.

Dad staggered and pulled Michael to his front in an awkward hug. Michael stood, enduring his father's hold.

What is wrong? Too big for your old man?

Just nervous.

Don't worry. We will catch up. I get to go.

Then Dad hurried away, and Michael was alone again. If not for him clutching a plastic bag skimmed with crumbs, empty snack package, and the medicine in it, he might have thought it a dream. He tucked the bag under his shirt and walked upstairs, alert for any signs of gray. He entered the dorm and wards lounged around, some sitting on the floor while few paced, not used to having nothing to do.

—Should write a letter to Paul, Jose, Nancy, everyone. Could explain what I did and why.—

His chest creaked a little.

—Wish can have a machine that shrinks them and puts them in my pocket so can take them with me. In real life, I must leave them behind me. I could leave a part of myself. Even though writing I am not good at, I can try.—

182

He visited Paul in his room. When he let him in, Michael noticed how thin his friend looked and how sunken his eyes were. He perched by his deadweight legs, not bothering with false conversation.

What wrong?

"Can—um—can I have paper and pencil, if you gos 'em?"

"Why?"

He almost said 'write', but Paul might insist on helping.

"I figure maybe I draw. Gertie might gos something there. Smars to figure whas to do."

Paul wrinkled his brow and his chin jerked to his bureau. *I get the paper in top drawer and pencil. You can tear a quarter.*

Little but big corner.

Yes.

The bed creaked as Michael rose and went to the drawer to check. In the opened drawer, Paul's drying tight folded socks and underthings were spotted and damp but smelled of clean water. He found a few sheets of paper. The pencil stub rolled back and forth before he took both.

One corner, right?

Yes. Paul signed grudgingly.

He used the edge of his hand to measure and tore a ragged square and went to his room. On his own bed, he hunched over the sheet that was miles deep of white.

—What words to say? To tell all hurts felt and all closeness. With fancy grand words like Contitution and amen men that will make everyone even a Whysee cry when read. Or like Decaraton of Indpending that begins with Hear ye! Hear ye! And means not to depend on nothing.—

He held the pencil and let it tap the paper. He made a rooster scratch and pulled it away.

—What did Paul say about words? It don't have to be fancy like the Contitution and the amen men. The only thing they do is tell what the truth is, the right kinds.—

Dear Paul

I write not good But said what in me Mind. Dad was out here and I found him. I no know way say bye but wave. By time you get this me gone. I juswan say you been good. You served more then here and now. 1st Robby boy sure he care of. He boy with great signs big hart. You fin him in playgrond in cold days cuz Ms. L bitc. Sure you get hocey stic him an somun spy him out for me.

And on the other side of paper, he wrote:

No way to go I number for u. 1. Henry doin good signs and keep workin. 2 Nancyto care self Gertie keep drawin. 3. Tell Jose sorry me out he a good guy 4 Not enough room tell in hurt haert but do my bes. Tell Kasy I sorry for beein asshole abou himher. No more room so all best you all here. You made sad place home.
SinnerSicerly
LoyourfriendMIchael.
P.s. I miss him.
P.S. 2. Nat Rickie Kelly asks tell them I said they not only hit by ugly stic but it beat the shit out of them.

He smiled at the last line. A tear surprised him, sliding on his cheek. He wiped it away, folded the paper, and tucked it in the pillowcase. For the hundredth time this year, he looked under his bed to check on his wooden handle with the old and battered blade. He stared out the window.

—Oh, yeah, baby. Go!—

Michael counted the days backward. Excitement troubled his sleep at 2:00 a.m., and he lay awake each night. Sometimes he would go for a run to tire himself out. The pills his father had given him eased his cold. When he woke late, he would lie on his bed, imagining the outside world.

—(Glistening meat patty between soft rolls, crispy fries, salty dollops of ketchup Heinz, red rap on the 57 to make it flow, pizza crusty bread, tomato, melted cheese, hot, slick on tongue, cold grape soda in long slow sips, long slow dance, skin long legs, soft hair rubbing over female secret places. Kechutt kut! BOOM! SHBOOM! goes the landscape as rifle chatters, sending scores of Whysees screaming to hell.) Yes, gonna do it all and join up in middle of U.S. of A.—

One morning in so number of days, the lights woke him. Wrenched from sleep, he saw Henry peering out the door. Michael got up and put his hearing aid in his ear.

"Whas happen?"

There was just the pitting of flashes, no buzzes, clangs of bells and alarms. Henry opened it wider and pointed at a cluster of Whysees in the hall.

"Th–ah–The–They push him down."

"Who?"

Michael pushed him aside and looked. Whysees surrounded a hulking form. They tormented a large slab of marble before he recognized the boy who sang every day.

—I know the words to the *Rock of Ages*. Paul told me them even though I know he did not want to:

> Not the labors of my hands
> can fulfill thy law's commands
> could my zeal no respite know
> could my tears forever flow
> all for sin could not atone
> thou must save and thou alone

So many holy words in that song.—

The leader knelt by the larger human form, forcing the gigantic chin on neck to stay down. Hold unbroken, the colossal head could not rear upward. The leader did not gloat. Just acted sick. Blackness glittered from beneath his half–closed lids. His arm wrapped the large neck, and another twisted around the bulging coiled of the elbow as if he rested on a fork of a tree. It was the singer who was trapped, tears brimming his eyes. A few doors away, Paul shrank back in his wheelchair.

Michael sidled over to him. *What?*

Tell you later.

He heard the hoarse sobbing sound in the quiet.

—Jesus.—

The leader gave the broad back a soft slap and stood. He spun and strode to the exit door. The other Whysees filed out after him. As they passed, the blonde one gulped. The exit door shut off the dull light from the window outside, and the bloodshot eyes of the blonde Watcher squinted at him before he followed the others. Paul wheeled over as Jose and Kasy helped the boy to his feet. The boy's woolly hair brushed against the ceiling. Holding his palms out, the boy mumbled. Paul signed for Michael.

Sorry s–o sorry. I get up early find R–E–D–D–Y in D–O–Y–A–L Dorm. He around on metal legs so I walk with him. Now he is not here. He is just not there! I pull the alarm down to get them coming. All they do was hurt my stomach.

Tears fell from his soft brown eyes, and he clutched his stomach, grimacing. His thick hands rose to his face as he sobbed harder.

—Got to get out of here. Hold on six days more. Haven't been able to stand and just watchin' his eyes all scrunched shut like that, big arms trembling.—

Paul wheeled himself closer to the giant of a boy. He patted him on the side and spoke, his voice soft and gentle.

"Whas going on, Paul?" Michael said, his voice hoarse. He let out a breath that he had been holding with a whooping sigh.

He is L–I–O–N–E–L.

Him?

Paul pointed to the teenager, and the youth had a shy smile. He faced Michael and lowered his head until his eyes stared at the floor. Paul signed as the boy told his story, his tone gentle.

Yes L–I–O–N–E–L. We, me and R–E–D–D–Y, we hide in church and there pipes all over. We run when the people came in and many time, the pipes bop my head. I try carrying him underneath tunnel of church. He scream at me to leave him, run hard. I ask him why so mad, and tunnel under church fill with our neighbor and police. He cry because I was too slow to hide the way he tell me. We are here because inside my head is thick, and R–E–D–D–Y tell me to be strong! And I am!

Lionel held up his thick arms, sculpted out of stone, the veins, pale stalks of engraved leaves stems. He laughed and wiped drying tears from his face.

"Why you sing all time?" Michael asked.

Lionel talked, his face bunched with thinking, looking at Michael as Paul signed.

I sing for me, I sing for you, I sing when my song, and I sad, and glad, make people happy and strong.

"Place cool use los of singing, I think."

Lionel only chuckled again. By the time they left the dorm for breakfast, Paul and Lionel were conversing. Michael could tell how Paul's face started out confused, then wary. Paul questioned him and seemed to have Lionel repeat some things. Paul nodded.

Michael, we need to talk.

—Please God, nothing about Dad. Did Henry go through my things? Better not show Paul the letter or kick his ass good, right, Sam? Sam… hurts to think of you. Will think of you all.—

187

It was unreal how they lost someone and gained another. Nancy came out of her dorm and waved at Henry. They hugged before joining the others walking to the cafeteria. They ate their watery oatmeal and dry toasts. Nancy chattered, her voice trebled with pleasure. As Nancy spoke, Henry dipped his head, his face blushing. Then he promptly stood and left as Paul stared at Nancy, his smile faltering. Lionel giggled and lowered his head, licking the oatmeal from his thick fingers. Paul said something harsh that stopped Lionel giggling. Jose looked confused and worried. Gertie nodded, self–satisfied.

"Whas goin' on, Paul?"

"No!" Gertie snapped. "It's for grownups only!"

"Shus up, Gertie. Paul, whas sae then?"

Later.

"He'll explain to you later so you will understand," Gertie said.

—Shut up. I know plenty more than you. Like how to get out. Know my Dad going to take me out. Just didn't know what you guys are saying, that's all.—

Paul talked to Nancy, who kept stuttering something, her eyes wide and panicked.

—Why they upset? Sam is gone. I miss him too but got to be hardheaded to join up when Dad gets me out of here.—

Michael finished his toast and waited for Paul to finish talking. Nancy had her chin tucked as she nodded, mute. Gertie said something rapidly. Lionel smiled, his face hopeful.

What you guy leaving me out of?

Jose tapped Nancy on her arm.

S'UP?

Nancy, dazed, tried to finger spell, *W…. A…. I….* but Jose gave a firm headshake and signed, *TELL NOW. TELL ME.*

She tried again, but her pudgy hands would not flex the way she seemed to want, so she slammed her palms on the table and shouted at Jose, who cringed. Gertie shouted at Michael while Nancy blundered to her feet, her stomach banging on the edge of the table. Still hollering, she stalked away, her voice trembling with rage and fear. Paul buried his head in his hands. Lionel, with a wan smile, asked him something. Paul gave a headshake and replied. Jose's lips blubbered, and he wiped his nose. His black eyes fixed on Michael.

ME KNOW NOTHING.

Me same.

"What said?" Gertie demanded.

"It's something importans abous you buh forges is."

"That's not funny!" Gertie screeched. She slammed her hands on the table, and the plates clattered. She flounced off, her puckering lips mumbling words Michael was beyond understanding and even caring. Jose calmed, sniffling. He got up and left them. Paul slumped in his wheelchair.

Let get out of here, he signed and wheeled himself from the table. Michael followed. Outside, Paul crossed his arms and shivered.

Winter is coming.

"Paul, whas going on?"

By the naked bush farther away, Jose moped, brushing his hand against the thin tips.

—Poor kid. Haven't seen Robby either. Hope he's all right. Should ask but might push me. Will look for him later time. Will go over there tomorrow. Must tell him about Sam.—

Paul stared at Jose thoughtful for a while before he said anything. Lionel brushed past and walked to Jose, his hand up and signing the letter L. Jose smiled through his tears and showed him the sign for J. Lionel patted Jose on his thin back, and they both sat on the curb around the bush comparing hand signs. Paul smiled.

Good, we are pulling together for a change.

Michael felt an urgent need to sign, so he shifted language.

O.K. Are you going to tell me what happening?

Thing are worse. Gate just gone bad.

189

What Paul said compelled Michael to look around at everything.

Serious?

I mean, more than that. I can survive what with now, but I don't think they want us to.

Jesus, what you talking about?

—(The leader's face is somber and thoughtful, staring down from the fourth floor.)—

Michael, two ward missing. Those who know them can't find them around. L–I–O–N–E–L can't find ready, I mean R–E–D–D–Y.

—(Eyes looking up from the metal bin. Small mouth opens and closes. Sam's eyes, one pinpoint and the other, a pit.) Oh, Jesus.—

What you think happen to them? Michael asked.

Michael, what are we going to do? Paul asked.

—Feel like cryin.' Screamin' also. Not for me, but for Paul and others. What's going to happen? He'll be alone. You know. Cut and run out of here, right? Yes, sir, *loco* Michael gonna quietly pack and cut and run with Daddy dearest.—

Paul shrugged, his mouth slack and threw up his hands, helpless. A soft wind brought the promise of cold. Something inside Michael burned to cinder.

And N–A–N–C–Y, Paul signed, his face tight. *All in a natural way.*

"Huh?"

—You know! Her and Henry. In her room. Ugh. Don't think of that. Was she on bottom because too heavy to be on top? Did her stomach squish on Henry's stomach? Eeew! Stop thinking like that! But sure respect Henry for gettin' some.—

Of all the stupid thing… Paul signed to himself.

"Um…. When is due?"

Never! They will rip it out! Just other. She don't have a chance!

Paul clenched the armrests, his knuckles white. He signed, his face wretched with misery. *What going to happen to her? What going to happen to us?*

Nothing. Cannot do nothing.

By the bush, Lionel and Jose were tussling, stirring up dead old leaves. Soft, dust billowed about their feet. Jose let out a delightful shriek and pedaled his sneakers against Lionel's knees with his heels, his high, sweet laughter carrying over to them. Soon the hiccupping laughter became thin and reedy until it burst into bubbles of giggles.

Michael woke early, sleep snapped as if a broken twig. The orange light of dawn bathed his room, and streetlights on the plaza glowed in the window like small moons. He became confused if he'd had conversed with Paul about the missing wards. It was just the unease of daily life unsettled by the loss of rhythms. He thought Jose's dissolved laughter was just a dream. Since his eyes would not close, and his heart kept hammering, he decided to go out for a run early to tire himself out and get rid of the fear that kept his belly jellied. He knew the locks on the doors would disconnect in the morning.

—Might do that now on. Rid my body of bangin' with being stuck here. Maybe get me hungry for that crap they still serve for breakfast.—

He found himself alone in the hallway, the still lobby, and outside the plaza. Although he did not know the word for it, his feelings were apocalyptic, as if he were the last person on earth.

—Wouldn't be such a loss after way things are goin'. Hope if the last person will find a girl. There's no choice for her but to spread long legs and I'll dipsy–do–dah right in there and won't need no rubber. Hah! In fact, I wish there's no one else except for live breathin' girl. Or two or three. Got to be good lookin', though.—

The thought cheered him on and, not able to help himself, he grinned. He stretched his legs a little before starting at a slow–paced jog downstairs to the underground parking lot. He thought of what it would be like to hold female flesh in his hands, to feel her against him, and he felt himself growing hard.

When he made it to the playground, he looked toward it and realized it was empty.

—Robby! Where are you? What about you? And to tell you of Sam… oh God, can't think of him now.—

When he slowed by a Whysee at one post, between the gate separating the playground and Farrow Field, he was surprised to find relief that he was not alone on this earth and things were the way things were. That Whysee even good–humoredly made a snapping motion, signaling him to run faster.

"Hah," Michael said, running faster from the Whysee, who merely shrugged then clasped his hands behind his back. He ran harder, his legs pumping, and Farrow Field lay flat before him. He breathed the rich air, and dusty lights glimmered dull beads on damp grass. His legs stretched with his increased pace, and his arms, toughened by exertion, swung. When he reached the football field, taking the long way around the broken–down fence that surrounded the tennis court, he noticed movements by the goal post.

He slowed, stopped.

Five figures, fine features melded by distance, moved in the dawn. Four were in gray sweats, the Whysees. The fifth had the tentative movement of a ward. Something inside him, not thoughts, sounds, nor images, but a startling impulse through his nerves, made him back until he was peeking around the corner of the crooked green fence around the tennis court. One was, of course, the leader with his muscular form. Far away, the form gestured to the other three Whysees, and one of them held a coil of gold–line rope around his shoulder. It took them minutes to direct the ward to stand beneath the bar between the posts. Someone threw the rope over to where other Whysees waited. The leader nodded and made a rising motion with his hands. Two other Whysees fastened the other end around the ward's neck.

—Playin' joke. Scare him, that's all. Right?—

The rope around the ward's neck, the two other Whysees joined the third, holding the other end. They pulled hard, once, then again. The rope went taut. Hands grasping his neck, the ward backpedaled, making the rope slack. It tightened again. Soon the worn shoes skimmed the grass, and his hands scrabbled at his corded neck. It seemed they were testing an exotic flying machine and the bars, made golden by the rising sun, seemed to be the wings of a giant bug for the ward to fly on them. But it was only the ward moving upward. In another minute and three hard pulls, the ward hovered about a foot from the ground, legs kicking. The body jiggled and arms flopped. The hands groped, the mouth a tiny dent in the distance. Arms drooped. Legs stiffened, and at last, nothing moved. The leader held up his hands, bidding the three Whysees to wait. Three of them clung to the rope, arms straining, and the morning sun shone on one of their necks, slick with sweat. The leader's hands swept to his hips. They lowered the body, and for a lunatic moment it seemed as if it still stood. Then it plopped to the ground.

The leader crouched by the body, pressing his head to its face. The leader waited. His head raised from the ward's face. Then his fingers trailed the underside of the chin. The leader stood. One Whysee trotted away toward the three mini skyscrapers that housed the Whysees. While the others waited, the leader at the bleachers unzipped a black bag. He took out a book, and Michael, who cringed farther out of sight, guessed it to be the notebook that the leader carried with him all the time. The leader used his pen from the pocket of his pant and made some notes.

—Our numbers in there, our numbers!—

When the Whysee returned with a plastic bag, the other Whysees busied themselves, pulling it over and under the body prone on the football field. Michael turned away and ran, giving the field a wide berth. No one saw for their heads bent, intent on pulling the bag under and over the ward. Without thinking, Michael took the same route back and passed the same Whysee from earlier. He saw the good humor that had been in his eyes had dwindled to a neutral gaze, such as the blank uncomprehending glance of an alligator toward a sinking stone. Michael returned to his room, lay on his bed, and hugged himself. He waited until his breathing slowed. Minutes passed before he came out to the cafeteria for breakfast.

During breakfast, he did not mention what he saw at Farrow Field. While he finished his sour milk and moldy bread with stale peanut butter, Paul mentioned he saw a little boy in the playground with bandages on his wrist knobs with the other children as he traveled to the library. Almost dribbling the milk upon himself, Michael set the half–filled glass on the table.

"I gos to go now," he said as he left them.

He arrived at the playground a few minutes later and jogged to the gate to reach over it and lift the latch. A group of children gathered near the concrete stairs. As he neared, he saw over their heads. A girl bent to a huddled boy, both lost in a mess of ratty hairs and earnest poses of the other children.

—Is that the one with the scab on her chin? Yeah, that's her. Cheeky kid talkin' back to me last time. What they doin'?—

"Ssss…" the girl coached the boy, her teeth clenched.

"Ssss…" others echoed.

He leaned over the small, hunched backs.

"Whas going on?"

The girl did not see him, so he waved at her face. She looked up, her face solemn with concentration. The children stood, their eyes squinting at his intrusion. When the crowd parted, he saw him sitting on the steps, arms crossed, and the startling sight of his missing hands even though he knew it to be. They were just round lumps of folded skin and scars, covered by rust–colored bandages. His face was still, soft eyes staring at nothing.

—Never forgive.—

R–O–B–B–Y?

The boy's eyes widened in recognition, and he frantically moved his arms, then stopped. His stumps raised, his face worked to look amused, but it turned out weary, and his eyes brimmed.

"Now, he gotta tawk!" the little girl said, satisfied.

Michael gave her a gentle but a no–nonsense push on the shoulder. "Time you move on."

The girl glared and flounced away. Others followed. One filthy boy wearing a torn sweater looked at Robby, then back to him.

"Kuh–"

"Whas you wans now?"

The boy's hands shook. *I don't know A.S.L., and he teach me. I want to said, 'I feel sad he not teach me more.'*

Sorry, Michael signed.

Robby smiled and jerked his head, dismissing him. The boy frowned with uncertainty. Robby waved, his left arm brushing him off and pleading for understanding with his face. The boy wandered away. Michael faced Robby, still on the step, both awkward from how passing of days kept them apart. He sat next to him.

Sorry, I do not see you soon.

Robby stared at the other children clamoring on the jungle gym. His bandaged stump pointed at a space next to him. He guessed who should occupy the space. A cloth brushed him on the shoulder.

—EEEK, the lump under Robby's bandage. What is under that? Is the bone sticking out? Robby holds his right hand–oops, his wrist. Points at me again. Then invisible someone by me.—

"Oh, Sam."

Robby wrinkled his face at him.

S–A–M?

Robby nodded.

That night…

Robby stopped nodding and waited.

Anyway, when they…

195

He gestured at the emptiness that surrounded Robby's wrists, and Robby lifted them, his mouth pressed as he smiled thinly.

When they do this to you... Sam was upset... he just go... I don't know... he get all mad, but you know scare and he and this Whysee you know Whysee?

Robby nodded.

He get into a fight. There was an accident. He... fall and he gone.

Robby shook his entire body hard, and he tried croaking, "No." but it came out "Nuh! N–uh!"

Sorry.

He looked back at Michael, started sobbing and grimacing through his tears. His narrow shoulders shook. His thin legs drew up to chest level, and he pressed his face to bent knees, shaking harder. Before Michael could lift his arms to hug him, Robby leaned and threw his arms around his chest.

—Stinks of dirt, oh Goddamn it, and never gonna say, sorry Jesus. Got a right to hate you for it. Stand up there, run things, make me and him deaf, Henry retard, Nancy, and Lionel and make Paul all twisted legs. What's your point, huh? And hey, know what, God? I don't care about you anymore. Just me, my friends, so forget it, Jesus. My throat hurt. You don't know how much I hate you, makin' everyone this way. You know, you're just a Whysee, run things, do things to me, Sam, and Robby. I don't give a damn for you, aren't goin' pray to you anymore, but put my arms round Robby's back 'cause you not do your Goddamn job, Jesus, God, or whoever you are up there, lookin' at us down here, down on a kid who needs a home, cry his eyes out 'cause someone who's just nice to him died. That's his idea of nice, someone who doesn't belt him in the face for signing. So, you up there look down on us. I just must hold on to him, 'cause you're nothing compared to Robby. Nothing! You get to die a grown–up, and he gets to be hurt as a kid. So, suck with you. Don't care if you jam a lightning bolt up my ass and send me to hell. Look at you with your strong jaw and white beard, gettin' pissed off, huh, God? Or who you are. Don't care. Hell is better than here.

Michael, don't act so high and mighty. You're the one who's cuttin' and runnin' on your friends.

Oh yeah? You just… hell, I don't care anymore.—

Robby slowed his crying to sniffles. He sat up, wiped at his runny nose with his forearm, and sniffed. They sat, and the children looked over at them.

—Stop look. You're all same. Deaf like us. Don't care if you talk good or know more. You're the same. Stand, play, loud shouts, and games, and make others feel bad by sayin' nah, not him, he's not with us, not good enough, so go back to your play and leave him alone.—

The others resumed playing. The girl was leading another group, using her voice to shout orders.

—Looks like playing a speech teacher. Brat.—

Robby shivered, crossing his arms.

O.K. now?

Robby nodded. Michael wiped off the streak of dirt on one cheek, and there was snot smeared on one of his nostrils. Michael wiped that also and rubbed his hand on the concrete steps. He checked his palm again.

I get to go.

Robby poked his side, his eyes up at him and hopeful.

—Two days left. Will hate me if I don't come. Hope others will.—

Michael gave a slow headshake and lifted his hands and shoulders in a shrug. Robby swept his bandaged lump hard along the side of his forehead, his face registering confusion. Michael guessed what the boy's phantom hand said.

WHY?

I can't tell.

Robby crossed his bald arms. Michael turned away. His chest hurt too much.

—Will not forget him. That is for sure. Will tell 'This is for Robby.' when empty gun in soldier's face. Will join up, first thing that is for sure.—

197

Michael left and walked back to his dorm his stride defeated.

The Day inched, numb. It was hard to know the time. That morning, he lay in his bed only to go into Paul's room to find just thirty minutes had passed. The eternal breakfast, among the buzz of his hearing and deaf friends, lasted five minutes before Michael lost patience and fought to keep from fleeing the inward impulse a steaming kettle. He controlled himself, picking up his plate and cup to take them to the conveyor belt. Lunch became easier when he wrung out his last moments with his friends.

Outside, he and Paul watched Nancy, Gertie, Jose, Lionel, and other wards play tag. The goal post was base. Jose was it. Michael saw a rope tied to the post and the other end snaking to the corner of the field. Gertie was near the corner, and when Jose started for her, she shrieked and snatched up the rope, using it as part of the base.

CAN'T D–O THAT, Jose signed.

They argued, Gertie in words and Jose in signs. Soon Henry and Lionel wandered over to see what the trouble was. Nancy crept along behind them and, giggling, ran over to the goal line and slammed her hand on the metal post.

Up by the bleachers, Paul gave a negative headshake. *Can't get together without arguing.*

"Yeah…"

There was silence.

"So, Paul…" Michael said, pumping his fist. "You um ever ges any?"

Paul wrinkled his face. *No. You don't either.*

Paul must have read his facial expression for he hastily added, *Sorry, but it bother me as much as it bother you.*

Serious?

Paul nodded.

"I though you don's nee to 'cause…" Michael gestured limply toward Paul's legs.

Paul laughed. *You think down here too much. Some can get it up while some can't. Mine still do. And there other use for hands and tongue beside talking.*

"Huh?"

—(Sam at fourteen: 'Hey Michael. You gotta *pum–pum* girls other than that flaccid dick of yours.'

Sam's tongue worms out to wriggle obscenely between two of his fingers.)—

"Oh."

"Yeah, oh," Paul echoed.

Awkward silence followed. Michael spoke.

"Sam sure dick a los of girls. As leas he die knowing thas."

"That doesn't mean it's fair."

Paul continued to rant, not seeming to realize that Michael was still there.

—What's saying now? Family, home…—

"Hey, Paul, whas saying?"

Talking to myself. Only no fair how they take everything from us.

"Yeah."

—Will take me away from Paul. Poor Paul, not fair. Unfair of me.

But I got to take my chance. I'm sure Paul would've done the same.

How would you know?

I think he would, all right?—

"You think abous him?"

Paul's eyes lowered, then raised to stare at him. He nodded. *All the time.*

Michael looked away and whispered. "I love him, you know. Nos like a queer bus like a close frien'." He felt his cheeks stinging. "Wish I tole him, though. He deserves thas."

"I am sure he knows, Michael."

"Yeah, bus he shool hear from me you know?"

Paul sighed.

"I wish we all were free."

I am.

"Whas you mean?"

No one make me think like them. No one can do that to me.

"Buh, you gotta work early in morning and wheel aroun' gettin' books for Whysees."

Yes, but I get to read and go into another world for a while. Nothing can stop me from flying like that. Sometime I lay my head back and dream of life that I want. I can think the way I want. They can't take these think in me away.

"That's neas, Paul. Wish I coul think thas way."

Michael?

"Hmm?"

Why do you want to talk to me?

—Tell him the truth! You're going away.

But what if he wants to go with me? I can't take him begging me.

You are a chicken coward!—

He scanned about before signing to Paul.

I go out early for run.

Yes.

I know why ward are missing.

I know too. G–E–R–T–I–E tell me she go off to here to watch them take each one every morning.

P–A–U–L?

What?

Sometime I wish they will hurry. I don't like the way they make me feel about me.

—Oh, you filthy liar.—

I understand. Paul replied.

When they come for me, I will just go with them. It is just a few minute, I think.

Better than this?

Yes. Afterward, I will see your and my friend again. And I'll be like everyone else.

200

—You Goddamn traitor. You sold him out. Goin' tra—
la–la with Daddy.—

Paul did not answer but gazed toward the field where
the rope lay waiting. Michael could read the look on Paul's face.
He had seen it a few times in the mirror, mostly when thinking
about girls. Paul was looking at it with longing.

During the day of the escape, he grew restless and
could not focus on what his friends kept saying.

—Today is the day, my man. Today's the day.—

When evening came, he was already outside the dorm.
He wiped his damp palms on his pants.

—What would they say to me on a night like this?
They'll know I'm up to no good. Wait, take your time. God,
can't believe I was looking forward to this. Can't believe how
I got mad at how slow time moved. Should have spent it better
instead of layin' around. Got to make it happen. Yeah, oh yeah,
baby. Today's the day.—

"Today's the day."

The cold scratched at his forehead and arms as he
leaned against the entrance door. He had pushed it open
around 8:45 p.m.

—Wish has a coat. Poor Paul. Hope he gets that letter.
Henry should see it soon. Better go now. Wait.—

Two Whysees came, arms swinging in unison. Michael
pretended to go back inside, but they did not even glance.

—Stupid asses think I am too dumb to run. Sure need
Dad, but hey, I got out last time, did I? Huh? *Loco* Michael
going out for second time. Hope second time is charm
though.—

He let go of the handle to sidle down the steps, and the
curving lane, keeping from the streetlights. Another group of
Whysees on the way back to their dorms passed, some stealing
looks at him, making him cringe. The wards lounging had
become background scenes on the sidewalks and fields since

there was nothing to fill the days now and nowhere to run. Michael headed to the Monkey House. Further along the road, a station wagon waited nearby. A profile of an obese man filled the side window. The last Whysee left so Michael crept to the car and tapped the window. He giggled when the man's eyes bulged in terror, then closed in relief. The car door opened, and two plump legs stepped onto the ground as the man heaved his bulk outside and crouched closer to him.

—Gotta lose weight. Looks like gotta yank his guts to take a leak.—

The man's lips moved. "Louis is my name."

He then waved his puffy fingers toward the back of his station wagon. He blundered past, and the back door squealed open.

—Quiet, they'll hear!—

Louis leaned over and pulled the carpet off from the interior of the trunk. Below was a flat, wide board. He moved it and it clunked on the fender. In the interior, Michael noticed a large sawed-in pit, the steel curve of the fuel tank, and the back axle of the car.

"You gos to be kinning me."

Louis nodded encouragingly and gestured toward the hold. Michael wedged himself into the pit and folded himself, his hands bracing on the cool steel of the tank and the bottom of his sneakers pushing against the other end. The board slid over, and if he peered, he might see the road beneath him. The car door clunked shut. He waited and then felt the car settle with Louis's weight. The car started and the road below turned into a bleary blur. His teeth clacked with the vibration of the car and the odor of the corn oil wafted in his face along with the heat. One hand lost hold, and the other scrabbled for balance, grabbing the edge again, feeling dizzy.

—What if I fall, my head hitting the road? I could break my neck or crush my head.—

Gravity pulled to his right and the whorls of the tar ran together below and straightened as the car slowed. The road stopped moving. He held his breath, for they might check at the booth at the front entrance. The road rolled again, and he waited moments before releasing his breath. His metal coffin lurched, making his head thunk against the curve.

—All gotta hold metal edges and soon be free. Will see Dad and be far away from this. I'm asking for pizza and grape juice later, but if have something else, don't care as long cut the rumblin' in my stomach. Will I have to go to school? Maybe won't have to. But how get work? Can work dirty jobs but with pay this time. So many things to talk to Dad. Had carried loads, pushed thousands of wheelbarrows, raked leaves, and got up early in the mornings. Even led a group for defense. People might admire that. Lot of people might need a guy who works long hours, uncomplaining. Will have to talk with Dad about that. Damn it, how long to Union Station? The road rollin' beneath and an occasional bump.—

The rolling came to a stop. As the engine idled, he waited. He held his breath, not moving. Above, something squealed, and the floorboard rattled. It shifted and slid away. Lights hit his eyes as he froze in despair at the gray shirts above him. A hand reached in and seized his shoulder. More hands joined the first. His head clunked against the rim as he was pulled out of the trunk. A dull throb in his skull, he tried resisting fierce holds from several hands. Michael struggled, mewing as his body lifted from his hiding space.

—Coward! You! You! You shit!—

Louis leaned his bulk against the hood of the car, not looking at him.

"Whas you do?"

Louis's blubbery head lowered. Michael looked and three older and hard weather–beaten faces of the Whysees surrounded him. Another man stood by the chain–linked fence, his hands in the pockets of his black coat. The man stared, the eyes empty. Then the unknown man nodded to another Whysee by him. The Whysee hustled over to the entrance and signaled. The iron gate opened. When it did, Michael saw traffic passing on a two–lane road. Cars slowed along the fence, some motorists rubbernecking. A police car arrived, a familiar figure hunched in the back of the car.

—Dad! No Dad!—

The gate drew shut behind the police car as it pulled up near the station wagon. It stopped and the police officer stepped out, fingers drumming on the rooftop. Three more Whysees hurried from the building near the gate. At first, they were disembodied gray clothes. The ends of the shirts became hands and faces, milky eyes and teeth over collars. One pulled Dad out of the police car. The other one joined the first in hauling Dad further from the fence. The unknown man nodded at the police officer, who gave a casual salute before getting into his car. When the gate slid open, the police car backed out and waited for a break in traffic before screeching forward to merge. Dad's mouth sagged, and his eyes blinked in disbelief.

Dad noticed Louis and lunged toward him, screaming. Louis's bulk crossed arms and rocked in the red glare. His father thrashed, but the Whysees kept their holds as if manacles, their bodies ringed with orange as they struggled in the dull glow of the taillights.

"Dad! No! Jus be still!"

Dad only struggled harder, and the unknown man nodded to Louis, who got into his station wagon, his voice pleading. The station wagon door closed and moved forward into the street. One Whysee signaled to have the gate closed for the last time. Hard hands grabbed Michael by the elbows and dragged him around the building. The hearing aid allowed him to hear Dad's heels scuffing. Their footsteps clomped as they rounded the building, and Michael was separated from his father. The two Whysees pressed Dad against the wall. Dad shuddered as the unknown man whispered. He reached into his coat pocket, took out a document, and showed it to Dad.

"Please," Michael called out.

One Whysee's head turned to Michael and muttered. The man glanced at Michael as if seeing through a thick plastic wall and turned back. He kept reading aloud the document as if in a ceremony, something formal and important. Michael could not grasp all these long–winded words. Dad twisted to Michael.

"Sorry," he lipped. He stepped hard, and they lost their hold on him. Dad tore toward the outside world, running with his hands handcuffed behind his back. He slipped to his knees on the sidewalk and stayed helpless. Dad did not even look at the unknown man as he unstrapped a short handle from his belt and aimed. A red dot of light glowed steadily on Dad's forehead. Dad's lips twitched and then his chest started hitching. It hummed in the man's hand.

—Goodbye Dad. I'm so sorry you got into here. Better close your eyes. You won't see this.—

He could feel the gravel beneath his sneakers, and his squeezed shut eyelids, the lashes mashed together. His hearing aid so well made that he could hear at close to lower–than–average decibel level, could puncture in his eardrums, the spittle sound of Dad's boiling eyeballs.

From the time his father went Sam's way, Michael fell into a stupor, lost to everything but for the respite of wandering thoughts and images. When he came back, Paul talked about how he had drooled and how hard it was to keep him fed. Jose imitated his catatonic trance, his head cocking quizzically. Gertie repeated how hard he had made it on everyone.

He fell into the memories of home. Everyone remained hushed about how his heart had stopped beating to be free of this life. Or for how long they could live.

—A dream. It's only a silly dream with scary pictures. You're safe. (Smells of bread, the purple trickle of grape juice, sticky scent of syrup, butter, and cinnamon. The curtains that block the morning light from the kitchen shadow Mom's face. Dad's seated form is smoke. Can't get your eyes on him right. Sore toes. Did you stub them? Your soles feel lumpy, as if rocky under them. Oft! Something hit your knees. A gentle voice calls, begging to tell what happened. Remains of bad dream, so forget it. Just forget it. It's realer here. You can swing your legs here. Later, play hockey with Peter. If Dad says *O.K.* Dad doesn't even sign, *stop that, the sound is making me nervous.* A twisting pain in the right foot. Shh, don't cry out. Don't want to bother Dad. Mom's plate. It's all empty. Dad's plate is empty. Mom and Dad sit there, no feeling, no luster in their eyes. The elbow spasms. Watch the glass, watch it, no! The glass clatters on one side, splashing grape juice onto the table. Purple juice spreads in pools. Mom doesn't move. Tell them you're sorry before they get mad!

Sorry, sorry!

Mom just smiles. No one signs, *'Michael! That was careless'* or *'Why are you sitting there? Clean up!'*

Mom and Dad are not moving.

It is better to clean up. Careful. Why? Don't know, just be careful. A push from the table, the chair scrapes. It is all quiet, just walking around the kitchen with strange sadness. You sleep at night. Did not let morning creep in, didn't need to face another day without rest and a dream. The white kitchen cabinet. Paper towels in there, and better get a chair all high up, no place for a seven–year–old boy. Wait. The cabinet right in front of you, not way high up. You are so big. Big in, oh no, filthy clothes and, yuck, your undershirt stinks. Might have to take a bath tonight. Even though nobody could get filthy while sleeping. What dream was that? About a horrible school filled with melancholic sights and sounds, sighs, and signs, weeping and flailing. Of pain. And the gray people. They kept acting perfect, but all they are, just gray. You hate those people and wish you could be strong like Dad. Dad's still like that fake person in the dress store window.

Cabinet. Open. And just the wooden back and the frame that holds the cabinet. Nothing else. Wait! The table. It is all empty! Something had cleared it all up. Maybe Mom had gotten up and cleaned the mess. But she is still in her seat, shadowed from the curtain hiding her face.

Mom's hands rise. *Do you want to take a walk outside?*

A presence. Something presses against your back. Stop pushing! Pushing you all the way down a long road. Legs buckling.

Take a walk outside?

A vague outline of Mom's teeth in the dull light. Through the window of the kitchen, a full moon hangs in the sky. Did time go by fast? Did you sleep too long, dream a long dream, almost living in the bad dream? Don't wanna go out.

"Mom? It's dark in here."

Your voice is deeper. Mom stares and seems she is bigger. Taller. A worn, sagging bed shimmers behind Mom and fades into the gloom. There's no bed in the kitchen! Then the kitchen becomes dark. Falling into bed after a hard day of playing hockey and then doing homework. What are you supposed to do? Can't remember.

The chair beneath Dad squeaks as he gets up. His figure is hard to read, all hazy and incomplete. Like a ghost.

Time for a walk, Dad signs.

The side of the kitchen blinks blue as if someone is taking a picture. A hand shakes your shoulder hard. The door has already swung shut. Maybe Mom and Dad in the den. Why don't they wait? A kitchen door push open and in the living room. Dad stands by the couch. Someone brushes by, Mom going over to stand with Dad. The living room bathes in warm light. Even from the window of the front door, darkness comes. Feels a little cold. A bitter foul taste and something pries into the teeth. There's a voice from the boy in the wheelchair, a blur of movements from him.

One swallow. Just one, the boy in the wheelchair signs. He wears glasses. Someone else, a boy with a flat face, pokes his hand in. Jeez, that thing in my mouth? God, rotten bread! It's all blue spotted. Tastes, oh, get it out! A swallow. Just shake your head. Just last of that bad dream, Michael. There. See Mom and Dad standing in the living room?

Ready for a walk in wood? Mom signs, her smile sad.

Dad has a pitying look, biting his upper lip as his eyebrows lift. His hand grasps the knob and turns.

Don't open! Don't open the door. Shut it. Yeah, forever, even if never go outside for the rest of your life. The. Rest. Of. Life.

Mom signs, her eyes wide, but her face still looks sad, a mixture of joy and sorrow.

Michael P–O–O–L–E. It time to go, my beautiful boy.

Her face grew bright, as if a candle held up before her.

We're finish, Dad signs. *You have only just begin.*

The door opens.

The bleak sky weighs heavy, the moon a pearl in the dying day. Who is taking your hand? The touch of Mom's hand is supposed to be warm, but you can't feel it. Mom and Dad are here with you on the front lawn.

Two choice, Mom signs, smile melting into somber lips. *What or what not.*

On the front lawn, Dad nods. On the driveway, Dad's red car, Chevrolet Sleeper, is parked behind Mom's station wagon.

Remember this, Michael?

Yeah, but make you miss everything more. Everything's all still, and no sense of motion. No windows from other homes glow, no car drives past, and no one passes.

Understand? Dad asks.

I don't… my chest feel heavy. I don't want. Sorry.

Is alright, Mom says, *what is another place far away, and the what not here.*

Where?

Don't cry, Michael.

Feel too old, tired at home, you miss Mom and Dad. Here's more than a house. It's home. Dad never looked so serious and why, he looks as if he is trying not to cry too. Dad's talking now.

You know where, Michael.

"Da, please."

Your voice's all whiny like a baby's. See nothing so final as Dad's nod.

What not, Mom signs. *Here is a place where you wait and rest forever and what is where you once was.*

Stay or go? Dad asks, his face pinched.

You wanna stay. Don't go from here. It's safe here. Stay.

Mom, I want to stay here. I have not be here for too long.

I know. None of us stay for a long time.

I will stay.

Dad exhales and his body sags. *You can, but no change here. We are not real. Only what not remain, just nothing in the past.*

Don't care.

What about P–A–U–L? Mom says. *What about the other?*

Mom's and Dad's images waver and blur in the evening. Right there, you feel the colder air, the solid concrete beneath you. There is the moon above and it has a face, and it swells bigger and bigger. The face is haggard, the gray eyes desperate. It has glasses with beads of tears sprinkled behind the lens. A terrified voice comes from far away, and everything becomes clear. There is the soft rotten breath of the moon, screaming.)—

"Breathe!"

The moon's face hovered in the sky.

"Breathe! You stupid—"

The weight of a body, dead legs, lay heavy on the limbs, and he felt Paul's elbow jamming in his ribs. The wheelchair above was empty. Paul clung to his shirt collar. His eyelids fluttered again. Up and it was Jose's sneakers landing on the sidewalk again, him signing as tears streamed on his face.

WAKE! WAKE! WAKE! WAKE!

His chest locked harder, and his throat swelled. Like popping a cork, he blew air from his mouth, startled whooping gasps and cries.

"Don't leave us, stupid! Don't you light out on us!" Paul scrabbled at Michael's collar. "Never leave me."

Paul blubbered, his face wrenched and helpless. Michael stared at the Whysee library where Paul must have come from the entrance. Above, worried wards' faces looked down at them. Paul heaved himself off and lay on the walkway sobbing, his arm over his eyes. His askew glasses dangled on a pink ear.

—Tears in eyes. Squeeze them shut, don't let them fall, and sleep again, trying to get back home.—

His eyes opened, and it was still cold and raw outside.

"Oh no, I am here." Michael's voice felt rough and kept cracking. "Oh Gos, I'm still here."

At seventeen—in prime of his life—stuck next to a mobile—disabled ward, and a deaf ward with a mind that could not keep pace with the outside world. He sat up and looked miserably to the roadway where few Whysees walked from their school building, books in hands, not sparing them a glance as if they did not exist already. His close family was gone now, and he was still here. The air seemed to be filled with clumps of salt. About them, snowflakes that would usher in late December fell, burying everything in sweet nothing.

Afterward, Michael spent most of his time in seclusion like an animal suffering a grave wound. He stifled his sobs into his worn pillow so Henry would not hear him. Jumbled memories of Sam, his father, and his mother filed through his mind until he could not tell for whom he was crying. Each day he slept, missing meals until Paul was forced to send Henry in to wake him so he could eat. He went more often, sullen at being poked and prodded by his well–meaning roommate.

The memory of Dad, like Sam, receded. Though the pain congealed under his feigned indifference, it remained. He did that because Paul kept quiet about the fact that he almost left him behind for the second time. Back in daily life, forgotten in memory, it was hard to live through the boredom broken by brief bouts of terror. Often, he wished for these brutal slow moments to pass quicker until his turn to go out with the Whysees and never come back. Deep inside he still clung to the good parts of his memory, with Sam's voice chiding him and shades of his father's image glimmering through naked trees muffled by burial of snow.

Several meals throughout, Paul would interpret what Gertie was saying since she was the only one in the mood to talk. Gertie had developed her own routine to replace the lack of structure in her life. She was seen each morning on a solemn walk with a small band of deaf and hearing teenagers born with various forms of intellectual disability to see each ward off to the spirit world. Their point of meeting was at the top corner of the slight hill that lolled toward Farrow Field, the best vantage to view each day's taking.

She said sometime she will grow so sad that she will cry, scream, roll on the grass, and shout goodbye to the soon to be take ward. If she had speak to that person at one time, naturally, she will be more upset…

Gertie prattled, her eyes starry and shining with her telling. He saw the image in his mind.

—('Goodbye!' Gertie yaps, waving her spidery hand in the air.

Others take up her cries, in warbling voices and signs. *Goodbye!* I'm sorry! 'so lonnnng! Gonna miss youuuuuul' *BYE!* 'Oh noooooooo! Please nooooooooo!' Bye–bye!

Soon as this day's unfortunate is being pulled up, the last image seen might be of few wards tumbling on the frosty hill by the bleachers under the faded sky, sprawling and groveling in their makeshift grief, limbs flailing. The sound of Jose's tinny wailing among the low sobs could carry over with the hearing aid, or not at all. When the hanged ward is beyond seeing and listening, they would get up and flee back to their dorms, faces flush and eyes gleaming. Every dawn they play the same wild, stupid, sorrowful game over and over until their turn.)

Soon, I hope. Dad would have slapped Gertie hard for being so stupid.—

Michael thrust his hand up and looked away, not wanting to hear anymore. Paul folded his hands, unsure, while Michael fixed his eyes on the window, still on the agonized losses and wonder of still going on with everyday life. Minutes later, the discomfort became too much, so he went outside for air.

Outside, he noticed stirring by the brownstone buildings on Hill Road. Deaf stragglers, who left the cafeteria before he did, headed the slushy road and passed Farrow Field, moving toward the front entrance of the Gate. They disappeared around the corner on their way to bigger and important buildings. Their signs were firm.

STOP THIS MUST.

KILL NO MORE.

TELL AUTHORITY STOP MUST.

CAN'T DO THAT WHY SEES MAKE US STAY.

DEAF IMPORTANT AGAIN.

PROTEST AGAIN.

He looked back toward the cafeteria. Lights flashed through the large windowpanes. It was not the steady blip of the blue siren on the ceiling. Lights skittered from the alarms on the walls inside, same as the wake–up morning lights. It seemed like the interior filled with lightning. The doors crashed open, and the crowd streamed out. Michael sidled away on the steps.

The first was that heavy set deaf from Halloween, his face joyful, shouting in a garbled voice, "Ho! Let's go! Ho! Let's go!" A gaggle of deaf waved and signed with occasional outbursts of excited grunts and hoots. They all moved, a flesh flood heading toward the brownstone buildings. The double doors continued to spew wards, spreading out onto the plaza in frenzied marches. In the tide he picked out several things: a deaf boy guiding a lanky blonde ward with bulging eyes and an awkward dazed grin for being part of something, Richie pushing a wheelchair careful not to spill the waxen body of a girl, and a sharp–chinned deaf signing.

AFTER PROTEST TAKE T–O YOUR ROOM?

Richie's response was a lewd wink and a noncommittal shrug. Pasty twin, the same girls from the day the Workboard had been turned off, hurried outside, grins of gray teeth, their small chubby arms linked. A thin girl with an angelic face toted a tattered cardboard sign written in red crayon.

StOp the HaNGS. NO!

He thought of offering to carry the sign for her, but a cherubic–faced boy slapped her on the buttocks and her mouth opened in silent laughter, her cherry tongue sticking out. Next was Nat, who parted from the tide, his face twisted by a deep frown as he strode toward the dorms. He stopped by them.

"Get to your room," Nat snapped.

"Back off. If I kick your ass before, I can do again."

Nat mimicked Michael's reply before stomping away. Kelly came out, next holding hands with Dimitri, her face awed by the way the entire crowd moved. Behind them, Paul was being pushed by a chubby deaf and a skeletal deaf, both often seen in Nat's crowd. Next was a deaf with a sloping forehead and a scar on his chin.

What are they doing to us? Please let me know, Paul signed to the deaf with the scar.

The deaf with the scar beamed and gave a sympathized shrug. *ME NO SPEAK S.E.E.*

Gertie followed them, waving and shouting, "Go! Go! Go!" with Nancy, who huddled behind Henry, his face fixed in determination.

—Thinks he's a hero protecting her.—

The stream of the crowd seemed unstoppable, so Michael followed Paul and the group of deaf, who urged him to go along with them. A smaller group broke from the main crowd to help wards in wheelchairs and metal braces down the ramp. He counted twenty, helping a dozen of the hearing disabled teenagers on the concrete ramp that circled toward Farrow Field. He came to the rescue.

O.K. I am suppose to help him down, he signed to one deaf.

He was grateful to see Richie's burly head further in the front did not turn. The deaf ward holding the handlebars did a familiar brush–off sign, with the tips of his fingers off his shoulders, and moved aside. The deaf with the scar nodded encouraging and even slapped him on the rear. Michael grimaced and grabbed onto Paul, who looked up at him in relief.

They D–I–D not ask if I want to go. They act now than when S–A–M die. Paul let out a bitter laugh.

Michael pushed his friend in silence since it hurt Paul's neck to sign up at him. He heard an occasional monotonous shout as various deaf let out an "Ugh!" "Huh!" or "Hoo!" Most of the time, just clomps of their shoes on the tar could be heard. Several conversed in signs.

MUST CALL SILENT PROTEST.

NO SILENT. WHY SILENCE BELONG DEAF? DEAF PROTEST ENOUGH.

NOT SILENT IF ME D–O THAT "det." The deaf, a red–haired boy with squinty features, let out a yell.

"Huh!"

Somewhere near the front, someone answered with a "Hoo!"

They reached the base of the ramp, and by then, most of the protesters had gone around the brownstone building. Michael shivered as they made for Landid House near the front of the Gate. Another deaf cried out, and he only pushed Paul on the slippery frozen road. Someone else hooted, and there was an answering cry in the interval between crystallized silences.

At the site of the protest, the edges of Paul's wheelchair bit on the snow–battered grass around Landid House. By then, wards squatted, lounged, or sat on the wintery landscape. Withered naked trees surrounded the courtyard, and a few deaf wards packed snowballs and tossed them toward the house, not daring to hit the clean windowpanes of the offices. Michael could imagine Dad working in one building.

—(His head stooped, graying hair, hands shuffling the broom, pasting on a placid smile if a Whysee turns to speak to him. Ears cocked for a deaf ward who got into trouble in September and put on report.)

Did he meet with that tub of shit who got him arrested and executed in the same job?—

Better go back, Paul signed, shivering.

Michael shook his head. *Bad idea, deaf will revenge us.*

Through the windows, several Whysees looked out. One hunched over a retro landline phone.

Better get close to the other, Paul signed, his lips pressed. *This sound bad from me, but you deaf are starting wrong trouble.*

"I know."

Michael sighed. He hugged himself and searched for Jose, Nancy, Henry, Lionel, and even Gertie.

—What about…

He's gone. Like Dad, remember?—

He spotted Henry snuggling with Nancy and saw Lionel by one tree. Jose stood near the front, signing animatedly with one deaf ward near the front.

"Foun' 'em," Michael said, pushing and working Paul's chair through the snow toward them.

EXCITE? Nancy signed. She pointed to Jose, who must have taught her. Henry said something. Nancy smiled at him and said something, and their lips brushed. It struck Michael how extremely adult they looked, being together.

—Wish I have my own.—

Paul rolled his eyes in disgust and faced Landid House where one ward stood in front of the crowd. The ward, waving his hands for attention, prepared to speak. The ward was the same one who had joined the others in making Paul go down the ramp. He grew more purposeful with attention, including Michael's own. His self–righteous sallow face swiveled on his grizzled neck, left to right, then right to left. He peered through smeared glasses and did the silent handswave. Most answered with their own handswave before he signed.

FIRST INFORM US WE HERE WHY? THEY WANT PROTECT US FROM GENERAL POPULATION. NEXT, THEY INFORM US GENERAL POPULATION NEEDS PROTECTION FROM US. NEXT, THEY ASSIGN WHYSEES FOR? PROTECT US FROM US. NOW THEY HANG US. FOR? T–O PROTECT WHYSEES FROM US? NEXT WHAT? NOW WATCH WORD PROTECT CHANGE T–O PROTEST!

He signed the last word, a fist thrust hard in the air. A burble of shouts greeted him as he stormed into the crowd, fist still in air, his mouth contorted into a jeer. Signs and shouts rebounded.

"Yeah!" *RIGHT.*

"Yuh!" *WHYSEES CAN'T DO THAT.*

"Huh!" *YES!*

"Hoo! Hooooooooo!" *ME KNOW.*

The ward who spoke plopped himself on the soggy ground, his arms crossed and his face stubborn. Michael turned to Paul, who was speaking to Nancy and Henry, his facial expression neutral, explaining what the speaker had said. Gertie and Lionel were set off, their thoughtful faces toward….

—Ugh!—

Kasy, who was doing the same as Paul. The next speaker was the girl with the cardboard sign, who got up front and signed: *MAYBE T–V CAMERA US! WHY? PROOF!*

The same boy, obviously her boyfriend, came up to her. The girl squealed, lifted herself aloft on the boy, and rode him piggyback, waving the sign over her blonde hair. Next was a hearing boy with a befuddled face, who thrust his fist up imitating the first speaker. Good–natured handswave responded. Michael grinned, amused at the ward being accepted by the deaf. Then he felt the rear of his neck prickled. Inside the windows of the Landid House, there was no one. Movements appeared from the rear of the Landid House. He noticed the scurries of the disabled hearings stealing away, the hearings in braces doing their best to haul those in wheelchairs, including the waxen girl.

"Paul?"

Paul looked up at Michael. *I think must leave.*

"Um… bis late for thas."

At that, a row of Whysees marched from behind the house, naked foreheads shining from the reflecting sunlight on snow. They lined from the outside corner of Landid House to the trees a hundred yard away. In their leather–gloved fists, they carried shiny spirals of barbed wire. On the opposite side, another row of Whysees lined the road that the wards had taken on the way to the protest.

"Michael? They're holding sharp wires." Paul's voice and signs both quavered.

"They're waeing. Why they waeing?"

Who know? I think they are waiting for a signal.

Before Michael answered, the line by Landid House moved, their steps intent. Naked faces, devoid of emotion, they marched, steadying the barbed wires, corralling the crowd and bulling the nearest wards. The sharp coils touched the first, that ward jerked away, his face a mixture of surprise and pain. He backed, torn places in his shirt showing puckered and bleeding cuts. More backed away and ran, yelping or grimacing when the wires brushed their bodies. The wires worked as a bulldozer, pushing mounds of moving bodies toward the road. Many had dazed grins on their faces. They all moved back toward the road that led to the dorms, wincing at the shouts along the road.

I am going now, Paul signed before he turned his wheelchair and worked himself over to the road. Michael stayed a few moments longer to make sure his friends and Gertie were unharmed, all moving toward the road. After checking, he gazed toward the remaining wards for the girl with the sign, who might need a bit of rescue. Amid the crawling bloodied wards who dared to stay, he saw the sign battered and smudged on the muddy snow. He moved farther away and when he was more than a dozen yards, he saw her by the outside corner of Landid House. Three Whysees surrounded her, and her head lowered in dismay as one checked the barcode on her wrist. The boyfriend was nowhere.

—Asshole should try to save her.—

Michael kept moving. One Whysee by the road stepped out of the rank of bellowing and arms sweeping Whysees. It was the blonde one still tormenting him. Michael did not even try to lip–read the shouts to know he was to keep moving until he cleared the Landid House and was already heading on the road to the dorms. Once he was far enough, he craned his head and saw that the Whysees had put coils of barbed wire on the ground. Another Whysee had taken off his leather gloves. It was the leader. The leader went to the three other Whysees and the girl who was due tomorrow morning. There was nothing more Michael could do.

Soon he was already walking alongside Paul, who kept wheeling himself with no one to help him back up the ramp.

"Whas matter? You still mas?"

Paul kept his eyes on his progress, working the wheelchair upward.

"Nee help?"

Paul shook his head, his face tight.

They reached the lobby and went inside. Bits of snow encrusted on the tires of the wheelchair sprinkled on the tile, melting into tiny puddles.

Michael, can I said something about your people?

Sure, but they are not my people before today and not tomorrow.

Right, do you see the way the deaf drag all the other with them?

"Yeah, every hearing goin', 'Whas you doin' to me? Whas you doin' to me!'" He laughed since the whole thing was funnier in hindsight.

Why today?

I don't know.

Why not yesterday? Why not last week, when all this start?

I don't know.

218

Remember when you and... Paul's face creaked and Michael thought of Sam.

It hurt to talk about it. S–O don't.

O.K. but think Michael. Who was the last deaf to get tag with the C–O–D–E?

—(Your hand in your mother's hand, feeling the gold ring on her finger. What people streamed out last that day? Most deaf, they know each other, and even Mom knows where to go. The few disabled or retards would be last. You are both in a comfortable mound of moving in the middle. Looping beyond hundreds of deaf children from institutions for the deaf, a blonde twelve–year–old girl waves two of deaf friends of hers ahead and signs, *ME G–O LAST. WHY? ME DEAF STAY HERE MOST SHORT TIME.*)—

P–A–U–L? People who come in last, get highest number?

Paul nodded. Michael continued.

And they are starting with highest and counting down. And because it was that last girl turn, it was exactly when many come out.

Paul's face remained bleak.

"Guess nos work ous goor, huh?"

It must have.

No. Whysee stronger than us.

No. We are not strong because we do not pull together. Wrong time.

When right time?

The very first day, the very first one, then we will have win. Not physically, but in M–O–R–A–L. Not now when it deaf girl turn. It will have been glory, one thousand and seven hundred ward coming on F–A–R–R–O–W Field D–O–Z–E–N of B–A–N–N–E–R–S one crowd, one hope, one word 'no!' No one worth dying, no one worth killing then, everyone will understand everyone count. No matter color, shape, intelligence, but this stupid, you stupid deaf, only until it happen to you or someone like you to realize you count too. Your ignorance brought politic into it and turn the whole thing sad and ugly. You just give them another reason to think O.K. to kill us.

Paul paused, then went on signing.

If we have go out that very first day, our action will live in the face of the Whysee who witness that day. Instead, our worth die along with each person who do nothing. They will justify themselve for it. That girl who sign A.S.L will inherit the deaf A–R–I–S–T–O–C–R–A–C– Y through her deaf Mom and Dad, but it will not matter. She will die alone tomorrow.

His lips pressed with weariness, and the futility of it all, he rolled himself away. Alone, Michael stood in the bafflement and shame that he had not risked his life to rescue her, and he should have done what Paul said they should have done. It should have mattered days earlier to that deaf blonde girl who had bestowed her grace upon Gertie. If only to borrow a crayon to scrawl a feeble line on the worn cardboard sign to stop the killing. Soon it would not matter to her.

—(In the earliest red morning, Gertie comes to a dangling form, strands of blonde hair covering a stooped head, sandals below in air and swaying beneath the bar. Her hands will never pick up a crayon or to sign to her boyfriend.

'Ohhh good byyyyeee! I'm sorreeeeee! Sooooo lonnnnnng!' Gertie howls, exhilarated at being intricately connected to her if only for the loan of a crayon.)—

Still tomorrow morning will come. Then soon this will not matter to him either.

Duck.... Duck.... GOOSE!

But it mattered to the Whysees. On Saturday, roll call was different. Michael felt it as he was prodded with the others to Farrow Field. Soggy shoes stamped in the slush, spreading the grassy and muddy patches of ground peeking between shifted snow, and they shivered, herded in by the Whysees, striding around, making all wards face one goal post. Past stained bodies and ratty hairs by the faraway bleachers, the leader stood with hundreds of other Whysees. Their faces, eyes hidden under the brims of their hats, were gaunt and raw with the aged look of experience. Hard, merciless faces had replaced the doleful gentle ones of the plebes in their first year. An adult, Whysee, the man who had executed Dad, stood with the leader.

The man nodded and took the concrete steps to the gate where a dozen Whysees waited. The short Whysee who had been left to guard Michael, Paul, and... that long time ago in September, snapped a salute and opened the gate. Then the man strode to the goal post, boots squishing on the grassier part of the ground. Twelve Whysees broke from the main line along Farrow Field and followed. Slush and snow crackled beneath boots as they halted and lined up by it, hands clasped behind backs. Their movements stayed synchronized, and it was like watching a short parade.

Michael looked from the tight line of disciplined youths to the leader with the remaining Whysees on the fourth row of the bleachers. The leader was a faded shade, a glimmer in the distance, and it reminded him of the first hanging he had seen days before his father was killed. The posture of the leader signified nothing for now, so Michael shifted to check the post. By then, the man stepped forward and barked a single word: I, Why, Die, Hide, Bye no one knew. Scattered signs broke out from the deaf.

WHAT SAY?
DIE HE SAY ALL DIE?
WHY WE HERE?
UP HIMSELF.

The man's face looked pained, and Michael idly watched the leader, who gave a brusque signal to the blonde Watcher near the main group. The blonde one nodded and hurried near the front of the crowd, searching for a person who knew sign language.

—What's about Paul?—

Michael spotted him and as their eyes met, Paul shrank back into his wheelchair, trying to hide behind Lionel and Gertie. Fortunately, the blonde Whysee overlooked him and selected one nearer the front of the crowd. Standing on his toes, Michael could see over one heavyset shoulder and over the scabs of another's balding head. It was the Girlman, Kasy, who was marched out of the crowd. The man's brow furrowed, and he squelched a shudder before speaking. Kasy signed in S.E.E. as the man thundered.

You are not happy with our decision. I have decide to make some improvement. Our duty is to help each every one of you go in peace. Before, our way was to start with the highest number and now some you may think we are terrible people.

—Serious? You think we wanna stay here longer? Nice hangin' with you guys. Bah—bye.—

S—O today I allow you to pick for yourselve. Today you decide who go today.

The man nodded to the Whysee at the ten—yard line behind him. That Whysee stepped forward and his face reddened as he bawled, "Last one remaining on the ten—yard line will be taken. Last one remaining on the ten—yard line will be taken."

222

Kasy's face turned ashen, and he murmured to the Whysees. The Whysees allowed him to shy away and go into the crowd. The tide of the crowd moved backward, and Michael checked his surroundings.

—Okay. Four rows of guys in front of me.—

Bodies pressed backward. Most Whysees lining the sidelines of the field started pressing from the sides, shouting at the crowd, squeezing all inward until one dollop of ward could be forced onto the ten–yard line. The front row buckled as wards tried to edge their ways back into the safe anonymity of the crowd. The Whysees from the end zone yelled orders, and Michael guessed they were the same as before. Several hands conversations erupted in spots of the crowd. Someone giggled. Struggling matches started as the nearest wards bulled their way into the crowd. Paul was safe near the rear. But Jose, near the front, jumped onto the tenth yard line and back into the pocket of the front row of gentle pushing wards, a daring grin on his face.

—Oh Jose, you moron.—

Michael moved toward the front, treating the crowd as a swallowing sea of hands, cloying fleshes, trembling torsos, panicked faces, and gritted teeth. He did not move directly to the front, but at an angle, for if he ever moved straight, he would be propelled onto the ten–yard line. He moved sideways, for a distracted ward would not push someone toward either side in numbed haste for safety, only backward. They would think of moving each other as a makeshift shield between themselves and the arms of the Whysees. He moved in a slow zigzag to get near Jose, who kept leaping back and forth. A plan, to not push back but do a slow dig after getting Jose, formed. He groped past a deaf shuffling with a large deaf, and his hand reached toward where Jose should be landing. Proud of his ingenuity, he imagined himself saving Jose.

—A sure hand reaching between the wards, two cunning blue eyes twinkling, then a snag on the back of astonished Jose by the shirt, and a slow weave back into the rear of the crowd.

THANK!
'No prob, man.'—
Jose made his next leap back into safety, one Whysee reaching out. Michael grabbed at the shirt on Jose's back and pulled hard. The weight stumbled both. He fell, pulling Jose after him, and scrambled to get himself standing. In panic and trapped under Jose's struggling body, he sensed the spread of emptiness. The comfort of the crowd gave away, and vertigo rolled the room—the field—in his vision, making him catch his breath as if he had caught himself from falling from a hideous height. Several wards down, a couple caught everyone's attention. On the ground, Jose clambered off him, his face twisted with irritation and fear. Michael got up and glanced left, turning his head toward the scene that grew rushed. He caught the sight of a gawky red–haired ward. It was Henry helping Nancy back into the depth of bodies. He almost succeeded when the wards parted for her. However, Henry could not wedge himself back into the same crowd.

Someone giggled. Heads turned, drawn to Henry's movements as he struggled to brush past the front row. Nancy turned and her eyes widened. She sprung to get back to Henry, trying to reach between the interlocked arms of the deaf, and her plump hands clasped Henry's bony ones. A tall, chunky girl reached in to pull the grasping hands apart, prying them apart, an angry wail from Nancy, and the tall girl shouting a deaf yell, "Hoo! Hooo!" to two persons of color wards signing about what to do about the red–haired boy, one signing, his face resigned.

ALL RIGHT. RETARD NOT KNOW ENOUGH. HE OUT.
Both went over to the tall girl, Gertie screeching, running to the front, and yanking at the ward who had taken over the execution. Kelly, near the side signed to Gertie, *LET GO HE TURN LEAVE,* shouting at Nancy, who clung to Henry's hands, "Wrahhh! Aggth!" in voice. It went faster. Lionel edged toward Henry his immense form held back by other deaf wards and by his own placid nature his voice

murmuring pleads to the deaf Jose's face fixing in horror four to seven deaf prying the couple from each other the Whysees moving now one with the rope in hand noose round Henry's neck Henry's face unaware and his mouth agape Nat's voice hummed a song Dimitri smiled charmingly her hands snarled in Nancy's hair Nancy's gullet quivering in pain her head pulled backward at a grotesque angle hands spasmodically open letting go a deaf helping two Whysees with rope all three brows lowered in concentration a yodel from Eggy showing the gaps between his few teeth in pleasure. Then quiet. Panic spread, blood from a pricked skin, and things stopped. Then teeming bodies welled backward, uneasy smiles on faces, and Henry at last, alone, the center point of the laboring Whysees. They finished. Henry frowned and waded into the crowd. The front row united, interlocked arms and pushed Henry back as far as the crowd could swell forward.

—Stop this, oh God, please send a bolt down here and kill us all. We all deserve this. Do it! Just do it oh God oh God oooooh so silent now, kill us Goddamn it, strike us all dead! Damn you if you don't!—

Nothing happened and Michael struggled toward his friends.

—Will feel nothing. Please let me feel nothing from this. (…) Can't stand this! Get me out of this! I'm over you Goddamn piece of false God! Shoot the lightning and wash everything away, eat us up and stop this!—

"Henry!" Nancy screamed. Gertie flung herself on the grass, weeping, though Michael imagined her feeling triumphant that she was part of this circle of friends for an audience of thousands.

The man nodded at the eight Whysees holding the end of the rope looped over the bar of the goalpost. They pulled. Henry stumbled backward, gurgling, his face the color of prune. The Whysees kept pulling. When Henry slid back, the rope slackened enough for him to get to his feet again. After another hard pull, Henry flopped to his knees as if an invisible alligator's tail slugged the back of his legs. He twisted, hands grasping at the crowd that shrank away. Nancy buried her face in her hands, and her massive shoulders shook with sobs. Dimitri, with a dreamy smile, shoved her. Nancy managed a shocked "ark!" sound before falling on her buttocks. She drew her thick legs up, crying harder. Jose, with a snarl, hurtled past and leapt on Dimitri's back, clawing at her face. Lionel gazed upward at Henry, who was still beneath the bar, and his eyes filled with tears. In despair, Michael looked at this all and tried to squelch the last of his helpless rage in the farthest reaches of his mind.

 —Please God, take me now. Please kill us all.—

Afterward, a small group followed Nancy as she walked back, sobbing, her head stooped, stupefied like a tormented bear. Kelly darted in, signed *BOYFRIEND GONE*, making a raspy "ump!" with her lips and tongue. Jose attacked Kelly, shoving her hard, and Richie clubbed Jose on the back of his neck. Even without Sam, Michael found the old lunatic streak that made him ram his elbow in Richie's ear, and before Richie could take a swing, Lionel put a stop to everything, putting his sturdy body between all.

Paul and Michael followed Nancy and Gertie to the girls' dorms. They passed Kelly, who stayed on the ground, still clutching her elbow. Michael found that even as if Nancy talked fast and gesticulated to Paul, her eyes dimmed. Her stomach seemed bigger. She left with Gertie in tow, who explained 'to watch for baby.' Lionel left for his room, and they parted ways, Michael and Paul heading to Paul's room.

 "Why?"

Still wheeling down the hall, Paul signed with one hand, while pushing and bracing the rim of the wheel with the other.

Some show.
Sick.
They sure show us.

They reached Paul's room, and Michael opened the door for him and followed him inside.

"Why dis they do this to Henry?"

Just to show us animal willing to sell someone else for our live.

"That's stupis. If they think they better than us, why worry abous whas we think of them? We're supposeh to be nothin' to them. Why drag this ous? Why make us hate ourselves more?"

They thought they had to show us why they start with highest number.

"Whas thas? Huh? Firs come las go?"

It make sense. If the system is highest go, then Whysee following procedure. No enemy, no friend, who is dumb, who nice, who nasty, only highest number must go. There is no need for rationalization, just meat to be process and sent away. Just we do not control nature, which deaf no thinking no rule. Just the genetic L–O–T–T–E–R–Y we lose again because of way we was born.

"Bus, why make us do this to Henry today? Why?"

Because of the protest. They want to show us what to be them. Do you want to do that tomorrow? Find another not worthy to live longer?

"No!"

That what they want. They show us we do not have to live with our choice. They don't either. High to low.

The redden sunlight spread orange rays through the window. Paul's shoulders lifted in a weary shrug. He continued to himself.

How it happen? A single movement of air can control the pattern of thunderstorm. The ripple effect on a P–O–N–D. Chao fall to order and order fall to chaos. C–I–V–I–L–I–Z–A–T–I–O–N rise and fall. Belief rise and fall. I can think of these, but I can't tell you why. I can't tell how a person can get it in his head to think unnecessary with useless. Some special head person ruin the president's birthday party at C–H–U–C–K–E–C–H–E–E–S–E kid restaurant, and he long time hold that against us ever since. And people with the same wavelength start a think tank at P–R–I–N–C–E–T–O–N that rewrite the national health policy on U–T–I–L–I–T–A–R–I–A–N–I–S–M. How G–E–N–E–S mess with F–A–T–E and insignificant human action that turn into a force that change the world. Our future is set in pond, not stone. That is how idea change the world. But why I can't.

Paul's eyes looked lost behind the lens. Michael leaned on the armrests of wheelchair.

"We're stuck here, huh?"

Paul nodded, blinking back tears.

When will it be my turn?

With his fingertips, Paul wiped at his eyes, then he signed, *What your C–O–D–E number?*

123.

171 is mine. I will be gone when you are up.

Most of us will be up then.

Our day are number past.

Paul giggled, and Michael laughed. Then he asked again. *When?*

Starting November 15, if they do one a day and not increase number, we will have about starting with one thousand and six hundred and ninety–nine left...

How many in year?

Three hundred sixty–five–day a year in one thousand and six hundred and ninety–nine. Four year and seven month at least until all room empty.

Four year a long way off.

Paul grinned. *Yes, I just can't wait until it my turn either! It will be sooner, I think.*

Why?

I had the chance to look at the Whysee face when they take H– E–N–R–Y.

We take him.

Fine. The cover of their hat, you know, the part where...? Paul grasped an imaginary brim on his head.

Michael nodded.

R–I–M–S cover their eyes, all I could see their mouth.

What about mouth?

Most frown or set hard. Few... they smile in relief.

How long it going be, P–A–U–L?

It will be soon. I do not think they want to wait longer.

228

—Four years of same. Would see Mom and Dad soon. So silly, me afraid to die now want them pick up the pace. C'mon hurry! What if hang poor Henry, then deaf runnin' goin' 'Take me, take me out!'

('Take me ous! Take me ous!' Sam echoes.)

Then Whysees go 'Sorry, mister deaf, we only take one a day. Why don't you come back tomorrow?'—

Michael's snort sprayed from his nose and he covered it, stifling it.

What are you laughing at?

Same joke. Can't wait until they get to us.

There was a wan grin on Paul's face.

P–A–U–L?

What?

I think… If my turn come up, I will run away.

Why do that?

Hell with them. Make the asshole work harder. I got nothing more to lose.

Nice attitude. Hope you make it.

Think will not.

Hope they must work hard when your number is up.

They laughed again, and everything seemed to stop being so terrible.

The Last Few Movements

Snow fell and freezing wind swept the roofs of the buildings in the Gate and onto the raw frozen dirt of Farrow Field. The fence north of Handytown had been moved four streets closer to the Gate. Paul remarked to Michael that he could not sleep in the last few nights because of the humming sounds faraway.

OUTSIDE NEAR FENCE SEE LAST NIGHT THIN RED LIGHTS IN WINDOWS IN DEAF ADULTS HOUSE AGAIN HOUSE. Jose signed at lunch.

Nancy, paler and with a bigger belly, smiled, though her eyes were bloodshot. Wet hair clung limp around her forehead. Her face looked a little strained.

—How many adults left outside?—

The spoon trembled in his hand as he slurped more watery soup. Lionel moaned, crossed his arms, and spoke to Paul, who nodded, his face serious.

"Whas he sae?"

He see something run from the children dorm last night from the window in his room.

Michael did not ask and later went to the receiving dock.

—Might make a good hidin' place when they come for me around August or sooner. Yeah, stupid to make all the hurts go longer, but got to go on. Don't know why but got to go on. Feel the endless heartbeats of my breaths important.—

Piles of bricks rose halfway to the ceiling, towers of hard, crumbly corners. Red dust streaked the columns of the dock, and the inside looked like the remains of a ruined king's dining hall. There was a slight movement in the gap in the middle of the red stained deck.

"Think I see somebyee," he said to himself.

He crept to the hollowed–out gap in the deck and peered at a flurry of skin that scampered into the darkness. He squatted by the gap and noticed a tiny network of spaces.

"Hello?"

Someone sobbed. He reached inside until his shoulder pressed against the hollow parts of the deck and he could feel the cracks and the wear of the woods along his cheek. His hand snagged a piece of cloth and he grabbed it. Knobby flesh retreated further into the dock.

"Who? Oh, no."

He touched the folds of a shirt and pulled.

"Come on, please, come ous."

Robby croaked and scrambled back clumsily on his elbows. A guttural, raspy howl came.

"Nuh!   Nuh!"

"Please, Robby."

He grasped Robby by the pants waist and pulled. Small teeth sunk into his wrist and he shouted and reared back, his head banging under the deck. He fell on his ass. On the floor, he pressed his wrist against his mouth.

"Chrike, Robby!"

His wrist throbbed, and slight crescent and reddened half-moons dented his wrist. He grunted, scrambled forward, groped, and ruthlessly grabbed hold of Robby's legs. He pulled him struggling out of the gap.

—Funny how Robby's face gets all scrunched up when mad.—

His stumps beat Michael's chest, thumpthumpthump. "Robby, cus is ous!"

Angry, tearful eyes looked to him. His emaciated arms wrapped around Michael's neck, nose and mouth burrowing into the hollow of his shoulders, and the boy sobbed harder.

"Hey, is all righ."

He appraised him. Robby stepped back, rubbing at his face with his forearm. Small and defenseless in a too large undershirt and muddy overalls, dust filmed his forehead, and he had a scratch on one cheek. His face was thinner, less round.

What happen?

Robby held out his arms helplessly. He tapped the crook of his elbow with his stump.

Where are the other?

Robby shrugged. He composed his face to look like a teacher, with a self–satisfied expression with a vague smile. With empty wrists clasped to his cheeks, he imitated her overly concerned way of helping the deaf speak. He swept his arm sideways, an urgent parody of an adult encouraging imaginary little ones below his waist to go somewhere upstairs. His posture changed to a stiff one and his face turned jovial while his scarred knobs mimicked something around his neck. The stump pressed to his head, his eyebrows raised, meaning, *YOU KNOW?*

Michael replied by shaking his head. Robby's face turned miserable. Then he pursed his lips acting thoughtful and pretended to look over phantom glasses. He also pretended to carry something.

A purse?

The little boy raised a scarred wrist to his eyes and peered over it.

—A what? Something that listens to heartbeats or that scope thing?—

Doctor? Michael asked.

His face lit up, and nodding frantically, he tapped the crook of his arm with his stump.

What do that mean? Michael tapped his own elbow.

Robby's mouth twisted in frustration. He darted in and poked Michael hard in the ribs.

"Ow!" Michael shouted.

Robby nodded happily.

Hurt?

He nodded again and pressed the stump against the inside of his elbow, his face mimicking a grimace of pain and surprise.

—(Needle probing into flesh.)—

"Shos?" Michael asked, making an injecting motion on his arm.

Robby grinned and went through the whole routine again. The teacher beaming and bidding the children to go upstairs. He acted out a jovial doctor who waited at the top and the injection. He looked fearfully upward, crouching behind an imaginary object.

What next?

Robby made a running motion.

It was easy for Michael to guess that Robby must have run from the playground. He asked the final question anyway.

Where children?

His stump rose and erased the air. Tears streamed on his wrenched face. He kept trying to wipe them off with his forearm, but more kept pouring out. His body trembled in the dusky space of the receiving dock, his form obscured by columns of concrete reaching to the ceiling. Michael reeled and when he looked up again, Robby sobbed, and he guessed what he was signing.

HELP… HELP…

Robby's eyes filled again, tears falling as he kept signing with his bald limbs. Michael glanced upward at the ceiling, where the ground floor of Davenport Dorm rested.

—Could turn around walk out of here. No one will know. No one will blame me. If they do, they did not have to make the choice I do! He might last a few days. They might find him fast and put him out. Mrs. Luggin. Had she cried for the darlings? Plenty, sure, but for her own drama. Too rich to be prevented from forcing deaf to be like hearing. For herself she might weep, but for children. More likely her pets. Might look for Robby. What is might not be kinder. All gone from pain but forever gone. (Mrs. Luggin's fat, sadly pleased face at her brave struggle to teach the wrong kind.) Can't cry and rage against all of heaven and all unfair earth.—

His teeth hurt from his jaw grinding. He could not stop his hands from shaking. Frost skimmed his body, the color matching the surface of bricks near the entrance. Pink to rosy. Robby stopped and took a step backward, frightened.

They come for you.

Robby crossed his arms and shivered. Michael, on his knees, appraised him: a boy spent outside in merciless cold, lacked being cared for, who lived without hands, just scarred slits with little rolls of skins for wrists and the stink of unwashed feet.

—Yeah, okay, Robby. Can be done. A little missin' bread and melted snow for water. In fact, the Whysees did me a favor by givin' all time for nothing.—

Robby…. Here is the best place. I guess. I am going to be here for you.

Robby stood there, eyes wide and disbelieving in the gloom. With streaks of tears tracing his dusty face, he turned to go into the hole in the deck. Michael was about to get up from kneeling, his knees cricking from the concrete, when a small force struck his chest. Short, filthy arms wrapped around his neck, and Robby's tearful face snuffled against his shirt. He felt the arms tighten.

—Come on, gonna choke me. Robby lives, I guess. I will make sure of that.

Why Michael, how noble for a change!—

Michael put his arms around Robby's back and held him. Before he left him, he marveled at how Robby had to stand on the toes of his sneakers to let his stubby arms reach around his neck.

—Hope think little. Oh no, two of them turning around at me.—

With his own blanket wrapped around him a shawl, he walked along Farrow Field to the dock again, trying not to look at the two Whysees.

"Brr."

They continued to ignore him, sure figures growing smaller with distance. Before he made a turn toward the tunnel, he made sure that no one tracked him. He scurried along the slope to the square tunnel. Stooped and feeling ridiculous, he looked both ways before entering the receiving dock. Inside, he stuffed the blanket in the makeshift shelter. He pulled out a piece of bread from dinner and knelt. He pressed on, his head near the opening.

"Robby."

He reached and his hand brushed the overall. A small sallow face looked out. He put the bread toward the face. Michael put the pieces in Robby's mouth.

Hurry, don't know if Whysee come.

Robby nodded and munched faster. His teeth snipped at his hands.

—Kinda like feeding ducks.—

Tomorrow Christmas.

Robby's face turned suspicious.

Santa bring you something.

Robby shook his head good–natured, pulled the blanket over himself, and huddled on the floor. Michael crept away.

—Have to be hard on him. All is colder.—

Outside the tunnel, Michael patted some melted snow and looked about the interior.

—(No Christmas in *barrio* and Gate. All year, on roads, sidewalks, wards pass, each other's faces tired.)—

The remaining Whysees glared from their posts, the gaze prickling at his back, must be mad because of spending the holiday here.

—Need ten minutes tomorrow. Ten minutes to get the stick wrapped in ribbon.—

Nancy's face was distrustful outside of the plaza when he asked her later.

"Be careful with it. I'm asking you nicely not to rip it off or steal it!"

"Yeah, yeah, Nancy."

"Be careful, Michael."

She smiled when she said that, and he could guess why Henry liked her. Her trust and generosity made her more grown. Even pretty.

After Nancy went to her room to fetch the ribbon and bring it back to him, he went to his room to get his hockey stick. He smiled, thinking of how Robby would react if he gave him the gift.... again. On his knees, he reached for it and felt nothing. His grin faded. His head bent to reach farther, his palm brushed against the mattress from the bottom.

"No, no, no."

He stood thinking.

—It's him. Asshole.—

He ran out into the hallway and to the third floor, where Nat lived. He pounded on the door. Someone inside mumbled a reply.

"Nas, you ges ous of here!"

His head pounded and blood rose in his head.

"Nas, I am nos kidding!"

The door opened. Nat's harried face peered from the crack.

"What do you want?"

"The stick. Thas stick you stole."

Nat's eyes widened, and he protested something, the dialogue that Michael missed.

"Don's play dumb."

"Look, if I took something from you, I wouldn't hide it, dickwad."

"Who took? You see him?"

"I don't see him. Now get out."

"Fine, bus I better nos catch you with the stick."

"You won't because I don't have it. Now, go away."

Nat pushed him and slammed the door. Michael searched, desperate. He ran to the third–floor level and leaned against the railing. He shuddered and glanced at the lounge across from him on the second floor. Richie Trunk walked in from the second–floor hallway. Thick face flushing to grief, his eyes glistened wet. The blockhead grunted and looked heavenward, sighing. In one of his clenched hands, a hockey stick skittered on the tile.

—Terri is missing. What's her number?—

His impulse was to run screaming at Richie. The blockhead was too big to fight, so he stayed out of sight. The blockhead lumbered to the first floor. After Richie turned the corner, he crept downstairs after him. He moved behind the stair railing and leaned against the door that led to the hallway on the first floor. Through the window, he saw Richie going into the bathroom, it disappearing behind a closing door. He pulled open the second door and went in the hallway, hand brushing the wall. His shaking hand turned the knob, and the door squeaked as he peeked inside the bathroom. As he sidled into it, he kept himself out of sight of the urinals in case Richie was using one of them. He could hear Richie's snuffles in the stall.

—God, cryin' and takin' a shit. Jeez, guess he could do two things at once.—

It lay on the tile under the stall. He inched his way near and pressed against the wall of the shower room, hoping they would not see his sneakers. Tensed for sight of motion, he knelt, watching the heavy boots on the tiles. He leaned close, heard a moan.

—Terri gone? Can't feel bad about that. Better people had been gone before. Ought to let him have it. Yeah, way he showed you nice last time. Yeah, right.—

A hand pressed on the tiles, he reached behind the wall to the stick with the other. He snatched it and pulled. A sob cut off in a half–strangled voice, and the heavy boots scrambled, but Michael was up and running out of the hallway. He hurried back to his room and stayed there all day, clenching it in his sweaty palms. At night, he slept with his arm curled around it.

In the morning on Christmas Day, Robby watched the slate of the brick, his eyes careful and steady, and lugged the handle between his wrists as the blade scraped the concrete, his back swayed and his arms crossed.

Keep your eyes on it, Michael signed, his chest hunched over Robby's shoulders. Robby looked up and nodded earnestly, his face out of proportion from the nearness. The boy swiped at it with the hockey stick, and the slate skidded a few paces.

Good. Get it in the goal post.

The goal was two broken bricks set into place. Robby gestured at the bricks with his arm, eyebrows raised.

Yes.

Robby worked the slate over, hitting it a few times, wincing at every movement.

Hurt?

Robby replied with a headshake, and his eyes shone. He lipped "fun," and the stick pecked the slate into between the bricks. Michael could not help himself. He thrust his arms upward to the vast ceiling.

"Goal!"

Robby raised his arms, pretending to wave at a cheering crowd. He stopped, and his face became aghast. His arm swept in an aw–shucks gesture. He clasped his forehead with his stump.

Not matter, we are friend. I got to go back.

Robby lowered his head in dismay.

I get to go. Late now.

Robby nodded, his throat bobbing a little. His stump thrust toward Michael and back at himself. Michael nodded.

I will.

Robby made as if to go into the empty part of the deck. He paused and ran to Michael's waist and threw his arms around him. He ruffled the boy's hair and felt a lump in his throat.

Is everything alright?

Robby nodded and crawled onto the deck. The last thing Michael saw before going back to return the ribbon to Nancy was the gift rattling as it pulled into the hollow of the deck.

Early Light

He sleeps. Bitter images, melancholic thoughts, scattered voices, and all harsh sensations break through the brim of his subconscious. They floated upward to the surface like goldfishes in a deep pond, a slight ripple, and then gentle movements of swollen forms below before the next vague eclipse, when the liquid becomes placid again. Earlier today, for instance.

That day, Gertie had gone on about the three strange boxes set and fixed upon the concrete surface of the ancient tennis court by Farrow Field. Nobody could tell what the boxes were supposed to contain, especially from the way she described things or drew a picture. Paul, next to her, explained what Gertie said. Kasy was not present that day. Michael could not help feeling relief from his absence.

—Girlman gettin' me all shamed. Glad he's not here though.—

She talked about them, the boxes drilled right into the concrete, and this tennis court surrounded by a twisted square fence of green crisscrossed wires streaked by rust. It could not contain a ward because both Jose and Gertie had seen a deaf Black boy from the other dorm who had to go with the Whysees to Farrow Field this morning.

A place for body, Paul guessed.

Gertie shook her head and started babbling.

She said she see Whysee carrying a deaf boy in a bag to Monkey House after.

Jose pretended to be her, mock babbling behind her back, which caused Michael to stifle his laughter. Gertie still babbled, making it hard for Paul to keep up with them.

I risk my life to go there, and I go to the green box for tennis and look right in. I can have die then…

—Yet…. She is still here.—

I had my head a bare inch from the fence. I look real hard…

Jose clasped his hand to his chin, contorting his face into an astonished look. His eyes bugged out and Paul broke into snickers.

I think hard. I think 'Hey G–E–R–T–I–E, why do they have a box there? Do they need to keep the thing we goodbye left behind? Do they sit on it when they get tire of pulling the one they taking to the field?'

"Oh sure," Michael said. "Take a cigaresse. Oh boy, whas a long har day we have pussing one ous to dry." He puffed on an imaginary cigarette.

Jose pretended to put clothes on the clothesline, putting clothespins on each shirt. *SUMMER HERE NOW!*

"Hey, they take breaks now!" Nancy said.

—What would Sam say to that?

(Sam cocks his head up and whistles at the sheer wonder of looking up some girl's dress from below her.

'*Calmáte ese.* She's still good for five minutes more without oxygen. Think can do five minutes blow jobs without stopping for breath…. Hey, no, no, wait!'

Sam, mock frantic, pantomimes untying the rope around the ward's neck.)—

"Michael!" Gertie shrieked. "Stop laughing! This is a hard time for everyone today!"

"Anytime with you a har' time."

He also signed that for Jose's benefit. Jose collapsed back on the chair, laughing, and signing, *YES! YES! YES!*

"Any time with you a hard time," Gertie said. "Tell him, Paul, huh? Tell him that."

"I am, I am," Paul said and signed the same thing. Then he signed the next thing Gertie said.

Why you never go there? Answer me!

241

Nancy made wings with her arms and cackled. Lionel said something fearful, his hands over his eyes.

"Afrae?" Michael hooted. "We know whas there." He gestured toward the windows that faced the faraway Farrow Field. "Rope cheap! No poin. Nos worth too mush trouble."

Paul made a *loco* gesture and pointed to Gertie, which made Jose laugh again.

"Not funny!" she screeched.

"Nos funny!"

—('Nos funny!' Sam squawks.)—

Nancy rubbed her belly and smiled. She kept her eyes on Gertie.

Stop laughing, Paul signed as Gertie continued. *I was brave that day. I go all the way over there past F–A–R–R–O–W, go up to the cross wire green fence, and I look right through and D–I–D not even cry or nothing.*

Nancy asked Gertie something, her face impressed.

Michael remembered Nancy's defeated walk the other day. Now her eyes shone when she pressed her hands to her engorging belly. Paul still signed Gertie's story.

'Not a tear,' I tell myself. 'I do artwork and real art hurts. They hurt because artists don't pay attention to anything but their work.'

"Pay assenion to this."

Michael flicked his finger against Gertie's forehead.

"Owwwwieee!" she yowled. She flailed, her glasses dangling on one ear. "Knock it off, you dummy!"

"Stop is. I disn's his you thas har. You knock is off."

"Michael, stop it!" Paul shouted, holding his hand up to him.

Michael's own hand was up too. Gertie flinched and her mouth sagged with her naked eyes staring at it as if she were a mole.

—Forgot myself.—

"Please, no," Lionel whispered, hugging himself. "No Whysee, no Whysee, no Whysee."

"I'm sorry. I gos tire an' angry."

Still wrong, Paul signed, his mouth tight.

She shivered. Jose gently placed the glasses back on her face. Her eyes goggled through thick lenses.

Her voice was a reedy whisper as Paul signed. "You're sorry, Michael? You want to show me how sorry you are?"

"I'm sorry, jus–"

"Yes or no!" Her holler was strong enough for him to read her lips.

YOU NEVER WHYSEE AGAIN, Jose sorrowfully signed.

Michael thought and signed. Paul told Gertie what he said.

"Yes."

She muttered.

"Whas she sae, Paul?"

Go to tennis court on green fence. See for yourself.

"Thas is?"

No. Bring my work, this paper. Put it in the box. Right. In. The. Box. Then you will see.

With pale hands like woodcuts, she fished out a flimsy paper, streaked entirely in black, from underneath her shirt. There was hidden in the picture.

—(A vague craggy form with three holes.)—

She held it out to him, and he took it.

This picture is call 'Four Eye Inside Box.' Paul signed as Gertie continued.

"Whose box, yours?" Michael asked, examining the paper. "I know, I know, nos funny," he added after he heard Gertie's squawks.

After lunch, they split on the plaza Gertie going with Nancy to 'watch the baby in stomach' and Michael, Paul, Lionel, and Jose to the circular ramp that wound down to Hill Circle and to the road that ran along Farrow Field.

"Goos thing nos a map," Michael remarked, looking at the drawing.

"Can I see?" Lionel asked.

—(Just molds of black craggy edges, two smears of dents and a shade of hollow dip and blocking everything, careful streaks of scribbling.)—

"Sure, bus I gos to ges is over to box to make up to Gertie."

As Michael handed over the paper, he glanced downward at Lionel's feet. Thick socks with worn and torn areas wrapped in stained duct tapes encased them. Then he raised his eyes to focus on the huge hands holding the paper. Hands strong as iron, veins as alloy melting with steel before they forged with age. Hands snarled branches of a tree shivering in the breeze.

"Lionel?" Paul asked.

"Oh, Luh–Lu–Luh Lord."

His broad face jiggled, two wide bulbs of white with retinas shimmering. Lips peeling back to show yellow teeth, his hand thrust the paper back to Michael, who took it without thinking.

"Oh, Lord, help! Save me! Help me!"

His frame shouldered past, and he stumbled running to their dorm. They (except for Jose) could hear him bellowing.

"No! Not gonna! Oh, no! Please, oh, please no!"

His sobs faded.

"Sesuh Crip, whas the fuck was thas?"

Shaken, Michael turned to the remaining two. Paul's grin had weakened.

BIG BLACK MAN SCARE. Jose signed, his face showing the same.

Sure move fast for a big guy, Paul signed. *Make me think of that picture of people laughing and then word below 'Why are those people laughing?' then it will tell us what page for the endnote to turn to for the answer. But there is no page to turn to. 7*

Michael looked up toward the steps leading to the bridge by the Bline Memorial Building. Up there, the figure of the leader kept watch, his hands clasped behind his back.

—Oooo look at you. You are so strong! Oooooo!—

They took care to work Paul on the ramp, the wheels crushing the cracked ice. Paul's wheelchair skidded, almost pulling everyone down with him, but Michael steadied it. Jose took a moment to pretend to steer. Michael laughed to break the silence. The crackle of the paper in his hand occupied his attention.

—(Gertie does more than look through the fence boxing the tennis court. Her face scrunches when she wriggles past the narrow–opened gate. At one box, her raw redden hand pulls the handle. The dark space behind the door shows God knows what. Her eyes bug out in fear. Her back retreats as she runs.)

What's in the box? In the paper? Did she see? Why not look at the paper again? Something popping out with those pictures that you gotta stare at for five minutes or like from the eBook, not that one but the other one… *Look and Learn.* It is just a wild patch of meadow, whorls of droopy stems and leaves. Inside of laying roses, a bird peeks out, and longer you stare…

(The bird is a king eagle of all. He surveys his foot planted on the engraved red stone in a royal crimson robe. Across from the regal back, an earnest advisor mouse listens attentively to a melting toadstool lady. A shadowy faceless man seen from behind on the carpet, above them and from leafy blades of grass, stare hundreds of faces contorted into expressions of joy to agony. Tiny bodies huddle en masse. A leaf pirouettes, all fueled by the artist's paint strokes and imagination.)

—Remember when Mom pointed-No.—

Michael, what are you thinking?

"Thinking," Michael echoed.

He stared at the expanse of Farrow Field, at the withered green fence, past the football goal post and beyond it. In the slush he noticed six sets of footprints. Four sets seemed orderly, as if made in a march, revealing muddy dead ground beneath the slushed snow. An erratic set extended from the side of the green fence all the way across the field. They reached to the hill toward the dorms. In the next few sets, the farther they were from the fence, the farther apart they were, marking a person's sprint.

—(Gertie's face stretches in terror.)—

Michael examined the picture again but could only make out scribbles and three holes upon a rough surface. It looked as if Gertie had smushed her face on it and then scribbled it all in black.

"Better ges going."

They started on the icy concrete steps between the bleachers. They took turns almost falling, some causing heart wrenching tremors through their bodies. The way things are, the Whysees will not be so inclined to transport an injured ward to the Health Center. Near bottom, Paul's wheelchair skidded, making everyone except Jose, whose face turned distressed, cry out, "Whoa!"

Michael hooked a foot on the dry underside of a bleacher, preventing all from taking a tumble down the sheen of slickered steps. At last, he worked Paul on the last step and unlatch the gate. He swung it open, and they pushed their way to Farrow Field. Jose found a well–used path flattened by boot prints that extended from the gate all the way over to the warped green fence so Paul could move on his own. They slugged through the snow until they reached the green fence. With damp ankles of their pants and bodies tingling from the crisp air, they peered through the rusted chain–links at the three metal boxes resting in the middle of the concrete, covered in slush like three torpedoes.

Better get a move on, Paul signed, shivering.

Jose nodded and struggled with the latch before he could open and let them onto the court. Michael joined Jose in pulling the gate open, snow piling on the bottom. Finally, the gate scrapped open a sagging mouth, ready to swallow them whole. They stood contemplating one of the three boxes. Paul wheeled closer and bent to pull the door open. First, he flexed his hand, prolonging the agony. His fingertips pressed against the handle and curled.

"Go on," Michael hissed. "Open the thing, please."

Paul looked at him, eyebrows raised. His hand pulled the handle, and the door lifted. Slush slid and collapsed to the snow below. Through his glasses, his eyes bulged.

"Oh, Michael! Oh no, Michael!"

Heart seizing, Michael looked over Paul's shoulder. Nothing remained in the eggshell interior but a dirty slipper in the corner.

"A slipper! Oh, no, a slipper!" Paul moaned, giggling, his runny nose glazed from the cold. He rocked in his seat.

"Ha–huh! Like you're on a funny show!"

Jose had his hands over his eyes. He lowered them, revealing a baleful glare at Paul, and gave a slow headshake in disgust. Paul kept laughing and hugging his knees. Michael threw up his hands before slugging his way back through the snow.

"Hope you can go back by yourself!"

Ooo…. Leaving me all alone with…

Paul's signs trailed off to nothing. Michael realized he still has Gertie's paper crimped tightly in his hand.

I am going to put it in this one. Let us not open the second or the third.

The white of the snow slashed at his vision. He shaded his eyes and looked at Paul. Paul's lips twisted thoughtfully. His eyes stayed clear under the blue sky through his lens. Two more unopened doors, two more unknowns waited.

"Let's nos open another one, huh, Paul?"

ONLY REFRIGERATOR NOT BURY BOX, Jose signed.

Paul's elbows wobbled on his armrests. Jose drifted toward the second, and with a foolhardy grin, pulled at the handle to open. It opened. Jose's eyes comically bugged out, his mouth stretching open in terror. Paul screamed hard enough for all. Michael's head, without a will, dipped, and he stared over Paul's shoulder. Curly hair, lolling breasts, one slipper on a foot, another showing chunky bare toes, blood caked on the toenails. Its eyes strained wide, and lips peeled back to show teeth in agonized panic.

"Michael! They're here, they're here!"

He sensed movements from behind and turned. The leader stood, thick hand gripping the elbow of another Black deaf. Two more Whysees filed in from behind and entered. Between them, another ward's buggy eyes stared from her glasses. Her liveried lips spoke, and he remembered.

"It's my turn now, Michael."

He thrust the drawing at her.

"Dis my pars. I gos to go now, bye."

He let it fall from his hand. It fluttered in front of her. The leader's brow lowered in puzzlement. Paul panted, grabbed hold of his wheels, and did an Indy 500 spin, but the little wheel caught in the snowdrift by the path and locked. He teetered on two wheels, hands skittering the edges, and lost control, his body flopping in the small snowbank. Legs in a heap, he looked up to them. Slush covered his glasses.

"Oh, Michael, I can't see!"

Michael circled them all, sneakers crunching in the snow. He set his teeth and struggled toward the gate. The younger Whysees parted, and even the leader stepped aside. Before he could forge his way out, he looked over his shoulder at Jose, who edged along the inside of the fence.

"Bye–bye Michael," she said. "I won't come back."

She waved and turned to salute the leader.

He brushed against one of the Whysees, hurried through the gate, and out. Paul stayed crouched in the snow, glasses dangling over one ear and his haggard face old. Michael backed away, his eyes on the leader, as if he were an animal given to chase. The leader turned his back and guided her to one box while the other Whysees led the deaf to another. The last image inside the court was the small wheel rotating, then stopping its spin.

He concentrated on gaining as much distance as could between him and the sagging green fence. Something moved. Jose walked behind, stiff jointed and his face like a robot.

Ahead, the snow–crusted horizon rocked in Michael's vision, Jose racing past, his face devoid of expression. Both burst into a slippery, sliding run up the steps between bleachers, around the long circular ramp, taking the longer way to their dorm. Both in panic had forgotten that Paul was not with them to require the use of it. They struggled upward, Michael holding on to the rail and Jose's sneakers skittering on the icy concrete.

The dorm lurched into view, and Michael reached the door moments after Jose, even catching the door before it shut. Jose stumbled on the staircase and sat hard on one step, his body shaking with sobs. Michael collapsed, staring at the tiles that Sam had fallen upon, the speckles in them blurred from tears. A hard wail came from Jose, and he fled, his arm over his face. The door shut, leaving him alone.

—You left him. What happened to the cool, whoa fucked up *loco* deaf, ready to fight, fucked up in the head, no fear? What happened to him? (Paul, supported by Whysees' arms, is lowered in the empty box, glasses off his defenseless face.) Will they put the glasses in with him? (The door closes upon his frightened face. Then he is alone in the pitch emptiness, nothing to hold him, to care for him. The emptiness sucks out his life, bit by bit, invisible coils of constriction, squeezing his neck, stealing the whistling air from him.)

And you left him there all for Whyseess to take, you stupid piece of shit. And you're alone now. Was it worth it? Huh? Answer me, you dummy dum dum dum.

I don't… happened too fast to think. Wasn't thinking then.

Fine, go back. Get him out of there. Go!

Too late, may be gone.—

Michael gripped his head and stared at the floor.

—Get him out of there. Time drainin', go!

By time I get there, too late. How long before air leaves brain?

Five minutes.

You got here fast. You can go back fast.

The Whysees, they might put me in there too.

They should, you chicken dummy dum dum. You left him. Just like you did in the hallways. Now you're all alone. Happy now?

Get off, you don't know nothin.' I lost my Mom, then Sam, then Dad, and then I lost him!

You did not lose him. You gave him up, served him right on the big plate for the Whysees to eat up. They're gonna come for you next and eat us up, eat us up, eatusupeatus! Grind youdownchopyoursoultopieceseatuseatuseatuseatusueateeetyo upunuuhhhupppppt. (eet us up!)

Stop it!

(A sure hand approaches the handles on the refrigerator and pulls.

Paul has his hands clasped on his chest. His eyelids flutter.

'Michael?'

'It's okay, buddy. I'm here.'

Thank God I was getting scare. I think you left me.

'Never, buddy. That's a promise.'

Paul reaches up like a toddler and loops his arms around the neck.

'Ready, Paul?'

A nod.

'Ump, heave!'

A pull and Paul is halfway out of the box, his ice–crusted legs slumping.

'Go Michael! One more push!'

'Unnngh!'

Paul is out and slumps on the refrigerator, his eyes full of affection.

Michael.... He will have said you D–I–D good.

'Shh, I got to get you out of here before the Whysees come. Cool it, buddy, or stay chilly, my man.'

Paul looks around from the center of the icy wasteland, and a laugh escapes him. Then years later, a hard–of–hearing blonde–haired girl with round breasts, tan skin, and blue eyes widened, impressed at the story told.

'Then me and Paul, we took one look at each other, and he go at the same time as me, 'Hey, cool it, man.' And I said 'Hey, lay chilly, man.'

And I got him out of there. Later he came up with a great secret plan and then we–)——

"An' then here we are... um... we um..." he whispered.

Footfalls and hesitating steps, and he raised his eyes from the depth of his arms.

TAKE HIM OUT? Jose signed, his eyes red.

He shook his head.

WHY?

Late, too much waste time.

FRIEND LEFT. His lips glutted in contempt, making a soundless "ungh!"

You with me whole time. You bad like me. No excuse if you said you retard.

Jose's eyes lowered, and he nodded. Michael nodded and tried to find a way back inside his mind.

ME DON'T WANT DIE, Jose added. Michael noticed *DON'T WANT* as an image of something thrown away.

Me same.

MICHAEL?

What?

ME YOU GO.... NEXT DIG BURY.

Where?

WE LOOK FIND PLACE. WE DIG.

There was nothing more to say. They waited. Even Nat did not interfere. He had stopped in the lobby to say things of his mean–spirited nature, but Michael felt a stillness that caused a strange lack of fear. It was not from courage but the realization that although he could not think of a description for it, that he had little to live for, including Robby. He wished it were not true, but his developing self–awareness remembered that not one of his panicked thoughts when he ran had cried out his name, nor flashing images had his face. All he had seen was the rocking of skim snow and the dwindling view of Paul's betrayed form, lying there for the Whysees. That feeling must have shown, for Nat lowered his eyes and moved on. 8

Sunlight outside dimmed. The vague pink lights prevailed by the blue–gray darkness of twilight came when Michael and Jose crept out of their dorm, not stealthily, but like scared rabbits, jumping at every movement. Several times, he felt Jose's hand clutching at his elbow. They came to the far end of Farrow Field to face the warped fence.

WANT IN? Jose asked in the blue of nightfall.

Michael nodded, and his legs slogged through until he reached the latch. He pulled it up, hand stiffening from the touch of dry, cold metal. Because of the snow, he could only pull it half a foot open. He squeezed in, the chill of the metal numbing his buttocks and crotch. Light snow powdered the path, and he saw traces of curved skid marks where Paul had fallen. On the first frosted box, his hand slipped once before he opened it. The inside suckled at the air, and there was nothing but the eggshell color of the interior.

—Too bad Paul is not there, though I would have to deal with that for the rest of my life.

Oh, Michael, you are such a chicken.

Stay off, whoever is bringing that up in my head.—

He moved to the second box and pressed his fingertips against another dry and sticky cold handle.

—Let there be nothing there please. Please Jesus. Please God, huh?—

He lifted and looked. A soiled yellow sock in the corner that smelled of urine.

—(In the cafeteria, the pants leg on Gertie rides up. On her bony ankle, the edge of her yellow sock peeks out.)—

He let the door fall with a thump and stepped into the last box. Teeth chattering, he pulled.

—Are Paul's glasses in there? Are they?—

It turned out to be nothing at all. He looked at Jose, who had his anxious face pressed against the chain–links.

Nothing. Nothing. Nothing where P–A–U–L is.

Jose staggered back from the green chain–links, and when he lifted his head from the wires, red diamonds marred his relieved face, clear in the moonlight that reflected from the snow. Giddy, Michael struggled through the gate and joined Jose outside the court.

WHAT DO?

Michael shrugged. He examined the tracks that led from alongside them that ran across the field toward the receiving dock.

—Like that old–fashioned wabbit on Dad's old laptop computer.

(The ground caves in whenever Bugs Bunny tunnels to faraway places. Bugs Bunny pops from his rabbit hole and pores over the map.)—

When he looked toward the field again, he could track them. Several dents, some drag marks, and thin impressions stretched to the receiving dock. He stared at disturbed snow, a picture forming in his head.

—(The Whysees' retreating backsides, and two hands in the ground pulling dead weight, working his way outside of the tennis court. The straps, tied or twisted around his crusty pants, drag the wheelchair.)

Yeah! Go, Paul, go!—

He broke into a sluicing run, and Jose stood in astonishment before he gave chase. They ran to the square tunnel. They scrambled together, then separated into the receiving dock, piles of cold bricks brushing their bodies. Moonlight fell upon a wheelchair wedged against one of the concrete pillars. A thin blade of blue light reached the dock, where Robby knelt by a soaked heap that kept hugging the boy's knees for warmth. The wet shape kept shivering, although Robby had covered him with a blanket. Their forms were incomplete winter spirits sprung out of the chill.

—That is what you put him through, you chicken. Should've gone over earlier, you dummy shit. Ooo look, whoa messed up *loco* Michael, nothing to say or do now?—

"P–Paul?"

Paul's head turned, and without his glasses, his eyes seemed watery, and the rings around his puffy eyes were angry red. His head lowered.

"Time to go home, huh, Paul?"

He waved a weary arm at him.

"Taking you home, all righ?"

Michael looked.

Glasses? he asked Robby.

Robby nodded and his stump limb pointed toward the wheelchair, where he saw the twinkling lens of Paul's glasses placed on the seat.

Thank. O. K. Go bed now. Get sleep.

Robby nodded and retreated into the hollow part of the deck. Michael retrieved the glasses and placed them on Paul's face. He took off the blanket, and Paul hugged himself, narrowed eyes glaring up at him. He took it over to the gap in the deck and stuffed it in for Robby. Jose looked.

Get legs.

Jose crouched by Paul, ready to lift. Michael took his place by Paul's head, and his hands locked under his armpits. He nodded, and both heaved Paul in the air. They moved him several feet before setting him down on the ground.

"Heavy," Michael gasped.

FINISH CARRY REST D–O AGAIN.

O.K.

They maneuvered his body around the piles, and twice Jose had to stop to clear scattered bricks while Michael struggled to support Paul by holding his upper body against him while propping his lower body with his leg. Paul gestured toward the concrete pillar, but Michael thought nothing of it. Steam puffed from mouths as they worked their way outside the dock. Chilly air greeted them.

"Ump," Michael grunted.

Jose staggered when Paul's arms started their sleepy struggle.

"Shh, goin' home now. Paul, take it easy."

A murmured reply that Michael pretended he did not catch. They took the back road, and several feet further, Michael found himself drained. They lowered Paul again, and he remembered.

—(An aseptic clip of baby–faced soldiers in urban fatigues carrying a sagging blood–soaked plastic body bag.)

Oh, another little war on T.V. when I was little.—

Jose…. Get blanket.

NOW?

Yes. Find any empty room. Get blanket.

Jose scooted, a shadowy shape in the blue dark. Alone, Michael knelt by Paul, clinging to his chest, and feeling his shallow breathing beneath his chin. He looked up at the heavy sky, dull illuminations of billions of candlelight reaching from light years away to fall upon his eyes. Dirty snow clung to the tar of the road like rolls of lard.

"Paul, you okay?"

He mumbled, and his brow lowered. Michael felt his friend's hot and flushed head.

"Don's go, Paul. Please. Don's leave me alone, all righ?"

Another breath rasped.

—Please, Paul. I'm sorry. I'm losin' it all: friends, family, myself, bravery. And now I'm nothin.' I should have been in one box. How bad can it be? Like going underwater without gettin' wet. I'll just be chokin', and my head will squeeze me out. Then golden lights dancin' and I'm swimmin' in the deep, then break free surface and up through…

(Mom has arms wide.

'Come here, Michael. You're hurt.'

Melt into her arms, all personal defenses aside. Lay wide open, fall away and sleep. Rest. Close eyes and let cold world fade, last of sounds filtered through hearing aid like sorrowful tomes of a hollow dream. You are safe and warm. You're home. All is alright, and all is good. Dad is neither tired nor scared anymore.

'It's alright, you did your best.')

Should have stayed with Paul. I'll be a hero, die a hero, see everyone again. Paul will be here too.

('You did good. It was you who tried to save me. You did not know I crawled and crawled. I met your little friend. He tried to help, but I was gone.'

'Sorry I did not protect you, Paul.'

Sam's smirk.

'See, way to go *estupido*.'

'Shut up, Sam.'

Paul stands. 'I can walk now. In heaven, I can walk. You can hear. Yes, Michael, we can do anything here, be anything here.'—

Wool fell on him. When he surrounded himself to the comfort of sleep on a chilly night, even out on a harsh road, a poke broke in his dream.

WAKE! Jose demanded.

Michael nodded and worked the blanket under Paul, who squealed each time he was moved. They used the blanket as a makeshift stretcher, carrying him up the lane to Galton Dorm. They staggered to the entrance. A piece of Sam's old shirt had been wedged between the hinges and the doorframe, preventing the door from being fully shut and the bolt/lock aligned. The shirt stuck out a tongue, and they liked to make believe that Sam was here watching for them. Jose pulled the door open, and the smooth tile made it easy to slide Paul all the way to the door at the rear of the lobby, leaving a slick trail. The entrance door did not shut after them, and that was something the Whysees would have to deal with tomorrow. After the second door, they were inside the dorm. In silence he cringed, almost expecting the blue lights to jangle like before now. The light bulbs along the hall remained dead. 9

They made it to Paul's door, and Jose slumped against the wall while he opened it. With heaving grunts, they dragged him into the room and put him into bed. After he removed Paul's glasses, Michael looked at his soggy clothes and thought he would be warmer without them. He gave a heavy sigh for effect and rolled up Paul's shirt. There was his narrow chest, dented nipples, bony ribs, and a cluster of acne by his navel. Fine, light hair curled from the bottom of his naval to the waistband of his soaked pants.

PANTS OFF, Jose ordered.

"Nah…"

OFF.

Michael gave a reluctant nod, and his hesitating hands reached for the button and unsnapped it. Because of Paul's hollow gut, the zipper stayed mashed, and he had to pull harder, the snicks audible in his hearing aid. Paul's pubic hair peeked from beneath the rim of his graying briefs. With the blanket pulled off of him, he reached for the shoes. He untied the damp laces and pulled them off, and one sock stuck to his foot. After he peeled the sopping sock from an aristocratic, pale foot, the dank odor rose in the room. He waited until the sleepy movements stopped before pulling at the cuffs of the pants. It slid down, revealing smooth shriveled legs, pink from the cold, and the underwear slipped, showing his raw hip. He shucked down the underwear and saw that it had withered to a nut shape.

—Would hate wakin' up to this. No way I'm gonna squeezin' the tip 'til top pops out. He's on his own with that, man.

(Paul bolts awake.

You… along with leaving me, you touch my… Michael! I will rather die than have gay touching!

'I wasn't being gay. It just looked nubby, and I was tryin' to help!')

Nuh–uh no way not doin' it.—

SLEEP TOGETHER, Jose signed. His hands made two forms, sleeping together.

What? I am not gay!

MUST O–R FREEZE.

You do it.

YOU HIM LEFT.

You too.

YOUR FRIEND.

Your friend too.
FRIEND YOUR FIRST. ME SECOND.
Fine. Get out.

He unzipped and shucked his pants and left them on the floor. Then he took off his shirt. Lips pressed with the sheer horror of it, he looked at Jose.

HAVE FUN! Jose signed with a bright smirk before fleeing.

"You little dick!" he shouted at him, cross.

He checked to make sure the blanket was fully under Paul's body to keep the heat vapors from rising. Before he crept in, he took Sam's blanket from the bed across from Paul's. Even now he could sense his sweat, salty and of zinc. The pink light from the plaza outside showed the white dollops streaked near the middle dried, splattered paint. Traces of Sam.

—Jeez, Sam is just as bad as I am.—

He slid by Paul and put his arms around his slick chest and held him as if a child, two quiet hearts beating for a time. Paul's shivers ceased to twitch.

—Too bad he's not a woman keepin' warm. I would have kept warm with my mouth, hands...

(Tasting her well-shaped foot, trailing along one of her supple legs, the secret thatch between her thighs, tongue lolling alongside the hips, and the dirty part between the cheeks of her behind, her sighs, your own, the globes of breasts, hard nipples, and rub...)

Better get away from him thinking that. Will kill myself if sees me like this.—

Michael lifted his head from Paul's damp hair and shifted himself farther for five to six inches of distance. When the darkness in the room turned to a bleary haze, he got up and groped toward the door. His hand fell upon the light switch. The room bathed in depressing hums of fluorescent light. Paul's body shifted and his hand waved at the emptiness.

"Paul? You okay, Paul?"

258

He hugged himself and stepped closer. Paul's head turned, and his eyes were closed, hair sticking up, face like a sleepy wicked old man.

"Paul, you wanna be alone now?"

His eyelids flew open, and he struggled upright. His lips hollered.

"Whas sayin, Paul?"

Trapped in his underwear, he looked at Paul, who realized their nakedness.

You run out on me and now this? What the hell you thinking?

"Nothin', Paul. I swear, nothing!"

"You left me!"

"Please, Paul, I jus los my Mom, Das, and now…"

Michael held out his hands, helpless and his shaky voice kept on talking.

"I mean come on, 'esus Cris. I los all, Sam an I almos los you, an' there's nothin' I can do." His gummy throat worked. "I jus a boy an' saw Mom down like this. My arm hur so muss 'cause Mom pull me so har to ges away. Mom, only one in worl is away an' never comin' back an' no one's sorry. Das is gone an' when I wanna lay down an' sleep, you nos les me! You pull me ous an' you shool jus' roll on an' leave me to lie down an' be gone. You din's les me sleep in my home an' now I'm here. Thas whas I'm doin' for you, Paul."

"Don't say that!" Paul hissed. His hand clamped over his wet face and with his naked eyes wide.

"Yeah, true Paul. You shool les me lay down an' go. Thas, I dis for you."

You shit. You talk of letting go, we have your Mom trying to get you. She come with you. You have Dad look for you. They die, so you can go on. Where is mine? Where is my Dad? They forget me. Nobody care and you are all I have now. You left me! Get out, you piece of shit! I never want to look at you again!

Face red and teary, Paul collapsed back. His lips drawn hard, he mumbled. Michael could lip–read some blubbers. "No one cares… I want my Mom. Mom. Please, Mom?"

Michael collected his clothes, pleading.

"Please Paul, you don's know nothin'."

"You know nothin', stupid! Get out. Goddamn it, get out!"

Paul's lips started moaning for his mother again as he buried his face in his hands. Michael fled. The hallway blurred.

Back in his room, he dressed. His lips quivered, and he bucked toward his bed. He crawled on it, eyes leaking tears. Everything he felt, saw, heard, and touched; all repressed emotions choked him. The beloved dead, daily grinding nonsense labors, everyday casual humiliation, scattered stupidity of others (mostly his own), with nothing and nobody to explain it all. The only place of retreat was inside his head. Pictures, insistent hums, voices, and an occasional stuttering thought stirred. He wept. His runny nostrils dripped on his tattered pillow. Exhausted, he slept. His mind revisited thoughts from that triumphant moment in September to the day he abandoned his best friend to the flurries of Whysees' hands.

He sleeps and wakes. Wakes and sleep. Twice his body jumps and thrashes as he dreams of bitterness, sensations plummeting.

—I lost. This. I lost this.—

The energy that runs neurons in his brain threatens to shut down, drained of life, faith, and dreams. Again, he submerges. Again, until his throat feels strangled, only to break through the rippling skin of the surface, breathing.

—I'm gone. Please come.—

Sink like a stone.

—Mom… Dad… you please take me home. ('It's my turn now, Michael')—

All that is him gives. Fall and never gets up. And he goes willingly into the depths.

—(At the Norristown library computer:

The screen during days Dad is broke enough to call going to Gino's eatin' out.

Soldiers lead a mustached man to the bridge. Colors are hazy purplish and green with a play of lights upon leaves from trees over the bridge, even if the film is in black and white. The man is middle–aged and balding. One soldier ties a rope around the man's neck. Something happens and the man breaks from the soldiers. He is free, scrambling down in the water and fleeing. Stones and ground burst from gunshots. For a long time, man runs in the wet heat through halls of leafy palms. At last, he comes upon his mansion and runs on a large stretch of lawn. On the porch stands a young woman, her arms out. Joyously, the man runs and just before he can sink into her arms, he grabs the back of his neck in agony.

The film fades with the body hanging beneath the bridge, twisting in the wind.

Michael what happen?

He fool himself into thinking he trying.

What about you? Will you try very hard again and again?

Yes, Dad.

Dad's palm is up, and he says in voice, 'Gimme a five.'

Mikey at seven, being cool, laying chilly willy, so cool he can take anything. Even with the inside of his head skipping down the wrong trail from time to time.)—

When the final film runs off its reel, there will still be him, lying in bed, an arm flung across his face and in all unspeakable things in what world, he smiles. The hitching in his chest slows to a steady breathing.

—Going to be all right now. Wait and see we're gonna be all right.—

In real life he wakes up and moans out last ounces of grief expelled, and it would be a long while before his body could wrack itself through this day. The room cast in the paling light of morning. For a beat, he braces himself for those skitters of blue lights, but the bulb above his closet remains dead.

—Still got some time. My number goin' up, and if it goin' up today, so what? Five minutes of chokin.' Then break through black water, past the stars, and I'll see them. If it doesn't, it'll go up someday. Everyone's number goes up, even a Whysee's.—

Readied with that, he finds the energy to prop his body up and swing his heels over to sit at the edge. He looks at the damp sneakers.

—Go out and see the light in the darkness again. How 'bout that, huh?—

He rises, puts on his hearing aid, and walks erratically to the door, the room rocking in his vision. Faint lights twinkle at the corners of his eyes, and he did not know whether they are nova bursts in his head or from the morning's lights. His hand rests on the knob and turns, the door clicking open.

—Bad scare yesterday. Never close to that many dead: Sam, friends, people round here, Dad and Mmmmm.—

Fresh explosive tears pour, and he wipes his eyes with the back of his hand as he steps out into the hallway. His feet squish on the stained carpet, and in the still hallway, an open door investigates an emptied room. The next half– opened door shows a female ward who must have fled the girls' dorm. Her squat body, the size of an eight–year–old, lay on the rumpled bed. Tiny aqueous hands are tucked under her eggplant–shaped head. Her shaggy hair spread on the bed, and her stubby knees are drawn up. It hurts him to look at her face, her eyebrows rising in permanent worry, and her mouth aghast, just a gape. It seems her entire body is willing itself to shrink so that she can hide among the wrinkles in the sheet beneath her. Before he can call out to her, a thought flits.

—Her number is up today. Can't draw her out or she will die earlier.—

Michael moves on to the next door. Farther, the bathroom door is ajar, and a dull shaft of fluorescent light flummoxes from it. He enters, and with his hearing aid, he hears quiet weeping. In the flicker of the light, the back of Jose's head as he labors by one stall panel. His shaking hand scraps the last of the letters on the wall with a crayon that used to belong to Gertie. On the metal, fading blue jagged lines run together:

DoN Cry

KeE Try

All around the new words and old smeared messages, a craggy smiley face is drawn.

"Jose?"

Jose does not react, so Michael places a hand on his shoulder. The boy springs, his eyes frenzy with panic, then collapses against the wall.

Me.

Jose's mouth works, and he fights back another sob.

SCARE ME.

Michael tries a laugh but comes out a wheeze.

Morning come. Watch sun, get people around, show we not alone. *Watch sun?*

Eyes brimming, he nods, and before he goes back, Jose leaves the bathroom door open so others can come by and read the message. Michael reaches Paul's door and holds up a fist, ready to rap.

"Paul? Is me. Paul, please?"

—You forgot the damn wheelchair. Idiot. That's why Paul is not answering. (Sam slaps his head at the sheer imbecility of his *amigo*.)—

He tries the door. The door opens halfway.

"Paul, you okay?"

Paul keeps his face to the wall.

"Come on, look as me, huh? I'm sorry I ran. Whole thing got me rile up an' I have to sis an' think awhile. An' I'm sorry I took my clothes off an' gos in bes with you, but I was keeping you warm, not being a homo. If I homo, I wool take my underwear off too. Huh, Paul?"

Paul looks over his milky shoulder, his eyes wary. His raw face like a paper bag stretched over a skull.

"Huh, Paul? Whas you say?"

He turns toward the wall again and waves him away.

"Paul, do whas you wans. I'm sen' Jose back for the chair," and unable to help to inject, "whish me an' Jose workin' to ges you back home, I compleely forgos. Stupis me righ?"

No answer.

"Fine, do whas you wans. You sae they no control, you have your time in your mine an' I have mine. Me, I think I'm gonna go ous an' see the morning with people I know. We're goin' to Farrow Fiel, an' wae for the lighs to wake me up. To wake us up to this day. Okay?"

The damp back of his head is the only reply. Michael's mouth twists, and he backs out of the room. His eyes drying, he hurries to Jose to ask him to get people together for the morning to come. 10

The sky seems terminal, as if the sun has a battery running out when Michael and Jose reach the dock. Inside, they hunt for Robby. Michael snags him by the cuff of his pants. Robby's head pokes out from the large hole in the deck, his eyes heavy–lidded.

See sun go up?

He rubs his eyes with his stumps, and his head tilts up and down for a yes. He raises his arms.

"Cris, Robby."

Michael squats, his arms behind for stirrups. He feels him climbing on his back, and the limbs close around his neck. Jose dutifully grabs the wheelchair and looks furtively both ways before wheeling it outside the dock. Michael staggers outside with Robby and looks both ways for Whysees, even though he is not due until late spring. Jose is already gone. When he tires of the bony knees digging into his ribs, he sets him on the ground. Feeling him go limp, he props him up again, putting his sneakers beneath the smaller shoes, and walks him a few steps. He shakes his small shoulder. The back of his head presses against his waist and his face is up, a ghost smile on it.

Up, please. Ready?

Robby nods. Michael goes back to the deck to get the blanket for Robby. He comes back and at the entrance, he sees how the boy picks his way over the slick concrete to the road like a cautious dog. His form seems watery from the narrow sky peeking in from the squat entrance. After Michael wraps Robby in the blanket, they make their way on the slippery road to the field where others wait. Michael keeps his hand on Robby's elbow to prevent him from slipping. On the rim of the gravel road, Lionel waves his large fingers outspread.

—(Five hot dogs in moonlight, sweeping back and forth under the stars. In the mall by the food–court counter, hot dogs on metal rollers turn, glistening sweet meat in the heat.)

Mmmmmmmm!—

My few friend, Michael tells Robby.

Robby nods and hugs himself inside the blanket. They meet Lionel and their ragged footwears crunch in the snow toward the field, giving the court and the goal post a wide berth. Nancy is deeper in the field, holding Jose's hand as they gaze at the glitters above in the softening twilight. Jose sees them. He releases Nancy's hand and hurries over to him.

GET WHEELCHAIR FINISH. NOT KNOW P–A–U–L COME.

O.K. Thank.

Behind Nancy, a form comes down the road along Farrow Field, the head lowered and using the arms as axles to rotate the wheels.

"Paul?" Michael calls to the dark and a chilling breeze answers.

Paul comes and pulls past, his face set. Michael steps aside, for Paul deserves their friends' warmth more than he does. Jose pauses as if something has occurred to him. He signs.

CAN ME TELL STORY?

Sure.

SIT ALL SIT.

They do, seats of pants damp, skin numb. They huddle for warmth. Robby presses his quivering chin on his forearm.

*LONG AGO PARENTS UNCLE ME ALL CAMP
IN W–I–S. WE ALL SIT AROUND FIRE. ME UNCLE
STORY.*

Robby's eyes brighten as diffused light approaches,
aided by aerial lights from above.

*WIND MONSTER B–A–K–A–K APPEARS DO
BAD THING TO PEOPLE.*

Jose's face becomes softer and older. A few feet away,
Robby wraps his blanket around himself tighter, rocking to
stay warm.

*RABBIT SELF SPIRIT CHASE MONSTER. BRING
FOOD SET (up) FIRE RABBIT SPIRIT HELP BLIND SEE
INTELLECTUALLY DISABLED SMART MENTAL ILL
BETTER THINK PROCESS. UNCLE STORY TELL.*

What did you say? Michael asks.

*'ME DOUBT,' ME SAY. 'DEAF WILL HEAR.' MY
UNCLE TELL 'WHY DEAF NOT HEAR?'*

Robby smiles and seems to know what comes next.

"What did the Rabbit say?" Nancy asks, after Paul
repeats what Jose said.

Jose grins.

*ME TELL RABBIT COME IN ROOM TELL 'WILL
EVERYONE PLEASE RAISE YOUR HANDS T–O
SIGN.'*

Jose covers his belly and plops himself into the snow,
laughing hard. Robby giggles silently and rolls on his side.
Michael turns to the east.

In the vault of the sky, tangerine lights collect below
cumbersome clouds at the horizon. The edges of clouds seem
to catch on fire, colors from cotton to umber. Gold shades
shimmer between fingers of naked trees, along iron bars of the
fence farther down the field and spread on melting snow.
Michael raises his arms wide, gulps in new air, sweet and clear.
Robby's arm waves at the sky. Nancy, at last getting it, giggles,
her outburst a puff out of her mouth. Warmth comes with the
morning sun.

—Not for nothing. Sure, we all die, but we can't stop living. A day and another, a way or another, we'll run out of them. Like everyone, I die soon. You die soon. We all will be gone someday.—

All he can do is wait and see. He takes another breath and ignores the scraps of cold for a few seconds. The last of the darkness from yesterday moves on and fades.

THE END

The Monster At The End of the Book

<u>1</u> Fence

<u>2</u> Barcode

<u>3</u> Twilight

<u>4</u> Batons

<u>5</u> This happened.

Peter remembered an eBook he liked and read with his own mother when he was ten. The book was 1982, 2058 Childcraft Annual E–Reprint of *The Puzzle Book*. His favorite parts were the riddles. He liked the riddles because they had the answers right in the numbers, so it was not cheating if your finger swept by them. However, the answers to his own resided in his memory. They leap across time and back, answers elusive as water bugs on the surface of the pond. Even today, he could still string words that were keys to what it was like to be him. The riddles helped him form the images and sounds of the day that he first set his eyes upon the deaf boy with the blue eyes. He guessed that boy's age to be thirteen. It was the last time that boy was with his mother.

It was twilight and cold for spring. By the fence, he rocked on his heels, watching the new arrivals. His mother and father had not come back to see him as they promised, and he might never see them again. Arrivals came from faraway places, New York, New Jersey, and many from Pennsylvania. All the children were twelve to fourteen years old. When the buses from the train pulled to the curb along Farrow Field, the Watchers were already in motion, striding to each bus door and efficiently parting the children with disabilities from some parents with disabilities, putting them in two groups on the football field. Some children have no disability, so the Watchers prodded those mewing and sobbing children back to the buses, idling and ready to roll.

He was far, but he noticed the mother and the boy in the crowd dotted by men and a few women in gray shirts. The boy and the mother were close to each other's height. He saw the boy pressing a hockey stick to his chest as he moved to disengage his other hand from his mother's hand. A brief waver in the crowd, a yelp, a high cracking shout from the deaf woman as she fled the crowd, dragging her son, who seemed to have dropped his hockey stick. Two Watchers took chase. It was frightening how the forms of mother and teenaged boy swelled from clothes and blurred rosy faces to the haggard face of the mother in jeans and untucked red blouse and dragging a wide–eyed son, his face jiggling.

The boy dug in his heels and pulled back at the mother's towing hand, her other hand signing something frantically. The Watchers' faces became hard with grim urgency. They had their black brooms ready to sweep the mother and boy away. When the Watchers caught up with them, Peter was already thinking up the first few lines of his newest riddle.

　　　　Later by the bleachers, Peter ventured to talk to the boy. The boy's dullen blue eyes stared numbly at the spot where his mother had fallen. He saw a dime–sized bloodstain on the collar of the boy's shirt. The boy pressed his forehead against the hockey stick that he had recovered from one of the sobered Watchers.

　　　　"Hey, mister deaf boy. Got to go now." He tapped the boy on the shoulder. "Time to go now, soldiers mad now. Got to go."

　　　　A tear slid on the boy's cheek, and his lips quivered. A Watcher in the gray shirt started up the steps. Then shrugged and turned back after seeing Peter.

　　　　"Hey, mister deaf boy. Gotta go now."

　　　　He grasped the boy by the elbow and tugged. The boy startled and noticed him for the first time.

　　　　"Got to move now, gonna get in trouble."

　　　　Peter pulled harder, and the boy wrenched his elbow away, spraining his wrist, pain in head, the colors of silver and pink.

　　　　"Ges offa me, lemme alone!"

　　　　Peter stepped back from the boy's fury, the colors blue and cloudy brown in his mind.

　　　　"Wait, wait, just trying to get you on field."

　　　　"Jus stay away from me!"

　　　　Peter might have been angry or frightened, but he did not remember. He was trying to help everybody in this, even the boy who stood screaming at him. He struck the boy on the neck. The boy sobbed and choked. The hockey stick clattered as he dropped it, and he sat on one of the metal benches, his face twisted in misery. Then the boy buried his head into his hands, moaning with pain and rage.

270

"Hey, cut it out!" someone called. Peter saw a short, tan boy looking down from the top bleacher. The boy's left eye has a funny squint to it.

"I'm trying to get him off to the field, but he won't listen!" Peter called up to him.

"That doesn't mean you can heet him," the boy said.

Another boy rolled up in his wheelchair on the sidewalk. He wore glasses and gray eyes shone through his lens. Both were new arrivals, too. The short boy walked down the steps.

"Careful, Sam," the boy in the wheelchair called. "One of them is walking over."

The boy called Sam made a careless gesture. More arrivals walked past them. One Watcher leaned on the chain-link fence. "Hey, you come down. You don't want us coming up to get you." He stopped to watch the new arrivals stream through the four opened gates and did not understand the rude boy.

"*Ay me cague encima,*" Sam replied to the man. He nodded to Peter. "Take off. I'll take it from here."

"But I was here first!" Peter said. He thought the boy would be grateful and be his best friend. He might even help him stop talking so funny.

Sam drew himself up, although the top of his head only reached Peter's eyes.

"Great job. Now take off before I pound you."

"Aw, it's no fair," Peter said.

He was not afraid. It just was not a good time to fight.

Sam ignored Peter and leaned closer to the boy.

"Hey—" he asked him, his tone soft, "Can you read lips?"

"Come on! Lips are not same as riddles in books!"

Sam glared at Peter and then looked back at the boy. The boy nodded.

"Look at me," Sam said.

The boy nodded and sniffled.

"What's happened?" Sam asked.

"They bonked his mother on head! He and she didn't hurry," Peter cried.

Sam stood and his sleepy left eyelid rolled to a dead–eyed stare at Peter.

"Get moving."

Peter did. Down three steps he could hear Sam, a boy he had made up his mind to hate. Just like a bully squabbling at him and taking his new friend away just 'cause people say he's retarded.

Sam continued to talk to the boy.

"We have to move on. There's no place to stay here."

Peter walked down further to the gate, clumped by the arrivals. He looked at a blonde Watcher. He was cleaning off his baton, running the club along the grass, and Peter realized that the man was the Watcher who had chased the deaf mother.

"I try to get him down," Peter said to the Watcher, and the man nodded, his face still bland.

Peter saw the boy in the wheelchair being carried on the steps by two Watchers. Peter joined the crowd on the field.

"Hey," a blonde kid in an undershirt snapped. "What are you crying about?"

Peter sensed what kind of person the blonde kid was. Not that he was mean. It was just his eyes were empty looking, although he had a cherubic face.

"Me?" Peter touched his cheek. It felt slick to him. He put his finger in his mouth and tasted salt. "I don't cry."

He realized that the inside of his neck burned, and it was hard to breathe. The blonde kid sniffed before talking.

"You stink. Like eggs."

"Yeah?"

"Your name is Eggy."

Peter giggled. "No!"

"Yes."

"Yes."

The blonde kid looked like a girl with soft blue eyes and a delicate chin. Peter smiled, shy.

"What's your name?"

The blonde kid frowned, thinking for a moment. He nodded, his face serious.

"Nat. They didn't let me have my last name. I don't get none."

"I'm Peter Mellow."

"Eggy."

"What?"

"That's your name. Eggy."

"Why?"

The boy who called himself Nat sighed.

Eggy." "You have to have a name, so I picked one. You're

"Eggy."

"Right. You're Eggy."

Eggy smiled again, enjoying his newfound hatred. Peter, now Eggy, hated the tan boy called Sam, the boy in the wheelchair, and the deaf boy. He still hated them, looking outside the window of his dorm room the following winter as Sam played hockey with the boy on the ice–crusted plaza.

In thousands and hundreds of mornings' flashing wake–up lights of the hallway, he watched as the short boy grew bigger and stronger, the boy in the wheelchair learned to sign more words, and the boy's earnest face became more beautiful. Years later, he realized how much he hated them when he came out of his room into the flashing hallway.

He saw three of them on the carpet, faces shining, and the two froze. One lay shaking, two others crowded around the first. From the deaf youth's face came a look of revulsion so hurtful that he wanted to say something nasty to him.

"You're gonna get in trouble, gonna get in trouble," he said, and he fled outside into the unsensual morning to begin his own day.

6 A ward

<u>7</u>

Back Cover of Book

<u>8</u>

Nat, his bestest buddy, had not spoken to him in a long while. The blockheads also won't let him out. It was okay. They brought him food every other day. He passed the time playing at being a prisoner with the Whysees and blockheads as prison guards.

Now he did not know the day. He thought every year ends at the start of summer, since school closes in summer and opens in fall. The real end felt like Christmas except for the warmth, the love, and another gleaming action figure from *The Enhanced League*. He could not remember when his lungs and throat burned so bad. It was a cough that just won't stop, and now his head felt stuffed and swollen.

He watched them, the beautiful deaf boy, and his friend with the flat face through the window. Hunger gnawed at his belly. He only had thin soup and coarse bread with the bitter, rotten blue spots on them he had tried to eat round it. He remembered eating alone at one table in the cafeteria back when he was well enough to move. His reflection, a skin covered skeleton, made him imagine the ghost of the future from *The Christmas Carol*. The beautiful deaf and the flat–faced deaf straggled across the plaza, looking and jumping at each fearful step. Sparks in his vision made it hard to see their movements. As a rat scurried across the sidewalk near them, a lint in the distance, he giggled at how both grabbed each other's hands. He wished to go out to them but wouldn't be welcomed. Besides, he was tired all the time.

2

His arms, stick and not stones, a rhyme that told him he should not let others' harsh words hurt him. Except for the middle of his chest and the way it drained the strength from his body each time, Nat said a harsh word toward him. Others, like that bully, good riddance at ridding of him, that tan boy who would not let him be friends with the beautiful deaf. His shriveled legs trembled as he leaned against the window, staring at the emptiness of the plaza that used to contain the boy whom he still wanted as a friend.

Memories joggled his vision and other senses. How strong he was! The remembered images of those smaller or less aware on the ground, sobbing or pleading, faces rictus with pain used to amuse him. He even remembered the deaf when he stomped on his head. It was funny how his entire body seemed to sag on the concrete. Now it's not. He thought of Nat, Richard, the big deaf, or that spidery bur–headed deaf girl, or the beautiful deaf girl with the dead eyes who did not come back one morning. He remembered how they shove or hit him each time he did or said something wrong. The last time Nat shoved him was when he tried hugging him last November, and his blonde friend had hurried out. Through the wall, he heard running water and splashing. It was when he had coughed and sniffled. The faces in his head melted into his own.

He saw them past the ghost of his forehead coming back. They looked scared and carried a body between them wrapped in a blanket. The open part showed a red to pale face, bunched as if a crabby toddler. Glasses had been placed on the face.

"Buh. Buh–baby," he whispered to himself.

He dreaded the next rattle of his lung, and he coughed hoarsely. Yes, they squabbled in the cafeteria a lot, they scrambled back to the dorm without the wheelchair boy, but here they come now. Two walking wounded, carrying one more back with them, to the dorm. Despite the torch blazing in his head, he could hear them come in, the clank of the entrance door shutting. The sloshes of something wet dragged across the tiles. Slumping against the window, he heard the clunk of the hallway door open and shut. He wheezed away, and several bellowing coughs forced him to the stained mattress where he lay. Why he needed to get into the hallway, he forgot, then remembered.

He thought he could tell them he was sorry.

10

His body temperature rose, and it got cold and hot at the same time. Everything froze and burned.

"Hi," he said. "My name is Peter, and it hurts."

Unable to lift his head or let out another forceful cough, he could not clear the searing pain from his lungs. His hands reached out to the ceiling and lowered to clasp himself in a self–hug. It only got colder. The sickness boiled inside his chest. His head burned, and he could feel his brain swelling. The pain became an iron fist and endless in the next hour.

"Help me, God. I am sorry. Please stop hurting me."

He coughed again hard, and mucus crawled up his throat, blocking the air passages. His eyes hurt the next time he coughed. His lungs and inflamed bones were burning, he strained to cough another whooping cough. It stopped hurting. The next time he moved, he floated. He saw himself. Under the dwindling beam of the dull light in his room, a shriveled boy lay there on the filthy mattress, skin gray and ceased its breathing. Its eyes became hollow, and pink hues beneath the lower lids darkened. He floated higher. Gray shaded his vision, and the coarse pain that ran live wires through his body ceased. After the creature's chest stopped rising, he was beyond anything or anyone that could reach or hurt him.